MY NEWSLETTER

To be kept informed of new Miss Riddell Cozy Mysteries, sign up to my Newsletter here: https://landing.mailerlite.com/webforms/landing/x7a9e4

And to pre-order the book that follows this one, follow this link: Then There Were ... Two Murders?

NEWCASTLE-UPON-TYNE, ENGLAND. JULY 1953

THE THIN RAIN sparkling on the café windows in the summer sunshine didn't dampen Marjorie's spirits. She seemed to buzz with excitement, barely able to be still as she drank her tea and waited for the time she would leave to start her evening.

Sitting across the small, plastic covered table from Marjorie, Pauline Riddell mentally shook her head in dismay. She liked Marjorie, had done since that first day at the Gosforth Secretarial College, but couldn't quite understand how Marjorie lost her head over any man who gave her a moment's notice. This latest infatuation was the worst of them all.

"Marjorie," Pauline said, quietly for the café was busy with other women from the company offices, "you must take care."

"I always take care," Marjorie said, grinning. She opened her handbag to show Pauline the small, flat packet with its plain white cover.

Pauline reddened. "That's not what I mean," she said. "This man won't meet you anywhere public and doesn't want you to tell anyone who he is. Something's not right."

"Maybe he's married," Marjorie said, grinning at Pauline's shocked expression. "And we'll walk out together publicly when his divorce comes through." She smiled in a way that made Pauline want to slap her.

"Don't be a fool," Pauline whispered. "He's playing you along for what he can get." Marjorie had hinted at this more than once but never quite so loudly in a crowded place.

Marjorie's face registered immediate anger. "You've no right to say that. You don't know Eric," she said. "He's an old-fashioned gentleman and wouldn't behave that way."

Pauline was silent. She studied her friend: pretty, vivacious, with beautiful blue eyes in a model's face. Everything Pauline was not, as she often thought whenever they were together. It was the old story of the pretty girl and the plain girl, each helping the other catch the eye of the boys and she knew, wistfully, which role she would always play in this partnership.

What amazed Pauline most was that Marjorie came from a poor family in the city while she, Pauline, came from a better off farming family in the country. Not that anyone cared for such things nowadays. After two world wars and a depression, everyone was equally poor, classes were all mixed up and anyone could become someone. Still, it was hard to imagine a gem like Marjorie growing up in a rundown part of a fading city. She should have been an aristocrat's daughter if there was any justice in the world.

Her own background was easier to understand. Her brothers were either in one of Britain's navies, merchant or Royal, or they were tenant farmers, while her sisters were nurses. Unwilling to become a nurse or a teacher, the only options she was being pushed toward, she had gone off into the world of business and had already achieved some success. She'd been hired as a secretary for two lower managers before being promoted to the executive secretary ranks, all within a year. At twenty, she was the youngest by far of the executive secretaries in the company. She quickly learned how much jealousy existed in an organization. Had she been prettier, she'd have suspected an ulterior – or would that be an interior – motive by the director. As it was, she was sure she got it on merit. After all, she'd spotted a potentially devastating mess in communications and fixed it before it became widely known, saving the department director's job. He'd promoted her as soon as he'd made provision for his aging, now retired, secretary.

"Pauline! I'm talking to you."

"Sorry. What?" Pauline again realized she'd been miles away and missed Marjorie speaking.

"You could make an effort to listen," Marjorie snapped.

Seeing her friend was upset, Pauline said, "I'm sorry. It's been a hard day and I'm a bit shell-shocked."

"Oh, you and your important work."

Realizing she'd said exactly the wrong thing, touching upon her own recent promotion and Marjorie's still being little more than typing pool, Pauline tried again.

"What was it you were saying?"

"It doesn't matter now," Marjorie said, crossly, "I'll tell you tomorrow." She rose abruptly from the table, almost toppling the chair, and looped her headscarf over her head to protect her elaborately waved hair.

"Lunch time tomorrow?" Pauline asked.

"Why not. Maybe you'll be in the mood to listen then," Marjorie said. She took her coat from the peg, and with a brief dismissive wave to Pauline, walked quickly out of the café door.

Pauline sighed. She liked Marjorie a lot, but she was very up and down in her emotions. This brief exchange was an example. When they'd entered the café, Marjorie had been excited, too excited, at seeing her new man and was now, less than an hour later, explosively angry when she'd left. Pauline's inattention certainly hadn't helped, but Pauline thought that wasn't what had made the change. It was something Marjorie had said that Pauline hadn't heard. Deliberately hadn't heard, for she strongly disapproved of adulterous affairs, even ones that may just be pretend or a way to wind her up, but now Pauline wished she'd listened. There'd been something beyond Marjorie's usual prattle and now she felt uneasy. Foreboding was the word that came to mind.

Foreboding was probably too strong a word, Pauline thought, pushing aside the feeling as she gathered up the cups and plates, before returning them to the counter. When she'd first come to the city, the idea of clearing her own dishes in a café was a surprise. The teashops her mother saved so hard to occasionally enjoy and had introduced Pauline to when she was old enough to share her mother's appreciation of the treat, had waitresses who did that. Pauline had believed every teashop did. But those other teashops also had cotton table clothes and nice china, Pauline thought with a grin, rather than plain plastic covers and 'works canteen' crockery. And the dainty cakes, pastries and sandwiches they offered were also considerably more visually attractive than the fare in this small café in an industrial neighborhood, though they weren't any tastier.

She returned to her seat and peered through the window. Marjorie was marching up the street in a determined stride that threatened to take the heels off her ridiculous shoes, a gift no doubt from Eric, as was the whole outfit Marjorie was wearing. He certainly had good taste. The blue dress and paler blue coat had both brought out the color in Marjorie's bright eyes. Pauline watched Marjorie growing steadily smaller as she drew near to the farther end of the street and the major road to which it joined. In her expensive outfit, she was as out-of-place among the grim smoke-blackened brick houses as a hothouse bloom in a northern rockery.

For a moment, she returned to the thoughts that had so distracted her when Marjorie had started speaking: Stephen's letter, which had arrived yesterday. It was two weeks old and talked about the rumors of a ceasefire. He hoped it was so, and if it were true, they'd be together again soon. She hoped so too. These past months had been painfully lonely without him. Once, she'd have discussed it with Marjorie, but Marjorie was now so full of her new love there was no chance of that. She imagined Stephen smiling, grinning at the prospect of home and all its delights, one of which, he promised, was her. She smiled and looked around to see if anyone was observing her. If they were, she was sure they'd guess her thoughts, which brought a flush to her cheeks. It was time to go. Pauline put on her own thin, nowhere near as expensive, summer coat and left the cafe.

Outside, she hesitated a moment to see if Marjorie was still in sight. She wasn't. Whatever it was Marjorie had tried to share and which was now causing Pauline such unease, may have been justified, though you could never tell with Marjorie. She was so volatile. Unfortunately, Pauline had agreed without listening to what had been said and now Marjorie had flounced off in real anger. Pauline suddenly felt afraid. What if Marjorie were planning to do something rash, like trying to force her new lover's hand by announcing their affair publicly in some way? From the little Marjorie had shared, and Pauline had listened to, her lover seemed to be a rich married man who said he was going to divorce his wife. Pauline thought this unlikely. Men with standing in the world had too much to lose to take such a step.

She set off down the street toward the bus stop. The factory was along the river on the western side of the city and her flat was nearer the center – too far to walk, even on a bright summer's day like this. To her left, the terraced houses that stretched from the factory, where most of the men from the houses worked, up to higher ground and the West Road, were almost gay in the sunshine. In winter, the area looked forlorn, abandoned even, as she knew from her three winters in the city, but now with children playing in the streets and wives chatting in groups along the length of the terraces, it looked a happy place.

The bus wasn't long in coming after she arrived at the stop, for which she was thankful. Three young men in the growing fashion for greased back hair, long jackets, string ties, and trouser legs so tight they were nicknamed drainpipes, were jostling each other in what seemed innocent horseplay but Pauline knew would soon 'accidentally' involve her. She jumped on the bus the moment it stopped and sat where the driver could see her. Throughout the journey, she tried to remember something of what Marjorie had been saying.

It was no use. Marjorie prattled, there was no other word for it, when she was in love. And she was often in love, either with real men or the imaginary ones she saw in the movies, which she went to every week, either with a man, or failing that, which didn't happen often, with girlfriends. All this would have driven Pauline to distance herself from another person, but Marjorie was also open, friendly, trusting, generous, and good-hearted. There wasn't a waif or stray, human or animal, that Marjorie wouldn't rush to help, and as Pauline loved animals too, that kept the two young women closer than would be expected by anyone who only knew Pauline. But how much of Marjorie's prattling was fact and how much wishful thinking? It hardly mattered as Pauline could remember practically nothing of it. What must be true, however, was that Eric existed because Marjorie couldn't afford the clothes she was wearing when she left the café.

Her flat felt cool after the sunshine. She lived alone, though the building, an old stone home in what remained a grander part of the city, was now divided into 'maisonettes' – tiny two-room apartments. Her neighbors were, like herself, mainly better paid young women who held responsible positions in the factories and offices that were still the mainstay of the city. Not for the first time, she thought, as she looked around at her few possessions, she wished her life too was fuller, more exciting, more glamorous – more anything really. And not for the first time, she realized that deep down she envied Marjorie's easy way with people and her attractiveness. She looked forward to the day when her fiancé, Stephen, returned home. He was in the army, presently in Korea in a war that was thankfully winding down, but he assured her any fighting wasn't likely to involve him. He was a staff officer and well away from the frontline. She prayed it were so and he wasn't just saying that to make her happy.

As she prepared her evening meal, she considered what to say in her letter today. She wrote to Stephen every day: news from home, news of his parents, news about her work, anything really. What had started as a way to keep him in touch with her, and her with him, was now also a way of making sense of the times in which they lived.

Pauline examined her pantry for supper. There was one piece of Wensleydale cheese, brought back from her last visit home, lettuce, tomatoes and a rather dry half of a cottage loaf, which she would have to toast under the grill to freshen. The cheese and bread situations were a problem she hadn't found solutions to yet. Newcastle shops carried only Cheddar, the hard, orange kind whose only real virtue seemed to be its ability to keep for months. For bread the locals preferred their stotty cakes, a flat oven-bottom bread, to the hearty farmhouse bread she'd grown up with. Added to that the warm summer made the flat feel close and it had a musty smell.

She'd eat, go out for a walk, as it was such a beautiful evening, and then reply to Stephen's most recent letter.

Her walk was refreshing after her evening meal, but she got home late which left her listless, unable to concentrate, and the letter was put off until tomorrow. The first time she'd failed to write every day as she'd promised to do. But her conscience gave her no rest, so in the early hours, she rose and wrote. It would go by the morning post.

2

INSPECTOR RAMSAY

THE DOORBELL RANG and Inspector Ramsay frowned. Slumped in his armchair, dozing gently with a radio discussion droning softly from the table about what was still rationed eight years after the war ended, why it was rationed and why it had to stay rationed. It was midnight and he didn't want or need any interruptions to his solitary evening. The bell rang again. It sounded urgent, that is if a doorbell could sound urgent.

"I'm coming," he called. He stood, drew his cardigan across his ample frame, walked stiffly to the door and opened it. His deputy, Detective Sergeant Morrison, didn't wait for him to speak.

"We've a murder," he said.

Inspector Ramsay nodded. "I'll get my jacket," he said. "You'd better come in."

"I'll wait by the car, sir. It's a beautiful night."

It was, but Ramsay knew that wasn't why Morrison didn't want to come in. 'Inspector Ramsay wasn't house proud' was the kindest description Ramsay had overheard of his home and housekeeping. He had no doubt it wasn't the description Morrison would have used because his detective sergeant wasn't a sympathetic man. Ramsay could understand that position too; once he would likely have shared it. Grief should have its place and its time. The war was long over. It was time for Ramsay to move on in his personal life, and maybe at work too. He just found it somehow unnecessary to do so.

As an industrial city, Newcastle could have expected to be bombed by the Germans in World War II, but it wasn't. Or at least not like the cities to the south the German bombers could more easily reach. However, the shipbuilders and armaments factories along the River Tyne didn't entirely escape, nor did the homes nearby. For Ramsay, then a regular uniformed officer patrolling the streets on night duty, one such raid was a disaster. There were only three people killed that night when a bomb, intended for a shipyard, hit a terraced home. The three killed were his wife, Mrs. Aileen Ramsay, and their two sons, Robert and Alastair.

They were buried at the Presbyterian church the family attended each week. Numbed by the horror, he'd walked through the service in a nightmarish dream. A nightmare from which he was aroused to blinding fury when a well-meaning parishioner said his family had been 'gathered to God'. Ramsay had yelled back they weren't 'gathered anywhere', they were 'scattered'. The ambulance crews and he had found so little of each, there had hardly been bodies to bury. The funeral was the last time Ramsay went to church.

Inspector Ramsay, properly dressed in his jacket and tie, got into the waiting car and listened patiently as Morrison filled in the details of the crime.

"There was a fight between rival gangs after the pubs closed. One man was killed, stabbed. I guess, when they all saw what had happened, they ran. It was other people returning from their night out who found the body and reported it."

"Do we know who the victim is?" Inspector Ramsay asked.

"Not yet but somebody will miss him tomorrow morning when he isn't up for work."

Some mother will miss him, Ramsay thought sadly.

"He's quite a fancy dresser," Morrison said. "A spell in the army would sort all these lot out." It was a theme he often advanced as the regular crop of young men found their way into police custody after each weekend's drinking.

"Your army needs guns and ammunition, Sergeant, so someone has to make them. Not all our young men can be firing guns, some of them have to be learning to make them or the wars would stop. And we couldn't have that, could we?"

Realizing the old man had been brooding again, though he could hardly do otherwise sitting at home each night staring at the photos of his wife and kids, Morrison continued, "I think I know the gang he's with. Clothes are like a uniform with these kids."

"Then we'll follow up with them in the morning," Ramsay said. "Tonight, we'll do the crime scene, and the forensics, and get statements from the people who found the body."

The car drew up. They could see the uniformed officers holding back a small group of interested onlookers and the police surgeon crouched down examining a body lying on its side against the curb.

The detectives stepped out into the warm air. It really is a wonderful night, Ramsay thought, as he looked up at the starlit sky. We get so few of them here. What a night to die. He walked to the body.

"A single, but messy, stab to the heart, before you ask," the surgeon said, "and about an hour ago. Not your normal after-hours fight."

"No, thank God. We don't get much of this sort of thing around here."

The prospect of a night interviewing witnesses and scouring a crime scene didn't upset Ramsay. Quite the opposite, he welcomed it as a change from the insomnia that regularly filled the darker hours of his days.

"Sergeant," he said, "you talk to the people who found the body. I'm going to talk to the homeowners." Most of the houses that looked out across the street where the body lay, now had someone standing in the doorway and other faces at bedroom windows. He felt this could fill a good part of the night.

However, it seemed, none of the people who lived in the houses saw anything. Some admitted to hearing the disturbance in the street. "Filthy language," one elderly widow said. But no one had looked out until the police arrived or would admit to having done so anyway.

The young people who found the body were also quickly let go. They had gone from the pub to a nearby park because the night was so warm and when the lust and alcohol-induced glow began to fade, had set off for the bus terminal and the last bus home. They had seen no one except the body, and he could no longer be counted as someone, could he?

Ramsay was driven home in silence, disappointed that it was still only one o'clock in the morning. There were still six hours to kill before he could sensibly get on with his day, which would start by setting in motion the process of finding the young man's family and friends.

3
_____

PAULINE RIDDELL

ON THE BUS TO WORK, Pauline craned her head around to see what everyone was pointing at. It was a crime scene. Police cars had blocked off part of a street that joined the bus route. There was nothing to see, but as she heard everyone on the bus saying, it must have been serious because they'd never seen so many police cars in one place. From sleepy silence, the bus was now abuzz with speculation. Pauline's own thoughts had a different slant; would the Police discover that last night she'd walked through the park farther down that street and would they want to interview her?

Work too had the same buzz, for many had walked past the scene on their way to work and they'd questioned the police on duty there. It was murder, that was certain. Newcastle wasn't a big city, not like London, Birmingham, or Manchester, so murders were quite rare and ones where the crime scene were so close to the city center, rarer still.

By lunch time, people knew that it was a gang member killed in a fight with another gang. The depravity of modern-day youth was discussed and the baleful influence of the last War, the present Korean War, the Nuclear Menace and the Cold War was given by everyone as why the streets were now so dangerous. Pauline nodded in what she hoped would be understood as agreement when the subject arose but found it a curious line of thinking. Until today, she'd never heard of this rash of teenage gang violence that had apparently been happening all around her these past three years she'd lived in the city. As a teenage girl until only a few months ago, she thought she would have known about it.

At the café, waiting for Marjorie to appear, she ordered her tea and Sly Cake, more popularly known to school-children throughout the North as Dead Fly Pie or Fly Cemetery. Despite these names, it was a family favorite with Pauline and one of the few things she thought this café did really well. Not quite Yorkshire well, but good enough for a displaced Yorkshire lass.

When Marjorie hadn't arrived by the time she'd finished her tea and pastry, Pauline decided she'd better go and find her. She guessed Marjorie was still angry about yesterday when Pauline had been daydreaming instead of listening.

She discovered Marjorie hadn't come into work and hadn't sent word why not.

"Her mum could have found a phone box to let us know," the head of the secretarial pool said crossly when Pauline pointed out Marjorie's family wasn't rich enough to have a phone in the house.

Pauline returned to her desk. She could get the bus to Marjorie's house after work but how would that look? She was Marjorie's friend, and as such, she knew it was just too much partying that had Marjorie off work, not an actual illness. Yet, not to go when she was Marjorie's friend would look odd as well.

Something Pauline thought really odd, now she was looking at that thought head on, was that Eric was supposed to be an older, more mature man yet Marjorie had mentioned parties that clearly involved drink, drugs, and what sounded like orgies, at least in Pauline's admittedly limited experience of life. That last bit had seemed like boasting to Pauline; this was the northeast of England and not famous for Bacchanalian revelry.

Her work kept her chained, head down, typing furiously at her desk until her concentration was disturbed by the afternoon break and the tea lady with her trolley.

"Your usual, hinny?" the tea lady asked.

"Yes, please," Pauline said, "and one of those nice fig rolls if you have one left." She was one of the last on the tea trolley's rounds.

"I saved you one. I know how much you like them." The woman handed over the cup and saucer with the fig roll balanced on the edge.

Pauline found the money in her purse and handed it over.

"Have you heard?" the tea lady said. "There was another murder last night. Not just one, two."

"How awful," Pauline said. "Another one of those gang members?"

"Dunno. It wasn't a man anyway. It was a young woman but she could have been in the gang I suppose. So many are nowadays, aren't they?"

"I'm afraid so, yes," Pauline said. "Was it near the same place?"

"It was. So, I expect it was them. Revenge for killing the man, maybe, or maybe the man was revenge for killing the girl. Horrible." She said 'horrible' in a way that caused Pauline to suspect that horror wasn't the feeling that was truly being expressed.

"I don't normally but I'll buy a paper on my way home," Pauline said. "I live alone so I don't like to think of this kind of thing happening here."

"My old man would give them a good hiding if they tried any of that stuff around our place," the tea lady said. "He thinks they should all be in the army, not doing apprentice-ships. They can do that when they've grown up a bit."

Pauline smiled. "I expect he's right," she said. She knew from experience this was the kind of discussion that could go on forever once started.

The tea lady pulled the trolley back out into the corridor. "See you tomorrow," she said.

Pauline sipped her tea and nibbled her snack. An uncom-fortable feeling had begun to coalesce in her stomach that had nothing to do with her food. Now the police would really want to interview everyone who was in that area last night. Would it be best to come forward voluntarily? She'd met no one she knew on her walk so she didn't have to come forward. No one could give her away. But, a small voice in her head said, mum and dad would expect me to help the police. Plus, if she didn't come forward and somebody had seen her, it would look bad.

The office rumors would soon be saying the murdered girl was Marjorie. After all, how likely was it there would be two missing girls in Newcastle in one night? If the police came here, what could she tell them? Marjorie had gone off at four o'clock to be picked up by her mature lover in his expensive car before being whisked away to a party out-of-town. From her own point of view, she had to think there was no chance Marjorie could have been wandering around the city center near midnight and it was just a coincidence her not coming in today. Coincidences happened in real life more than seemed likely and this was an example of it. That was all she could say, if the police asked. The same reticence that had allowed her to argue against visiting Marjorie's house earlier now settled her mind. She had nothing to say to the police and nothing to fear by not putting herself forward.

Tomorrow was Saturday. If Marjorie wasn't at work in the

morning, she'd go around to Marjorie's house to see how she was and that would be the end of this uncomfortable feeling.

The evening newspaper Pauline bought on her way home might have changed her mind if it had had the name of the murdered woman. It didn't. First thing tomorrow afternoon would be a proper time to make enquiries. Until then, she would say nothing.

To put all this out of her mind, she re-read Stephen's latest letter. It was written more than a week ago, which wasn't encouraging. There were news reports of a ceasefire being arranged and she'd hoped that meant letters would come even more quickly than they had been doing. Maybe it was the opposite and there was a clampdown by the censors in order to prevent wrong information about the peace talks getting out. That might explain the delay. She sighed and filled her pen, noting the bottle was running low. When he did return they'd save a fortune on ink, she thought with smile. She had to write or she'd never sleep soundly, her conscience would nag. How much should she tell him about Marjorie? He'd met Marjorie so he would be interested to hear news of her, but right now, Marjorie had just missed a day at work. She couldn't suggest to him that her friend had been murdered.

If the murder victim was Marjorie how would Stephen feel, she wondered. While he liked Marjorie, he thought her too much of a tease. That's what he'd said. Pauline asked if she'd flirted with him and he'd answered no, it was just what he'd observed when they were in company. She'd been satisfied with his answer, pleased even, but was sad Stephen couldn't value Marjorie as she did, then. Now, however, she wasn't sure Stephen hadn't been right. Marjorie's desire for the admiration of any man she came into contact with was what had led to Pauline's present unease.

4

INSPECTOR RAMSAY

IT WAS the small hours of Saturday morning, barely sunrise, and Inspector Ramsay was dispassionately examining the bodies on the slabs. While murder wasn't common in his police work, dead bodies were and these looked little different to any other suspicious death. They looked pale, ordinary people except for the single wound in the chest.

"You can't say for certain it was the same knife?" he asked the police surgeon.

"It could be," the man replied. "The type was certainly the same. A switchblade, or flick knife they're often called. Much beloved by those who want to intimidate others for gain but also used by people who work for a living in a variety of fields: fishing, for example."

Ramsay frowned. Fishing and the Tyne were almost as synonymous as coals and the Tyne, or shipbuilding and the Tyne. In other words, not a particularly helpful piece of information.

"Anything to help us identify the young woman?" he asked.

"Nothing other than what was in her handbag and pockets."

"And that wasn't much," Ramsay said. "It's a puzzle."

"She wasn't dressed for gang warfare, you mean?"

Ramsay nodded. "She was found in the same area, killed with a similar knife, is of an age to be one of the gang's girlfriends, but she's dressed for a high society cocktail party. No teenager wandering the streets with a gang of tearaways dresses the way she was dressed. And she's not one of the regular girls who frequent the city center, we've checked with the beat police."

"Someone will miss her soon," the surgeon said. "She's not a runaway. There are none of the usual signs."

"No, I fear she's just some poor kid who was in the wrong place at the wrong time. Maybe she saw who killed your other 'client' and paid the price."

"The time of death suggests that's a possible, even likely explanation. Poor kid," the surgeon agreed.

"Well, thanks, Doctor," Ramsay said and left the mortuary deep in thought. She was a puzzle, that girl. Her clothes and accessories were expensive but she wasn't a rich girl, he'd swear to that. He didn't mean she was from an impoverished background; she just wasn't from a well-to-do family. She'd grown up with the minimum needed to build a healthy body, thin but not skinny, and with none of the mismatches you saw in the real poor. On the contrary, even with all the life and color gone from her face you could see she was stunning, no crooked teeth, or misaligned nose or eyes. A regular girl from a family that had enough, but not more, and who wore clothes she couldn't buy with a year's wages. It didn't look or sound good to him. If he'd had a daughter, she'd have been about this girl's age and he knew how he'd feel if she was his. He may have left the church, but it hadn't left him. Its teachings were very strict on makeup and expensively fashionable clothing that flaunted the body the way these clothes did.

5

PAULINE

PAULINE STEPPED off the bus and looked around. She'd
caught one straight from finishing work at twelve. Marjorie
had never invited her to her home and Pauline could see why.
Here, on the east side of town, the terraced houses running
down to the river on her left, were in a worse state of repair
than the ones around the armaments plant where she worked,
and as a country girl, she'd found them unsettling enough. It
had taken her a long time before she'd realized the rough
voices and hard features she saw and heard weren't being
unfriendly; their accent was just harsher than the Yorkshire
farmworkers she'd grown up with. In time, she'd discovered
the people were nice enough, but she couldn't forgive their
lack of tidiness. Doors and windows needed paint, children's
toys lay abandoned everywhere, rubbish was strewn across
any empty space. She longed to box their ears and make them
put everything to rights.

She studied the street signs looking for the right one.
Personnel had been reluctant to give her Marjorie's home
address until she'd pulled rank as the engineering director's
secretary. Now, armed with the house number and street
name, she was lost in a strange part of town she'd never in a

million years have visited if it weren't for the unpleasant feelings that hadn't left her after an uneasy night's sleep.

Panic was beginning to set in when an elderly woman approached the bus stop. Pauline asked for directions and was pleasantly surprised she understood the reply. Often, she couldn't; the local accent was so strong. Thanking the woman, Pauline set off in the direction of the semi-detached homes to the right and found the street almost immediately. She found it a relief to know Marjorie's home wasn't among the terraced houses, and immediately felt guilty at thinking such an unkind thing. The sampler she'd sewn as a child remained with her always:

'Kind Hearts are the Garden'

'Kind Thoughts are the Roots'

'Kind Words are the Blossoms'

'Kind Deeds are the Fruits'

It was all very Victorian, of course, but none the less true for being that and she did try to remember and live by it. Only she found her innate reaction to the local people speaking was often fright. Sometimes a sudden speech could actually make her jump.

She arrived at the house and surveyed it quickly. Here everything was as it should be. No peeling paint or abandoned junk in the small garden. The garden was planted. Roses were in bloom and the tiny lawn was freshly mown. The path to the door had flowering borders of pansies and alyssum. Pauline opened the gate, strode up the path, and knocked on the door before her courage failed her. She wasn't at all sure Marjorie's family would be pleased at this intrusion.

The door was opened by a thin, anxious looking woman whose face fell even further when she saw Pauline.

"Yes?" she asked.

"I'm a work friend of Marjorie's," Pauline said. "I came

to see if she is well." It sounded lame, put like that. Did anyone call to see if someone from work was well?

"She isn't here," the woman said, and then asked, "Are you Pauline?"

"Yes, I am," Pauline was thankful that Marjorie had at least mentioned her to her parents.

"Oh God," the woman said and began to cry.

Pauline was stunned. "What is the matter?"

"We hoped she was with you," the woman replied and began to sob. Seeming to collect herself, she stepped back and signaled Pauline to enter.

The woman, by now Pauline was sure it was Marjorie's mother, led her into a small sitting room where an older man who'd been staring out the window turned to greet them.

"This is Marjorie's friend from work," Marjorie's mother said. "She came to see if Marjorie is well."

The man was ashen, his face the color of his receding hair. He stepped forward and offered his hand to Pauline, who shook it. His grip trembled in hers.

"Mother, I'm going to the police," the man said and he walked past the two women. In a moment, Pauline heard the front door open and close and saw him striding down the path.

"We thought she would likely be with you," Marjorie's mother said simply.

Pauline's stomach felt filled with lead. She found her hand was now trembling. Her worst fears were coming true and she didn't know what to say. She couldn't share them with Marjorie's mother, or offer her hope Marjorie was safe. She wished fervently she'd never come here. The idea her appearance would signal Marjorie was missing hadn't occurred to her. She wished she could leave but knew she couldn't leave Marjorie's mother alone, not at a time like this.

6

RAMSAY

AFTER A WORKING lunch of fish paste sandwiches and pale ale, Ramsay and Morrison stood in front of the blackboard set up in the incident room. On it was a chalk-drawn map of the area around the two crime scenes. Ramsay had insisted on the separation of the two murders until it was finally shown to be two parts of the same one.

"I see what you're getting at, sir," Morrison said, "but it would be an incredible series of events that would cause two murders to happen within minutes of each other using the same kind of knife and both at almost the same location. There's not a hundred yards between the two places where the bodies were found."

"I know, Sergeant, but something's not right."

"In what way, sir?"

"Well, what was she doing there? You know the area. Does it strike you as the sort of place where a party as posh as the one she was dressed for takes place? And why was she alone? You've seen her. Does a girl as beautiful as that ever walk home alone from a party?"

Morrison's expression became thoughtful for a moment, then he said, "Maybe that's the answer though, sir. She mistook the tone of the party, overdressed and instead of being the main attraction ended up being shunned by the others for being above the company. She left alone, early, heading for the Haymarket bus station. Unfortunately, the east side gang were running down that street and she came face-to-face with the thug with the knife in his hand."

"And he stabbed her? Why?"

"Because she recognized him, or he recognized her. It was late but still plenty of light left in the sky."

"Then he dumped her body in that garden, hiding the body under the hedge and behind the flowers in the herbaceous border?"

"Yes, why not? And took her purse because it contained cash, I guess."

"I agree it looks like that, Sergeant," Ramsay said, "but I find it too unlikely. I want to keep an open mind for a time. At least until we know who she is."

Morrison nodded. "She certainly looks more like one of them models than any local girl, that's for certain. There's nothing in her handbag though to say who she is. Any papers must have been in her purse."

"A model back from London to see her family, maybe," Ramsay said, thinking the thought over. He shook his head. "It's a puzzle."

The door opened and the station desk sergeant entered. "Sir," he said quickly, "a father has reported his daughter missing at the Byker station. They've just called it through. A young woman who sounds like she's our victim."

"Are they still on the phone?"

"Yes, sir."

"Put them through to me here and get a car ready."

The phone on the incident room desk rang, and Ramsay snatched it up. When he'd heard enough to be sure, he gave them his instructions.

"You heard all that, Sergeant?" he said.

"Yes, sir."

"Then you take the car and bring back the father and this young woman, the girl's friend, the mother too if she wants to come though I'd prefer she didn't. This isn't a job for a mother."

Morrison, whose wife had just had a daughter that was his greatest joy said, "Not a job for a father either, sir."

Ramsay nodded. "You don't need to tell me that, Sergeant. Now go."

7

PAULINE

THE DRIVE from Byker to the city center police station seemed interminable but it gave Pauline time to think. The detective's careful statements about the body they had and the circumstances surrounding it gave Marjorie's parents a little hope. After all, Marjorie shouldn't have been in the city center at 11 pm on a Thursday night or wearing expensive clothes. Pauline, who knew better than they, willed herself to say nothing though she knew their hope would only make things worse for them when they saw the body.

They left the car at the entrance to the police station and followed DS Morrison inside, where they were led into a sparsely furnished room where one elderly, portly man was waiting.

"Inspector Ramsay, this is Mr. Armstrong, Mrs. Armstrong, and Miss Pauline Riddell, a close friend of the missing girl," DS Morrison said.

Ramsay shook hands with each, openly sizing them up as if deciding which of them were the suspects and which the witnesses.

His grim expression and lined face didn't fill Pauline with a sense of warmth or goodwill.

"Sergeant Morrison tells us you have a young woman you need us to identify," Mr. Armstrong said.

"We have the body of a young woman, yes. We don't know who she is, and if you are able to, we'd like your assistance. This will be difficult, I know."

"I'll do it," Mr. Armstrong said. "We have to know."

"Thank you. DS Morrison will take you to the mortuary," Ramsay said, nodding to his sergeant. "Perhaps, Mrs. Armstrong and Miss Riddell, you will take a seat here and wait for Mr. Armstrong's return."

Pauline helped Mrs. Armstrong, who was growing grayer with each passing minute, to a nearby chair and sat beside her. Pauline put her arm around her protectively. The Inspector's grim expression made him look like he was the sort of man who would have no compunction about bullying people into a confession.

"Can we get you some tea, Mrs. Armstrong?" Ramsay asked, his voice much gentler than Pauline would have given him credit for only a second ago.

Mrs. Armstrong shook her head.

"Miss Riddell?"

"Thank you, no, Inspector," Pauline said. "I don't think I could drink anything right now."

Ramsay nodded.

Pauline decided he was sympathetic; it was just his face was against him. It looked as if sorrow had set up home in him, she thought suddenly. Maybe that's what a life of witnessing crime everyday does to a sensitive man. She got no further with her thought for the door opened and Mr. Armstrong entered, followed closely by DS Morrison.

One look at her husband's expression told Mrs. Armstrong everything she'd lived for was gone. She moaned, an eerie forlorn sound, and buried her face in her hands.

Pauline gripped her tightly in what she hoped was a comforting way.

Mr. Armstrong walked to his wife's side and patted her back. To Pauline, it was an incongruously inadequate gesture, but Mrs. Armstrong responded by wrapping her arms around his hips. Pauline removed her arm from the stricken woman and stood to allow Mr. Armstrong the seat so he and his wife could be closer.

Ramsay was studying the three people with the same expression he'd had when they first walked into the room. Cold, dispassionate, enquiring, studying, watching – waiting for a wrong move. Pauline almost shivered as she imagined the thoughts that must have been wandering around in his head.

"Miss Riddell," Ramsay said, "I think Mr. and Mrs. Armstrong may like some time alone. Would you be willing to come to my office and tell me what you know of the events leading up to this?"

Pauline nodded, hardly able to speak. A quick glance at the Armstrongs told her they didn't need anything from her so she followed the Inspector out of the room, down a short corridor and into his office.

She took the proffered chair and sat, gratefully; her legs felt like jelly.

"There's not a lot I can tell you, Inspector," she said, not waiting for him to ask a question.

"Well, let's start with when you saw your friend last."

Pauline explained about meeting Marjorie as they left work and the short time they spent in the café.

"Was your friend dressed for a party?"

"Yes," Pauline replied. "She was meeting someone called Eric and going on to a cocktail party, I think. She changed at work and left the clothes she wore to work, at work."

"Did she say where she was meeting this man Eric?"

Pauline hesitated. This was going to sound evasive, she knew. "No. But she never did. She kept him a mystery, not like the boyfriend she had before. I heard everything about him."

"What was his name?"

"Bob Hindmarsh," Pauline said. "He's a young draftsman where we work."

"When did Marjorie and Mr. Hindmarsh split up? Is he the sort to resent that break?"

"About four months ago and no, he isn't that sort of person."

"What do you know about Eric?"

"As I said, not a lot. I gathered from things she said that he's an older man, quite well off, and someone important. I think he was married. I think his story was he needed time to manage his divorce appropriately, that sort of thing."

"This is what Marjorie told you?"

Pauline shook her head. "Not exactly. It's what I inferred from the little she said about him."

"Anything else?"

"He has a posh car, leather seats and wooden dashboard, you know the style."

"Make?"

"I don't know."

"Where did she meet him?"

"I don't know that either."

"When did she meet him?"

Pauline thought quickly. This she did know or at least could work out. Was it before or after Marjorie split from Bob? After, she thought, but not long after.

"About three months ago," she said. "Sometime around the middle of April."

"You're her friend. Where might she have met him?

Where did you go that would bring a wealthy man into contact with her?"

"Except in the early days, when we were students, we never went out anywhere together, Inspector. We were only friends at work, really. So, I'm afraid I can't answer that either."

Inspector Ramsay practically sighed with displeasure. Pauline knew he thought she was being unhelpful, possibly deliberately.

"So, there's nothing else you can tell me?"

Pauline shook her head. "I wish there were. I'm frustrated I know so little. I should have asked more but it never occurred to me. I didn't tell Marjorie everything about my life so why would I press her to tell me more about hers?" She should have done, of course. Marjorie had been very descriptive about her relationship with Bob, a little too much so for Pauline's temporarily unpartnered state of mind. That she said so little about Eric, which Pauline had tried so effectively to ignore, should have set alarm bells ringing.

"Would you be up to looking at the clothes your friend was wearing when she was found?"

"If it will help."

"I don't know if it will or not, Miss Riddell, but something might come of it."

Pauline followed the Inspector back out into the corridor and past the room where she could see the Armstrongs were recovering their composure and into yet another small, bare room. There were two sets of clothes laid out. One set clearly that of the male victim and on a separate table, the clothes Marjorie was wearing.

"Do you recognize any of these?" Inspector Ramsay asked.

Pauline nodded. "These are the clothes Marjorie was wearing when we met after work. She said Eric bought them for her when he was in London because he wanted her to have nice things. She could never afford anything like this."

Pauline had known the clothes were special but the truth of them was bewildering. The cocktail dress bore a Balmain label and the shoes came from the same level of fashion house, though she didn't recognize the French name. She'd thought the brooch on the dress was just paste but it was Cartier. The whole ensemble, which Pauline had thought beautiful before, was like something from the Vogue magazines Marjorie loved to flick through. When Pauline and every other woman could only aspire to the now fading Dior 'New Look', Marjorie was wearing Balmain! Whoever Eric is, he must be loaded to afford these items without his wife noticing the spending.

"Your friend didn't mention saving to buy these?"

"Inspector, we work as secretaries at the Vickers plant. Neither I nor Marjorie could save for these in a million years. It was her friend, Eric, who bought them for her. He's clearly someone with a lot of money."

"That was my thought too," Inspector Ramsay said simply, "but I'm not an expert on women's clothing."

"When I asked Marjorie, she told me he'd bought them in London," Pauline said. "I didn't realize…" She stopped as she realized why Marjorie had become so angry. It was the clothes. Marjorie had told her proudly where they'd come from and Pauline had answered in such a distracted way that it told Marjorie she hadn't been listening. Marjorie had expected Pauline's usual concern at this extravagance and its implication of Marjorie being a kept woman, as the saying went, and when she didn't react, Marjorie took offence. She'd wanted Pauline to be jealous and found her only uninterested. Perhaps she'd thought Pauline's weak response was simply contempt.

"Didn't realize?"

"I didn't realize just how expensive these things were," Pauline said dully. She added, "Even in London, I think it would be easy to find who sold these."

"Yes, I had thought that too," Ramsay said.

Pauline looked at him sharply and was surprised to see in his expression something of an ironic smile. She flushed. He thinks I'm playing detective and is amused at me, she thought. It made her bristle.

"Well, have you checked?" she demanded.

"I have people checking," the Inspector said. "It's too soon to have any answers."

"Of course," Pauline said. "Sorry. I'm more upset than I realized."

"I understand. Would your friend ever hang around with others, a 'gang', if you like?"

"I shouldn't think so, Inspector," Pauline replied, not adding she wouldn't have been Marjorie's friend if she'd thought she hung around with gangs.

"But you don't know?"

Pauline flushed at the implication she was being evasive. "As I said, we were work friends mainly. She certainly never mentioned to me going about with a group of friends or a gang."

"Thank you for your help, Miss Riddell. Now, I'll have someone help you with your statement before you leave, while I follow up with Mr. and Mrs. Armstrong."

"Can I go once my statement is done? I'm not sure what help I can be after that."

"Of course. Will you wait for the Armstrongs and leave with them or not?"

"I don't really know the Armstrongs, Inspector. I imagine they'll want their own family and friends to be on hand, rather than a stranger like me."

"You'd never met them before today?"

"No, I hadn't. Marjorie never invited me to her home. I think she was self-conscious about it, but I don't see why. It was a perfectly nice home."

"Then I suggest you say farewell to the Armstrongs now and leave right after your statement is signed."

Pauline turned to leave but stopped when the Inspector spoke again.

"If you do think of anything, Miss Riddell, you will let me know, won't you?"

Pauline frowned. "I've told you everything I know, Inspector. Really, I have."

"You'd be surprised what people remember when they least expect it," Ramsay said. "It may be there's something and it will come to you. Anything you remember, no matter how small it seems, we want to know. Will you do that for me?"

For a moment, the Inspector's expression seemed almost friendly and Pauline found herself saying, "Of course, I will."

Outside, she wished she hadn't agreed but what else could she have said? Not agreeing would have made them suspicious about her and she definitely didn't want that. She also wished she hadn't said she thought that Eric was married. She didn't really know that. She shouldn't have shared guesses, particularly guesses that might make the police think badly of Marjorie. And what if they shared her 'guess' with Marjorie's parents who didn't seem to know anything about Eric?

She was unnerved by her own actions. She'd told the Inspector that Marjorie had never talked of going about in a 'gang' but when Marjorie was with Bob Hindmarsh she regularly told Pauline about the gang he and she went about with and the fun they'd had. But in Pauline's mind, the gang Marjorie was talking about was just a group of friends, not a 'gang'. And what these friends did hadn't sounded much like fun to Pauline but she assumed others found it so and none of it sounded criminal. But why had she held that back? To save Marjorie's reputation? Madness! They would question others and soon learn Pauline had lied to them about the gang, and if no one else knew about 'Eric', then they'd think she was lying about that too. Far from having a bad reputation in the police's minds, Marjorie might appear a happy, outgoing young woman while Pauline would be a malicious liar, which would raise even more suspicion in their minds about Pauline. Far from getting back to them with anything she remembered, she decided, she'd made such a mess of things her best hope of not being hanged was to never speak to the police again.

SHE SPENT the rest of the afternoon in a dysfunctional daze. She felt the interview she'd had with the police was one mistake after another and she couldn't understand how that had happened. It was like doing an exam at school or college and afterwards feeling you'd answered every question the wrong way.

She did her usual Saturday afternoon chores, shopping and laundry, and all the while seeing Marjorie's pale face on the mortuary slab, her body covered in an equally white sheet. Normally, she felt half her weekend was just doing the mundane jobs she had no time for during the week. Today, they seemed like a kind of therapy, her link to the world of the living. Marjorie would never do any of these ordinary things again.

During her first two years in Newcastle, she'd gone out on weekend evenings with other students from the secretarial college, usually in company with Marjorie, but one by one the others had found boyfriends who became husbands and now, only three years later, she had few people to socialize with. Her own fault, she realized. She wasn't the life and soul of any party and her few boyfriends had soon moved on to more lively companions.

She owed a lot to Marjorie, if she was honest. It was Marjorie who'd befriended her and introduced her to her wide circle of friends. Left to herself, she'd have spent most of her evenings in her flat when she was at college. And it was at a party that Marjorie had taken her to that she'd first met Stephen.

He was home on leave from the army and they hit it off at once. She'd finally found that someone who she could talk to for hours and, even more amazing, who would listen. And he felt the same way, he said. And they did talk, until reinforcements were needed in Korea and his regiment was shipped overseas. Now she could still talk to him, just using a pen and paper instead of speech. Tonight, again, she was having trouble settling herself to that and she couldn't understand why. This could be a great letter to Stephen, some real-life experience instead of hopes and dreams for the future. He was probably sick of hearing of future babies, their names, the color of the nursery and everything else she'd rambled on about over the past months. With a great effort, she sat down at her small table with a blank sheet of paper and began.

She was on the second sheet of paper when she realized why she was restless. She'd also told Inspector Ramsay that Bob Hindmarsh had been all right when Marjorie had dumped him. But that wasn't true. He hadn't been all right at all. He'd done nothing too violent, that was true, but he was angry and, being Marjorie's friend, she'd experienced that anger from him when he wanted her to make Marjorie aware of his feelings. Of course, she understood, it was all just the usual hurt everyone feels when a love affair ends. But she hadn't told the police about it. Worse, she'd told them that Hindmarsh wasn't the sort to hurt Marjorie and she had absolutely no reason to say that. She knew nothing about him other than she'd met him occasionally with Marjorie, and at work. She hadn't liked him, and she hadn't told the police that either. She wasn't the sort who hid things from the police, or hadn't been until today, and her conscience was smiting her accordingly.

She'd imagined writing to Stephen was going to be easy now that she had something interesting to say. In fact, it was hard. How to explain what she'd done, or hadn't done to be precise, to someone who was always so regular and correct about everything? She described the day and its events as fairly as she could, not overstressing her fears about holding back what she knew but mentioning them, along with her thoughts on why she'd done that. It didn't make comfortable reading, even to herself. Maybe Stephen could give her advice. Sometimes his return letters came very quickly. If his reply to this one did, she'd at least have an outsider's opinion, though perhaps one who wasn't exactly neutral.

She was finishing her daily message when a thought occurred. Stephen loved cars and motorbikes. Maybe if she described what Marjorie had told her about Eric's car, he might be able to identify the make of car or something more about it. She wrote what she remembered, realizing it was pitifully little for him to judge by and ended with hugs, kisses and the hope they would soon become real embraces.

She placed her letter in an air mail envelope for posting in the morning, made and drank her Ovaltine nightcap, nibbled her homemade Shrewsbury biscuit, and retired to spend a night of unsettling dreams interspersed with long wakeful periods. By morning, she knew she had to find for herself some evidence that would salve her conscience for not telling the police everything about Bob Hindmarsh or at least provide her the justification she needed for going right ahead and doing so.

8

RAMSAY

BY MID-MORNING SUNDAY, uniformed branch had rounded up most of the two rival gangs involved in the Thursday night trouble. Ramsay spent the day interviewing those who seemed the most likely to be implicated in murder or most likely to give the game away if questioned long enough.

It was a miserable task but better than sitting home alone, which is how he spent most Sundays. He felt the results were promising because he'd gained a good understanding of the events of Thursday night and he was able to fill in the timeline on the incident room chalkboard.

The gang from the western end of town had come to hear a bunch of musicians from London, soon to be the newest stars he gathered, who were performing, one night only, in the Red Lion public house on their tour of the north of England and Scotland. The coming new music was 'skiffle', apparently, and a man called Lonnie Donegan was its leading light. The gang had been in the pub for the start of the concert at 8 pm.

The gang from the central area were already in the pub when the others arrived. Nothing much had gone wrong;

everyone was enjoying the music until around ten. After two hours of drinking, the jostling began to get out of hand. Someone said something to someone and a fight started. Bouncers had moved in and thrown out those who were fighting.

That settled things down inside until around closing time when fighting broke out again. The bouncers threw everyone out into the street, anticipating the cooler air would settle the kids down. It did for a time. The two groups moved off, still haranguing each other and then, again for no sensible reason Ramsay could yet see, the fighting started again. This time with a knife and one boy was dead. It took a moment for everyone to realize what had happened but as individuals began to flee the scene, it soon became a mass panic to get out of there. No one saw who had the knife. No one saw which way the person with the knife went.

The group that had run down the street past the small park where the second body was found – it was more of a walkway between two parallel streets than an actual park – didn't see any woman in expensive clothes. Nor did they see anyone hurt such a woman. No one knew anything, in fact. He'd dealt with people like this many times before, though not usually for murder. Someone always talked eventually.

The third group, the two couples who'd found the body of the boy, were much clearer in their recollections. They had been at the Barley Mow, a pub at the foot of the street where a well-known folk singer was performing to a packed house. There were so many calls for encores that the landlord had allowed the performance to go on past ten thirty, even as he'd closed down the bar, as was required by the Licensing Act. Ramsay suspected that bit wasn't entirely true but it wasn't what he was interested in so he let it pass.

The four had hung around after the show, at first listening to the performer as he'd answered questions from the enthusiastic audience. Then they'd left the pub just before eleven and hung around in a nearby parkette before heading up the street toward the bus terminal. All four were from out of town. They hadn't seen any of the gang members who'd run down the street only minutes before. When they came upon the body, they'd given it a wide berth thinking he was just a drunk passed out in the gutter. Only as they'd come alongside, did they see the blood and the stain on his light-colored shirt. Three stayed with the body, while one of the young men ran to the bus terminal where they knew there was a phone box or possibly a policeman.

So much for the eye-witness statements, Ramsay decided, as he made further chalk notes on the board. He'd let them all go for the present. When he had the final forensic reports, he'd call back the ones he'd mentally noted for further questioning.

One thing that came out from all of this – the girl wasn't with either of the gangs. He hadn't believed she was but it was good to have that confirmed. The second murder victim then must have been walking along that street though he still couldn't for the life of him see why. He hoped something would come out of forensics that might answer that question.

It was growing dark by the time he was finished collating the evidence to his own satisfaction and time for his next step. PC Goddard had been the one who had walked through the small park that night as part of the search for evidence after the finding of the first body. He should have seen the second body. Why didn't he? Goddard was on duty again tonight and he and Ramsay were going to retrace his steps to see what he could see.

The two officers arrived at the park at 11 pm. The sky was still light, but inside the park the trees and shrubs cast deep shadows.

"What time was it on Thursday when you arrived here?" Inspector Ramsay asked.

"I can't say exactly, sir," Goddard said. "We arrived at the crime scene about 11:15 pm and it was only about ten minutes later we set out to search for evidence."

"It took us about two minutes to walk here from where the body was found so shall we say around 11:30 you would enter the park here?"

Goddard nodded. "About that."

Ramsay looked at his watch. It was still a few minutes early and he wanted to be exact, for the body hadn't been seen during the search. If she'd been killed by the murderer fleeing the scene with the bloody knife still in his hand and her body dumped, it would be reasonable that Goddard would have seen it.

Finally, the time to move arrived and they stepped inside the entrance. It was dark, no doubt about it.

"Your torch was working well? The battery was strong?" Ramsay asked.

"Yes, sir. Like now." Goddard moved the beam across the path and into the bushes, sweeping it side-to-side.

"The body was found under that hedge and behind the flowers in that border. Can you shine the light over there?"

Goddard did as he was directed. Inspector Ramsay studied the area from the path.

"Did you search in the bushes?"

"No, sir. There was to be a more detailed search when it got light."

"Which is when the body was found."

"Yes, sir."

He'd hoped for something to jump out at him from this re-enactment, but nothing did. He couldn't entirely fault Goddard, there was little evidence of any disturbance where the body lay, not even after the police and forensics had worked all over the area. How much less obvious would it have been to Goddard on that night?

Ramsay nodded. "Thank you, constable," he said, knowing the man would be almost sick with worry at being caught out in a dereliction of duty. "I'll let you get on with your beat. There's nothing more I need to see here."

9

PAULINE

PAULINE ATE her toast and marmalade while planning her day. She'd miss church this once because she first needed to visit the place where Marjorie's body was found. If she had to explain to the police about her solitary walk that night, she should be prepared to answer questions about the location. Second, she'd develop a plan to interrogate Bob Hindmarsh on Monday at work. That wouldn't be easy. They rarely came into contact; they weren't friends and he'd be suspicious of her interest, but she had to know if he was involved. Third, she needed to find Eric, whoever he was. There must be a way to do that, but the answer wasn't staring her in the face at breakfast time.

Finding the place where Marjorie's body was found wasn't as difficult as she'd feared when she'd set out from her flat. The newspaper reports had accurately pointed the way but the small, ever changing group of gawkers would have marked the spot even without the help of the press. She joined the rank of onlookers and stood in solemn silence studying the spot. It was marked by the boots of the police and their forensic experts and therefore had little to tell her. She walked back to the street to estimate how far from the other body Marjorie's had been. Not much more than a hundred yards was her guess. She'd been that close to the other murder. Only the time difference separated her from the events the police were investigating. If she told them she was there, would they believe that? Could she prove it in any way?

From the bystanders, she could hear a steady murmur of speculation as to what Marjorie was doing there. A lot of it was unkind, and unfair. Marjorie was loving and giving, not mercenary. Pauline had to bite her tongue to stop herself giving the speakers her opinion on their ugly words. After an hour of walking the park and street, she found she'd discovered little that would help her. The Barley Mow and the bottom of the street still had a poster in the window for the concert that had happened that night. Maybe that's why Marjorie had been here. Maybe her new male friend was a folk music fan. She knew Marjorie wasn't. Marjorie was all for modern songs, songs she could dance to. Finally, as it neared lunch time, she returned to her flat to puzzle over her next steps.

The most important next step was to see Bob Hindmarsh as early as she could on Monday, preferably before the police interviewed him. He would suspect her of telling them about him, if they didn't tell him themselves, and she needed to assure him it was innocently meant.

10

RAMSAY

THE CHIEF CONSTABLE had demanded a report by Monday morning. Ramsay had outlined the extent of the investigation and his theories about the murders before handing the report over. The Chief had listened in silence. To Ramsay's mind, that didn't bode well for his future on the investigation; it suggested the Chief wanted to get outside help such as Scotland Yard. The Chief read it, while Ramsay, sitting expressionless, waited to hear his thoughts.

His boss turned from the report and fixed him with a steady gaze. For a moment the two men looked at each other in silence, then his boss said, "If you're right that there are two separate murders here, shouldn't we focus on the local kids and a fight that got out of hand and leave the more puzzling one to people with better resources to deal with it?"

Ramsay wished now he'd been less conscientious and said nothing about his doubts. "I don't think that's warranted at this time, sir. The most likely explanation, that there's one murderer and two victims, will probably turn out to be true. I'm keeping the team separated as they investigate to keep the possibility of two separate murders open in people's minds, that's all."

"But you do raise good points, Inspector. The first death could even be manslaughter, the perpetrator's lawyer would certainly argue for that, heat of the moment and so on, but the second is truly murder. Why would even a panicked gang member raise the stakes so brutally? And the first stabbing was amateurish and messy, the second you say was clean and professional. How to reconcile that easily without a separate murderer?"

"The way I see it," Ramsay said, "it can be explained quite simply. The first looks a mess because it happened in a struggle, two similarly matched kids fighting so the stabbing was necessarily badly executed. The second was different. The woman didn't expect it so he had time to pick his spot and strike before she could take any defensive action."

"The surgeon says the second was expertly done, though."

"True enough. But that isn't as big an argument in favor of a second attacker as it might appear. Plenty of people have done their National Service and are trained in weapons of all kinds. And plenty have brothers in the army who've shown them how to do things like this. Others are in the Territorial Army; weekend soldiers they may be, but I'm sure they know how to handle a knife at close quarters." Ramsay paused, hoping he'd said enough to head off the Chief's desire to give away the best case that had ever come his way.

"All right, Inspector, continue for now. But if there's real evidence of something more sinister about that girl's murder, I'm calling in outside help."

He's frightened for his career, Ramsay thought cynically. Better to have Scotland Yard succeed, and take the credit for calling them in, than have his own officers fail and have to explain that upstairs. Still, he'd been given permission to proceed and that's all that mattered. If he cleared it up quickly, it would be good for the Chief, the Superintendent

45

and for Inspector Ramsay. There may even be a promotion in it for him. Chief Inspector Ramsay had a ring to it, something he'd long given up hoping for. Despite his success over the past years, and even if he was successful this time, he knew it was never going to happen.

"Thank you, sir. I'll keep you abreast of progress."

"See you do, Ramsay, see you do."

Inspector Ramsay made his way back to the incident room where DS Morrison was reviewing Ramsay's notes from yesterday.

"Any questions?" Ramsay asked.

"Why did he hide this body and not the first?" Morrison said.

"That bothers me too. All I can suggest is he left the male victim because he panicked. Also, in gang warfare you want it seen what you can do. Killing a girl though wins you no respect so he placed her out of sight."

"It was a risk. Taking the time to hide the body. A big man could have just dropped her over the hedge, I suppose, but an average man would need to carry the body through the gate and cross the grass to place her where he did," Morrison said. He'd given this some thought on his day off.

"He could support the body upright to the gate so it looked like he was helping someone injured or drunk," Ramsay said. "I looked at this carefully the other night. It is a risk, I agree, but once he'd killed her there was nothing else to be done if he wanted to get the body out of sight."

"It seems mad to me."

"Two stabbings in fifteen minutes doesn't sound rational either so it's possible we may have someone unbalanced on our hands," Ramsay said.

"Maybe we should check the local loony bins haven't released anyone recently."

"Add that to uniform's list," Ramsay said, nodding. "I'm not saying it's likely, but we should check anyway."

"What did the Chief say?" Morrison asked. He wasn't sure he wanted to hear the answer, but it was better to know.

"He says we have the case for now," Ramsay said.

"I'm glad. We'll have it closed before someone from London has stepped off the train."

"I hope so," Ramsay said. "It's just a case of getting one of the kids to talk. Have we all the forensic in?"

"Yes. The postmortem results just came in. They're on your desk."

Ramsay read each report and handed each on to Morrison as he finished with it. When they'd both read them, he asked, "Any thoughts?"

Morrison shook his head. "There's nothing here we didn't know. It was bad luck that thunder shower happening when it did, washing the bodies and surroundings pretty well clean."

"At least we know for sure the girl was placed there before the downpour."

"True, but it would have been too much of a coincidence for two separate murderers to leave two separate bodies within a hundred yards of each other on the same night so I'm not sure it helps us much."

"It's just another chip off my theory of two separate murders," Ramsay said. "It makes the one murderer and the 'girl in the wrong place at the wrong time' line of enquiry even more likely."

"You want to drop the separation between the teams?"

Ramsay shook his head. "Not yet," he said. "Anything else?"

"She wasn't dropped over the hedge. There's no post-mortem bruising to suggest anything like that."

Ramsay nodded. "Which leads me to thinking she really

had recognized the man and he had some feelings toward her. He took care she wasn't left on the road, anyway."

"So, maybe the murderer lives on her side of town, went to the same school, same pubs, dances, or works in the same place?"

Ramsay nodded. "Get the team following up on background checks of these hooligans and the girl. What about the other victim?"

"His fists show signs of bruising, so he landed some blows but there's nothing to say on who." Morrison said. "Plenty of them have bruises."

"This one is a straightforward enough case," Ramsay said. "Except for the stabbing, it could have been an after-hours fight any weekend in any town up and down the country."

"And the second one will turn out to be the same. When we find the culprit," Morrison said.

"I fear you're right, Sergeant," Ramsay said. "But I'm still hoping for something more. I'd like us to have something to show what we can do."

"I'm with you there, sir. I could do with the extra pay a promotion would bring."

Ramsay smiled. Morrison now had two small children and, daringly for someone of his level, a newly bought house so he imagined it would be a welcome step up.

"Then, Sergeant, we should stop daydreaming and get back to work."

11

PAULINE

HAVING MISSED Hindmarsh as the workers filed into the factory and offices at the start of the day and the new week, Pauline went looking for him at lunch. Many people brought sandwiches and on fine days like today many took their lunch on the riverside embankments. It got them out into the sun, when there was any.

The River Tyne at this point is tidal and smelled of the sea when the tide was high, which was a lot better than the smell when the tide was low. Farther inland, the Tyne was a place where anglers cast a fly over deep pools but here, near the estuary it was dark, polluted and practically uninhabitable for fish. Both sides of the river were lined with factories, coal-fired power stations, shipyards and the remains of former buildings of the old industrial city. Houses and roads, too, sloped down to the river and the runoff from streets, sewers, and yards all ended up there.

Still the local people were used to it. 'Where there's muck, there's brass' as the saying went and they didn't mind it as much as Pauline did; she'd grown up in the country with clean fresh air from the moors. And to be fair, even to Pauline the view down the Tyne toward the sea was worth the smell. Newcastle's bridges stood proudly astride the river, particularly the Tyne Bridge, with its distinctive coat hanger shape. And beyond them, the shipyard cranes towered above houses, factories and even the biggest ships being built in the yards. It was a sight to fill anyone, not just local people, with pride.

She saw Hindmarsh at once, leaning against a pole talking with a group of factory floor workers. She didn't recognize any of them but then it was hard to distinguish the factory people for they all wore the blue coveralls, which they called boiler suits. They were young, final year apprentices probably, and consequently loud and pushy. His back was to her and it took a moment to catch his attention, he was so engrossed in the conversation.

"Bob," Pauline said, louder. He looked around, saw her and moved away from his colleagues.

"Pauline," he said. "Long time, no see."

"Have the police talked to you?"

"What about?" he sounded genuinely puzzled.

"About Marjorie. You do know she's dead, don't you?"

"Yes, but what has that to do with me?"

Pauline flushed. "They talked to me," she said, "and asked about Marjorie's boyfriends. I told her what I knew. That her present boyfriend is called Eric. They asked about past boyfriends and I gave them your name."

"Why?" His expression was a mixture of shock and anger.

"What else could I say? It's the truth. And why should you be concerned? It's months now. You can't be suspected."

"They'll want to pin it on someone!" He was almost shouting now.

"Hush," Pauline said. "Do you want everyone to know what we're talking about?"

"I can't believe you ratted me out to the police. What have I done to you to deserve that?"

"I did nothing of the sort," Pauline said, growing angry herself. "I was asked a question. I answered it with information that doesn't incriminate you in any way. I don't understand why you're behaving this way."

He struggled to regain his composure. "They're going to think I killed her because she dumped me. Don't you see?"

"If you behave like this when they do interview you, that's exactly what they'll think. My coming to tell you gives you time to compose yourself and explain your movements last Thursday night in a calm and rational way. I'm sorry you can't see that."

"It was you who separated us. You told her she was too good for me. You poisoned her against me. We'd still be together if it wasn't for you."

As this was the reason he'd been so angry with her before, none of this outburst was a surprise to Pauline. And there was truth in it, she had to admit. She didn't think he was good enough for her friend and she had taken every opportunity to open Marjorie's eyes to his weaknesses.

"Marjorie knew her own mind," Pauline said. "I may not have been your friend but I could never have separated you if she hadn't also seen your faults."

"Rubbish. She looked up to you. She thought you were clever. Your words destroyed us. I hope you're satisfied because she would be alive if it wasn't for you."

The truth of his words pierced her as surely as the knife had pierced Marjorie and she turned away before he could see the tears welling up in her eyes. She walked quickly, afraid if they talked any longer the rage in him would spill out and he'd attack her. He was always hot-tempered and today was no exception. If the police questioned him, they'd find him easy to manipulate into an unwise statement.

Walking back to her office, she realized something about what she'd seen just now bothered her but what it was she couldn't quite say. It was true, office and factory floor weren't often seen together, but it was much less true for men. Many of the men in the technical offices, as Hindmarsh was, had come through the apprentice ranks. And, of course, the men he was talking to could be brothers or cousins; she knew nothing about him except he went out with Marjorie for almost a year. Maybe they were familiar because she'd seen them around, which was likely, even if she didn't recognize many of the factory workers by name. She'd seen them enter and leave the factory every day for over a year now. Perhaps, that was the answer, they were men she'd seen around but couldn't put a name to. She put it out of her mind. Bob Hindmarsh's whole demeanor, his barely suppressed rage, was enough to worry about.

Back at her desk, she sat breathing deeply. It had been an ugly incident and one she'd experienced before when he was still trying to get her to petition Marjorie on his behalf, which is why she'd never done so. She'd told Inspector Ramsay that Bob Hindmarsh wouldn't have hurt Marjorie. In truth, she hadn't believed it when she said it and she believed it even less now.

Slowly, her breathing returned to normal and her pulse too. She hadn't achieved what she'd set out to do, which was decide one way or the other if she'd tell the police she'd misled them when she said Hindmarsh wouldn't hurt Marjorie. However, she had in her own mind made a convincing case he could have killed Marjorie. Was it enough to make the police take it seriously? She thought not. She would need more, much more.

A horrific thought came into her mind; she'd now made a bad enemy of the man just by giving his name innocently to the police and her own life may be in danger because of it. She felt he really was that unstable. There was no going back; she had to tell the police. But, again, she had to have more to make them see what she felt.

12

RAMSAY

"MRS. HINDMARSH?" DS Morrison asked, when the door of the terraced house opened.

"Yes," the woman answered, looking from Morrison to Ramsay and back. "What do you want?"

"We're police officers, I'm DS Morrison and this is Inspector Ramsay. We'd like a few words with Bob Hindmarsh. Is he in?"

"He's not back from work yet. Why do you want to speak to him?"

"It's just routine, Mrs. Hindmarsh. We're speaking to everyone who knew Marjorie Armstrong."

"Hmm," Mrs. Hindmarsh muttered. "He'll be back soon. You'd better come in and wait."

They didn't have long to wait before they heard the door open and a male voice shout, "I'm home, Mam."

There was a muffled conversation in the small entranceway before a young man appeared through the door of the room. His appearance wasn't encouraging. He had black hair, moustache and beetling eyebrows set on a dark complexion and his expression was sullen. Saturnine,

Ramsay, thought. The two detectives rose to introduce themselves.

"What do you want?" Hindmarsh demanded.

"We're investigating the murders of Thomas Bertram and Marjorie Armstrong and we'd like any help you can give us. We believe you knew Marjorie very well at one time."

"Aye, what of it?"

"Can we sit and talk about her, who she knew, anything that you think might help us catch her killer, and of course, most likely Thomas Bertram's killer too?"

"Marjorie and I stopped seeing each other over three months ago. I don't see how anything I know can help you."

"But you would see her at work sometimes, surely?" Morrison said.

"Not to talk to. We fell out, you see."

"Why did you fall out?" Morrison asked.

"Her friend, Pauline Riddell, filled Marjorie's head with dreams of grandeur. She said I wasn't good enough. Marjorie could do better."

"I see, why did Miss Riddell think that?" Morrison probed.

"Because she's a stuck-up cow who thinks we're all savages up here," Hindmarsh said bitterly. "I was an apprentice pipefitter two years ago. I'm a draftsman now. In another five years, I'll be management, you'll see. Then her and Marjorie would be happy to have me, but they couldn't wait."

"You have ambition, Mr. Hindmarsh, and that's a good thing. Are you sure it doesn't push you too far?"

"Course I have ambition. Who would want to spend all their lives in this dead-end dump? I want to be somebody. I want to be where no one can squash me for their own amusement. Is that so terrible?"

"It's not," Morrison said, "unless it leads you to do something rash."

"Well, it doesn't. I stand up for myself when I have to, same as anyone else. I didn't murder anyone, though I would happily murder Miss bloody Riddell. She's the one who got Marjorie killed."

"Is that a threat?" Ramsay asked.

"Of course, it bloody isn't," Hindmarsh said. "It's the way anyone who's angry says what they feel about someone who's stabbed them in the back."

"An unfortunate choice of words, Mr. Hindmarsh," Morrison said.

"Don't be clever. You know what I mean by it."

"Very well," Ramsay said, "we'll change the subject. Maybe you know who her latest boyfriend is."

Hindmarsh shook his head. "No, I don't."

"Where were you on Thursday night, Mr. Hindmarsh," Morrison said.

"Oh, aye," Hindmarsh said, "I knew that's what you'd think. I knew this would be trouble."

"Well, not if you can give an account of your movements that night and have someone who can confirm them."

"I was at the Mucky Duck," he paused, "the Black Swan, down the bottom of the street. Stayed there till closing and came home. Went to bed and stayed there till I got up for work next morning."

"And your mother will confirm that?"

Hindmarsh shifted uncomfortably. "She were out when I came home."

"At ten thirty?"

"She sits with old missus across the way most nights. She's out most nights till all hours."

"I see," Ramsay said. "And there's nothing you can think of that might help? Nothing Marjorie talked of when you were together?"

"Nothing. There's nothing I know that could help."

"Thank you for talking to us, Mr. Hindmarsh," Ramsay said. "I hope you'll understand when we ask you mother if she can account for your movements last Thursday."

"I told you," Hindmarsh snapped. "She weren't home."

"But she would have seen you go out, wouldn't she?"

Hindmarsh agreed she would. They left him sitting, staring sullenly after them.

Mrs. Hindmarsh was outside gathering washing from the line when they asked her if she could remember what her son was doing on Thursday evening.

"He went to the pub about eight and he were in bed when I got home," she said.

"And what time would that be?"

"About one in the morning."

"You were out late?"

"I sit with Mrs. Elliott over there," she pointed to the house opposite.

"Wouldn't you see your son coming home through the window?" Morrison said.

"We sit in the kitchen, where it's warmer, and that looks out the other way."

"Mrs. Elliott doesn't sleep much, does she?" Morrison said.

"Likely you won't either when you get to be her age, young fellow," Mrs. Hindmarsh said sharply. "She were very good to us when our bairns were small. I repay that by listening to her talk about the old days now our husbands are gone."

Suitably chastened, Morrison and Ramsay said goodbye and left.

13

PAULINE

AFTER HER UNSETTLING meeting with Hindmarsh the day before, the pretext that the Engineering Director wanted to know the background to one of his staff gave Pauline the perfect opportunity to visit the Personnel Department and view Bob Hindmarsh's file. As an executive secretary, she was considered safe enough by the ladies in the personnel office to search the cabinets on her own, once the appropriate cabinets were pointed out. Pauline would have felt more gratified at this privilege had she not seen that it was just an excuse for the staff to continue a particularly engrossing conversation they'd been having when she walked in the door.

Whatever the reasons, they were perfect for her purposes. She found the file the director was supposed to want and then quickly found Personnel's file on Bob Hindmarsh. Looking up, as casually as she could though her insides felt queasy, Pauline saw the staff were still in earnest discussion and ignoring her completely. She skipped though the file, making quick notes in her shorthand notepad as she read. It wasn't illuminating other than to show he had come through the apprentice ranks before becoming a trainee draftsman. He had a number of notes on file for lateness and one for insubordination when he was a first-year apprentice. It wasn't the file of a murderer but it did show he didn't like following rules or being told what to do by others, which was enough to confirm her fears. He wouldn't like Marjorie breaking up with him or knowing that Pauline had influenced that event. She replaced Hindmarsh's file, signed for the file she was supposed to be taking back to the Director, thanked the women, who barely noticed, and left.

Back at her desk, she found she was trembling with the excitement of her small act of misbehavior. If this continued she'd become a criminal herself, she thought wryly, because she was enjoying all this a bit too much. Her next effort was less thrilling but more productive. She called the Drafting Department Director's secretary, an older woman who'd taken Pauline under her wing and helped her in the early days when she'd first been promoted out of the typing pool.

She explained her dilemma. She didn't want to get Mr. Hindmarsh into trouble with the police but...

The woman didn't let her finish. "Tell them," she said. "He's got a temper, that one. I can tell you." And she did. Clearly, there was no love lost between her and Hindmarsh.

After the tale had been told, Pauline thanked the woman and hung up the phone. It was like her own dealings with the man, he was surly and easily riled but there was no real suggestion of serious physical violence. He was beyond the normal young man struggling with himself and his dealings with others, but not so far beyond he'd ever seriously hurt anyone, so far as anyone knew.

Unfortunately, the people who *would* know, the police, were the people she couldn't ask. She was about to let the matter drop when she remembered she had a contact who might help. Stephen's cousin, Poppy, who was a young reporter at the Morpeth Herald. Not Newcastle, but she would

know where to look in the press records to find any unpleasantness in Hindmarsh's past. Only she couldn't call from
work, which meant she had to contain her impatience until
four o'clock.

Poppy wasn't in the newspaper's office when she got
through to them and she had to leave a message. Pauline
wasn't happy with that. A note dropped on a desk in a busy
office was sure to be missed or mislaid. She wished she knew
where Poppy lived so she could visit. Pauline took the bus
home more depressed than ever. Everything about these days
showed her how foolish it was to even dream of helping the
police discover who killed Marjorie, a foolish idea that kept
creeping into her mind. Her wish for adventure and excitement was encouraging thoughts of becoming a private investigator, like in books or movies.

Her evening meal, however, was eaten in solitary, silent
contemplation of how little the ordinary person could do in
solving crimes, which led to her thinking she should just let
the police do their job. Scotch egg and a salad of lettuce and
tomato were perfect for summer, she thought, but they don't
lift the spirits the way a hot meal does. She was clearing the
dishes when there was a knock on the door.

She opened it.

"Hello, Pauline," Poppy said, "remember me?"

Stunned, Pauline could only stammer, "Of course, I do,
but I've only just left the message."

"What message?"

"Aren't you here because you got my message?"

"No. I'm here because you're named in today's Chronicle as a witness in these murders. They may not have interviewed you yet and, if I interview you first, I have a
scoop."

Pauline shook her head to clear it. "I don't know what
you're talking about," she said, "but come in while I get my

shoes on. We're going out to enjoy this sunshine while it lasts."

While Pauline slipped on her shoes and pulled a cardigan over her blouse, sunny it may be but this was still evening in northern England, Poppy explained her visit further. They left the flat and headed toward the nearby park, Poppy still talking.

When she paused for breath, Pauline said, "How did you know where I lived?"

Poppy said, "You can't have forgotten? Stephen gave us each other's addresses when he went overseas. He wanted us to support each other while he was away. Just like him, don't you think, to imagine we couldn't manage without him." She grinned and tucked her hand under Pauline's arm.

"I remember now," Pauline said. She'd put Poppy's address out of sight. She knew why Stephen had given it to her and she refused to even think of such a possibility. It was superstitious of her but she honestly felt if she didn't see Poppy's address, Stephen would come home safely.

"There's a bench over there," Poppy said, tugging Pauline to hurry her along. They reached it just before a family claimed it. "We need to talk without being overheard."

"I don't know anything that can't be overheard," Pauline protested but sat down beside Poppy as she was bid.

She looked at Poppy in amusement, partly because of the conspiratorial air she was exuding and partly because she remembered when Stephen had told her about his cousin Poppy. A great girl, he'd said, and Pauline had imagined a colorful, beautiful girl. One that would warrant the name of Poppy. Her surprise on being introduced to a determined, pushy, ordinary brown-haired girl was immense. To be honest, she and Poppy could be sisters, was her thought and one Stephen had echoed, 'two P's in a pod', he'd joked. On enquiry, she learned Poppy had been born on November 11,

Armistice Day, known locally as Poppy Day and so she'd been named.

"So, spill the dirt," Poppy said, opening a notepad and extracting a pencil from her jacket pocket.

Pauline smiled again. Poppy was dressed like a reporter, a male reporter, in old baggy trousers, a shirt of nondescript color, and a worn tweed jacket. Her short hair, not well cut, added to the overall effect. The faint stirrings of jealousy she'd experienced when Stephen had spoken of his talented cousin Poppy seemed even more ludicrous now than they had before. She'd imagined a beautiful, worldly socialite who was a genius and found Poppy was just a tomboy who could write. It was like *The Wizard of Oz* but in real life.

"About what?" Pauline asked.

"How did you come to know the deceased?"

"We were at college together and then got jobs together in the same company," Pauline said.

"You were bosom buddies though, right?"

"I'm not sure what you mean by that. We went to dances together at first. Then Marjorie met Bob and I met Stephen. After that, we saw much less of each other. Even at work."

"But you were instrumental in discovering her murder, weren't you?"

Pauline shook her head. "Let me tell you what I know," she said. "Then ask questions. There's not much to tell."

She explained her part in the affair and Poppy took notes.

When she was finished, Poppy said, "So who grassed you up?"

"What?"

"Somebody gave your name to the Chronicle. It wasn't you and my guess is they're still trying to find where you live. Somebody gave them your name but not your address. Who was it?"

Pauline thought. Marjorie's parents, perhaps? Hindmarsh?

Could they have got to him yesterday afternoon when he was still angry with her and this was his revenge? It seemed unlikely. The police? Even more unlikely.

"I think it was probably Marjorie's parents. They knew my name but not where I live," Pauline said, at last.

"Probably. Now what I'm looking for is the 'Marjorie I knew' angle from the grieving bosom buddy, so keep going. What about her boyfriend, Bob, was it?"

"She broke up with Bob in the spring," Pauline said. "That's what I was calling you about."

"This is more like it. What did you want to tell me?"

"I didn't want to tell you anything. I wanted you to find out from the press archives if Bob Hindmarsh had a history of violence."

"You think he's the real murderer, not one of the gang members?"

"No, not really, but maybe, yes."

"It's just a feeling?"

Pauline squirmed. Put like that it was pathetic. "It's like the police say in the movies. I want to eliminate him from my enquiries, only I don't have any enquiries." She explained her difficulty with the man and his anger.

"Sounds guilty to me," Poppy said.

"You mustn't say that, Poppy. That's how justice goes wrong."

"I'm only kidding," Poppy said. "Give me his full name and anything else that will help. I'll see what I can do. In return, I want your grieving girlfriend story now, and everything you learn when you're making these enquiries of yours."

"I'm not making enquiries; it was just a phrase to illustrate how I felt."

"All right, leave it with me. Now let's get back to this

interview. I need to phone this in before nine tonight to catch the morning edition."

Pauline gave Poppy the details she'd picked up in Hindmarsh's employee records and her fears concerning him. She told Poppy everything she could remember Marjorie saying about Eric while Poppy scribbled furiously in her notepad.

When Pauline was finished, Poppy practically leapt to her feet. "I've got to get this phoned in," she said. "Tomorrow, I'll look into your preferred murderer."

Pauline began to protest. Poppy grinned, "I'm kidding, relax. Talk to you soon," she said and quickly walked away.

Pauline let the late evening sunshine soothe her while she pondered the implications. Earlier, she'd thought she could have no success investigating crimes. Now, however, she had a useful ally, one who could get the background. Maybe she could solve crimes, or at least help the police while they did. The sun became hidden for a moment and the warmth was gone. A soft breeze was blowing, and without the sun, it raised goosebumps on her bare arms. She put her cardigan back on and began walking home the long way, determined to get the most out of another fine day. There were few enough of them here in the north.

14

RAMSAY

"SIR," Morrison said, walking into the incident room with a newspaper, "you may want to see this." He handed his boss the Wednesday edition of the Morpeth Herald, opened at a half page article.

Ramsay read it and cursed. "What's that silly girl playing at?" he said. "If Hindmarsh is the killer, and he sees this, she's put her own life in danger."

Morrison nodded. "I thought you'd be interested," he said. He wanted to say 'pleased' but Ramsay wasn't good at irony or nuance.

Ramsay shook his head. "The only good news is the Herald isn't sold much in Newcastle newsagents," he said. "I think it's too late to warn her, the damage is probably done but I'll try to stop her making things worse for herself."

"Will you go around there this evening?"

"No. If she hasn't been pounced on by local reporters already, she will be the moment she leaves work. Get uniformed to phone her work and put her through to my office."

Morrison left the room, grinning. The boss was a sucker for kids, whatever their age.

The phone rang and Ramsay picked it up. "Yes," he said, curtly. He needed to set the tone of this right from the start.

"You called me, Inspector?" Pauline said.

"Have you seen today's Morpeth Herald?"

"No, why?"

"You gave an interview to one of their reporters. An interview that could get you killed if you're right about your friend's murder being by someone you suspect, and who has yet to be caught. Did that not occur to you?"

Bewildered, Pauline said, "I don't understand. What does the article say?"

"It's what it doesn't say, what it hints at, what it implies, what it suggests, you need to worry about. Not to mention suggesting the police have got it all wrong and you have it right."

"Inspector," Pauline replied, "the article has obviously angered you. I'm sorry for that. I understood it was going to be a 'the girl caught up in a tragedy' article. From your response, I'm guessing it isn't?"

"Read it and see. And don't give any more interviews. Why did you anyway?"

Pauline considered how much to tell him. She decided not to hide knowing Poppy. "My name was in the Chronicle's story and Poppy, who is a cousin of my fiancé, saw it, recognized the name and came to see me last night. She said it was just a different angle. It wasn't about the murder, just a person caught up in it."

Ramsay shook his head. How naïve can people be, he thought. "Even if your friend had wanted to write such an article, her editor would never have gone with it. They have to sell papers, Miss Riddell, and that means controversy if they can't have smut."

"I see," Pauline said. "Do you really think I'm in danger?"

"Read the article and then ask yourself what you would do if you were a murderer who didn't want to hang."

Pauline wanted to reply, *I wouldn't have to do anything if you were doing your job*, instead she answered calmly, "You think I've been naïve, Inspector."

"Yes. Naivety is charming in children but it can be fatal in adults, Miss Riddell. I fear this may be one such occasion."

"I'll buy the Herald on my way home," Pauline said. Her stomach felt like it had jumped from a plane without a parachute.

"Do! And read it! And don't talk to any more reporters!" This last sentence was almost shouted.

"I'm sure your advice is good, Inspector, and I'll do my best to follow it. Now I'm sorry, I must get back to work," Pauline said, and hung up the phone.

Ramsay replaced the handset on its cradle. He hoped he'd made an impression. She wouldn't like his shouting at her, but he had to stop her placing herself in the sights of a murderer. Like Miss Riddell, he didn't believe Marjorie's death was a response to a panic attack by a scared young thug. He was sure there was a cool rational mind out there who thought he was safe.

15

PAULINE

PAULINE READ the article that evening in her flat. She hadn't dared read it on the bus because she was sure everyone was already looking at her suspiciously. It was as bad as Ramsay had said. Poppy had thrown her into the center of a murder inquiry, and worse, had intimated she was investigating in her own right because the police were incompetent. Her mind flew back to the previous evening and Poppy almost running away from her. Not even a backward glance to suggest they were more than reporter and source. It hadn't bothered her much at the time, she put it down to a reporter's desire to meet a deadline, but its full implication now settled in. They weren't friends, they were human shark and victim.

She'd been resentful of Ramsay's tone after their talk, too much of father and errant daughter in the exchange for her liking, but now she found she was grateful for his indisputable concern. She was still angry at her 'friend's' betrayal. And she'd thought Poppy would be an ally!

It took most of the evening for her feelings to return to a state where she could continue planning her next steps. By bedtime, she was calm and able to plan. She doubted Poppy would deliver on her promise to research Hindmarsh, and if she did, it would appear in an article linking her name as the source. Ramsay was right. She'd placed herself in grave danger. Even if Hindmarsh wasn't a murderer, he could quite rightfully feel that she'd pilloried him and in return he would be within his rights to give her a beating – that was how things were done in the city. In truth, she couldn't altogether blame him. If the situations were reversed, she'd have felt the same way. What a mess. No wonder the police were always telling us to leave them to do their job.

And if that was what Hindmarsh would think about her, how did she feel about Poppy? She couldn't believe someone she knew, almost a relative, would knowingly take advantage of her. Yet, Poppy must have been party to the article going out. Pauline couldn't help imagining Poppy and her editor laughing themselves silly at the gullibility of such a simpleton as herself. That did make her angry and it was fortunate Poppy wasn't in the room to answer for her treachery.

Pauline drew a deep breath. There was no good in pointing her anger at anyone but herself. It was a lesson for the future. Not just to be wary of 'friends' who appear out of nowhere when they have something to gain, but also never to involve the press in anything she was doing.

Having firmly made that decision, Pauline immediately began wondering if, and when, Poppy might have an answer about Hindmarsh's criminal record. Recognizing the contradiction, she decided that what she'd meant by 'never involving the press' was she would never give them information again but would happily accept it from them. They had used her. Now she would return the favor. She already felt she was becoming a wiser, more astute, woman.

16

RAMSAY

INSPECTOR RAMSAY LOOKED up as DS Morrison burst into his office. He was obviously too excited to knock.

"Yes, Sergeant," Ramsay said, in a tone that settled Morrison down quickly.

"Sorry, sir. I have some good news."

"Aye, well, out with it now you're here."

"Remember my informant, Temperley? The one you don't like?"

Ramsay nodded.

"He says the word is out. A kid called Derek Cranston is the one we're looking for."

"That's the word on the street?"

"Yes, sir."

"Sounds to me like someone's fitting him up," Ramsay said, "but we'd better look into it. Have uniform bring him in."

Morrison left the office as quickly as he'd entered it. Ramsay could hear him ordering the desk sergeant to get the word out from all the way down the hall.

Despite Ramsay's misgivings, Derek Cranston arrived at the station with a solicitor accompanying him, which suggested he may well be the culprit. Ramsay let them stew in an interview room while he finished preparing his questions.

"Sergeant," he called after an hour had passed with Cranston still waiting in the interview room.

"Sir?"

"We'll talk to Mr. Cranston now."

They entered the room to find the solicitor calmly working on some papers and Cranston pacing the floor. Ramsay introduced himself and Morrison to Cranston and greeted the solicitor. They were well known to each other. The man defended half the tearaways in Newcastle.

"My client wishes to make a statement, Inspector," the solicitor said. "As you would have discovered if you'd done us the courtesy of being here when we arrived."

"Have you written it out?" Ramsay asked innocently, seeing the hand-written page in the lawyer's hand.

"I have written the statement based on the information given to me by my client," the lawyer said. He handed it to Ramsay.

Ramsay read it and handed it to Morrison who read it in turn.

When Morrison was done, Ramsay said, "Your client admits to stabbing Edward Bland in a street fight on the night of July 20th. Is that correct?"

"In self-defense, yes."

"Would you like to tell us more about the background to the events, Mr. Cranston?"

"Everything my client needs to say is in his statement, Inspector."

"I'm sure you know that the court will need more than 'Ted Bland was out to get me'," Ramsay said. "It would help you, and me, if we explored this further. A young woman was murdered that night using a knife that was very similar to the one used to kill Bland and the implication is strong it was the same knife."

"I didn't have anything to do with that," Cranston cried.

"Where is the knife? Maybe the pathologist can eliminate your knife if he can compare the blade and the wound."

"I threw it in the river."

"That's a pity," Morrison said. "You must see that makes things worse for you, unless of course it was your knife that killed the girl."

"It wasn't. I dumped the knife after we ran. I was scared. I ran down toward home and threw the knife away before I went inside. I should never have bought it," he ended almost in a wail of despair.

Ramsay watched him coldly. He really did look like a scared kid. Unfortunately, the Tyne is a deep and muddy bottomed river and the likelihood of finding that knife was practically nil. "Then tell us the background, Mr. Cranston. It may help us understand why you were even carrying such a weapon at all."

Cranston looked at his solicitor who, after a pause, nodded.

It was a garbled tale as old as time. Cranston had asked out a girl, not knowing she'd been Bland's girl. Bland had let it be known he'd kill the kid. Cranston, a small, slender young office worker would have been no match for a dock-hand like Bland. Bland wouldn't have killed him, of course, just given him a good hiding, as the saying went, but Cranston was terrified. He bought the knife to deter Bland, nothing more.

He'd gone to the pub with his friends to hear the music and there was Bland, grinning at him and running his finger across his throat. Cranston had been scared. He'd stayed back after the show, but Bland had hung around outside with his friends. Bland confronted him. He ran. Bland ran after him.

The rival gangs followed behind, looking forward to some blood being spilled. Just the usual weekend scene in every big city everywhere. Cranston found he couldn't outrun Bland, so he'd pulled out the knife and turned to confront him.

Bland thought so little of him as an opponent, believing him to be too afraid to use the knife, that he'd closed with him at once. Bland's punch had sent Cranston staggering and he turned to see Bland coming at him again. He'd stuck out his arm, more to ward Bland off than threaten him, and Bland pressed right onto the blade of the knife. He collapsed immediately. Cranston stood frozen in shock. When he heard people shouting, and saw them running, he'd panicked and ran as well.

Ramsay believed him. He was a timid looking young man, not at all the sort to enjoy street fighting.

The interview continued for a time, then Ramsay explained what would happen next. He left Morrison to make the arrest and left the room. Morrison deserved the collar. After all, it was his informant who'd broken the case. The only drawback, so far as Ramsay could see, is Cranston would not admit to the second killing and in that too, Ramsay believed him.

17

PAULINE

PAULINE HUNG up the public phone and exited the phone box. Once again, (she'd tried morning and evening on the day before as well) she'd had to leave a message for Poppy, who was, once again, out of the office, even though it was 7:15 in the morning, when most people were just arriving at work. Pauline was furious and didn't believe a word of it. She understood why; Poppy wouldn't want to talk to her because she knew she'd put Pauline in a killer's sights. She considered waiting to try again but she had to get to work.

Once she was at work, the problem of connecting with Poppy was forgotten. She'd barely hung up her coat when her boss asked her to step into his office. His tone and expression were definitely not welcoming.

"I met the manager of Personnel as I came in this morning," Dr. Enderby began.

Pauline's heart sank. She'd felt guilty about snooping and had expected to be caught every moment since she'd done it. She knew what was coming.

"She asked me if I'd found what I wanted in the file I took out, or I should say, you took out in my name."

"I can explain," Pauline said quickly, before he could get into his stride.

"I hope so, Miss Riddell. Snooping in employee's personnel files is a serious breach of company rules, not to mention security."

"As I'm sure you know," Pauline said, "one of our employees, Marjorie Armstrong, was murdered." She waited until he'd acknowledged he did know, before continuing, "Marjorie used to walk out with a young draftsman who works here, Bob Hindmarsh. I couldn't help wondering if there was anything about him that the police should know. I know what I did was wrong, but it was a spur of the moment decision. I just had to know. She was my friend, you see."

"And why should you think he might have killed her?"

"He was very angry when she broke up with him. I've been struggling with myself as to whether I should tell the police or not – and I acted badly. I'm sorry. It won't happen again, I promise."

"The point is it happened at all, Miss Riddell," Enderby said. "If you have information the police should know, tell them. Not doing so calls your own motives into question, both in the criminal investigation and now at work. I believed you to be a trustworthy woman and now I'm not sure I do."

"Sir, I swear, it was a moment of madness in a tragedy that touches me deeply. The circumstances couldn't be repeated." She willed him with all her might to forgive her.

"My concern isn't just the breach of privacy around these two files, the one you took out on my behalf and the one you read for your own purposes. We have had a number of files and papers go missing and turn up in strange places. We work in a sensitive industry, Miss Riddell. You may not realize that, but others do. We have security officers from the Secret Services in the factory right now observing us all. Your behavior may come to their notice. What am I to tell them?"

"That I replaced the file I took out without reading it and what I did had nothing to do with industrial or national secrets. I assure you it didn't."

Enderby's expression didn't soften and Pauline was sure she would be fired, or worse, handed over to security for interrogation. She had known they were in the offices and in the plant. There'd been a memo from the Board to the department heads announcing the program and explaining the reasons behind it. But she'd been so focused on her own quest, she hadn't understood how her actions would look to those charged with defending the company's secrets.

"We'll say no more about it," Dr. Enderby said slowly, "and hope your behavior will not become general knowledge. But if there's ever a repeat, or anything like a repeat, you will leave the company without a reference. I promise you that."

Pauline's heart leapt. It was all she could do not to leap over his desk and kiss him.

"Thank you, sir. I won't let you down again."

"See you don't. Now get me the file for my morning meeting and let's get back to work.

All day, she sat at her desk with her insides in turmoil. She expected at any moment that Enderby would return and tell her she was out or Hindmarsh would storm into the office and lay into her. At the morning break, she bought two pastries – a fig roll and a dead fly pie – from the tea lady. One she ate at once and the other she kept for lunch time. She didn't dare leave her office in case Hindmarsh was waiting. At the end of the day, she waited until the day shift were long gone before cautiously heading out. Her first stop was the public phone box where she called Poppy again. Again, she was not in the office.

Sick with fear – she couldn't pretend otherwise – Pauline waited for the bus and, when it arrived and opened its doors, leapt on it as if the pavement was on fire. As she approached her flat, she carefully looked about her in case Hindmarsh was waiting. Seeing no one, she entered and locked the door quickly behind her. Tomorrow, she vowed, I'll buy a chain and bolts for both doors.

Preparing her evening meal was enough to begin soothing her nerves. It was still warm weather so a simple salad with a slice of bacon and egg pie was all that was needed. She put Marjorie's murder firmly out of her mind by focusing on work and what she needed to accomplish tomorrow. Then, when that failed to produce a satisfactory feeling, she thought about Stephen's last letter. She sat down at the small table and began her meal.

His letter had been a happy one, ecstatically so from someone of his level-headed disposition. A ceasefire had been declared and they were hoping for a swift conclusion to the fighting. If that happened, he and the army would be returning home very soon. He wanted their wedding to happen quickly. His recent experience had taught him that life was too uncertain to waste in waiting. However difficult it may be, they should start building their future together right away. She'd read his letter over and over and was still not tired of hearing this. She couldn't imagine a life without him in it.

Slowly, however, as she nibbled the slice of pie, she found her thoughts wandering back to the murder and on to other possible murderers. Her focus on Hindmarsh had blinded her to other possibilities. Who was Eric? She understood why he might not have come forward upon hearing the news of Marjorie's murder, but he still had to be considered as a possible suspect. If nothing else, he had a motive and he was the last person to see her alive. Were the police following up on this? Or had they dismissed him from their enquiries?

Were there others? Marjorie's parents, for example. They'd seemed devastated but maybe they were devout or old-fashioned people with strong views on family honor. It didn't seem likely, she had to admit, but it wasn't impossible.

Did the police really believe it was the person who'd killed the gang member? Again, it was the most obvious solution and also the most likely. After all, what were the chances of two knife murders happening at the same time and same place if not by the same person? This was a depressing thought and one that made her own behavior toward Hindmarsh practically criminal, but she had to go on searching for answers.

A rapping on her window made her look up. Poppy was there, waving a sheet of paper.

Pauline opened the door to let Poppy enter and was just about to launch into a tirade of abuse when Poppy spoke.

"You were right," she said. "he is violent. He's got a record."

At once, Pauline's focus switched. "Show me," she said.

Poppy handed her the paper and Pauline read it quickly. She looked at her friend, "It's some time ago and he was very young," she said.

"It's eight years and he was in a juvenile facility for six months," Poppy said. "That's pretty serious. And it was for an attack on a girl."

Pauline considered, staring at the newspaper clipping. "It's good enough for me," she said. "Now, if I could find out where he was that night, I might have something for the Inspector that will make him take notice."

"They'll have his record and where he was already," Poppy said. "If you tell them about his anger, his bullying you when he thought you could make Marjorie come back to him, then they'll have something like a motive. That's the bit they're missing, Pauline."

"Knowing this," Pauline said, "don't you think the article you wrote was dangerous for me?"

Poppy shrugged. "You have to understand, the more exciting the article, the closer to the front page. I didn't say anything that wasn't true. I didn't quote you as saying anything you didn't –"

Pauline interjected, "But you implied things. You insinuated I believed things. You made it sound like I was on the trail of this man when I was just unsure about his behavior."

"And that's what I said," Poppy answered.

"If he reads your article, or someone who knows him reads it, he'll come for me."

"Then tell Ramsay what you told me and do it quickly. He'll get you some protection."

Pauline's nightmare, where Poppy would be hired by a paper in Fleet Street in London on the strength of her reporting Pauline's murder, returned and her anger flared.

"You've put my life in danger. I wouldn't need police protection if you had behaved responsibly." She was pleased to see Poppy look guilty.

"Look, I'm a reporter," Poppy said. "I have to write what sells papers. I followed the rules of our professional ethics. Sorry, but that's how it is."

Pauline glared at her, unable to decide whether to throw her out or ask her for more help. Her earlier thoughts about how a regular citizen could investigate mysteries if they had the support of a press reporter came back to her.

"All right," she said. "The damage is done and can't be undone. Do you know any rich men in the area with the name of Eric? Can you research and make a list of them? Marjorie was meeting a man called Eric."

"I can try but his name might not be Eric. After all, he went to a lot of trouble to hide his private life from her. Eric may be a false name."

"Maybe, but we can't rule out the chance it is his name."

"I'll do it," Poppy said. "Hey, why don't we visit the

scene of the crime right now. I might see something others have missed. Reporters develop an eye and a nose, for things, you know."

Pauline nodded. Anything was better than sitting alone or walking in the park alone tonight. "Let me get a jacket and we'll go."

However, Poppy's reporter nose and eye provided no new thoughts at the scene, or later as they walked to the bus terminal. Pauline waited until Poppy boarded the bus home and then walked slowly home alone in deep gloom. She had to tell the Inspector what she'd not said, and it wouldn't be a comfortable interview.

18

RAMSAY

IT WAS late on Friday when Ramsay ordered the team to go home. People had families and, in truth, the investigation into the girl's murder was stopped. There was no new evidence. There had been people answering the police's request for information relating to the time and place of the killings but what they had to say wasn't hugely helpful. There had been cars on the street near the park where Marjorie's body had been found but the two people who came forward couldn't remember anything about any of them. Cars had passed through the area and maybe had stopped. There was nothing remarkable about them and no one remembered a number plate.

He wasn't surprised. While the kids at the skiffle group concert were too young to own cars, the fans of the folk singer at the Barley Mow were a different matter. The singer was well-known and had many fans who might have cars; they were university or college lecturers, militant pacifists of various political stripes, even police officers like DS Morrison, as he'd discovered. And if they had driven into town to see their hero, they'd have been driving away at around the time in question. Maybe the man Miss Riddell had mentioned, Eric, was one such person. Certainly, adulterers were all too likely to be of the same type of people, Ramsay thought sourly. His Calvinist upbringing tended to make him dislike people whose sexual behavior was out of the norm. He was well aware of it and did his best not to prejudge, but he still didn't like them.

"Sergeant," Ramsay said, as he saw Morrison heading out. "There's no chance the Barley Mow kept a list of who bought tickets, is there?"

Morrison shook his head. "It wasn't that kind of do, sir."

"It was a faint hope," Ramsay said. "Before you go, last thoughts on our suspects, Sergeant."

Morrison paused in the doorway, clearly irritated at being delayed. Ramsay knew he wanted to be home for the children.

"Well, sir," he said, knowing instinctively the boss was talking about the young woman's murder, "I'm not sure any of them are suspects. There's Hindmarsh who had a breakup with the girl three months ago. He had a weak motive but we've no evidence for means or opportunity. Then there's this Eric Miss Riddell told us of, but no one else has been able to offer additional information about him. He might have had a motive and means and opportunity. We've not been able to even prove his existence. That leaves Cranston, who had means and opportunity but a weak motive."

"You mean because there doesn't seem to be any link to him at all?"

"Exactly, sir. Our idea is that he recognized her and knew she would identify him so he panicked, killed her and hid the body but, so far as we can tell, it doesn't fit. He didn't know her, or not that we've discovered anyway, and he ran the other way from where she was found, though we've no witnesses to confirm that either."

Ramsay nodded. It was where his gloomy thoughts had

taken him; he'd hoped hearing someone else spell it out he might see something he'd missed.

"Thank you, Sergeant," he said. "Now get home and read those bairns of yours a bedtime story."

Ramsay gathered his jacket from the hook and followed the men out of the station. It was a beautiful night. The sun had set but the sky was still light, as it is in northern parts if there are no clouds. He set off walking home. It was too good a night for buses and he needed to think.

Turning a corner, he saw Miss Riddell and another young woman. They were walking the other way, deep in conversation, on the other side of the street. They didn't see him. There was nothing remarkable about the two women but, like so much in a policeman's life, small glimpses into the lives of others often came in useful and he felt this may too.

19

PAULINE

WORK THAT MORNING was tedious for Pauline. She now knew what Hindmarsh was capable of and she had to relay what she knew the police. She didn't know how Hindmarsh came to be where Marjorie was after the mysterious Eric dropped her off, but she was sure he was and the police needed to find out how. Somehow it had happened and that had given him the idea and the opportunity to do what he'd wanted to do for months. That's what she had to make them understand, but she didn't feel she had enough to make them believe her. Could she find something more?

She developed a plan. When work ended at midday, instead of going back to her flat and doing the laundry, she'd follow Hindmarsh and learn about him. Where he lived, who his friends were, what he did outside of work. Somewhere in all of this would be a clue. Something would connect and she'd know what happened. Then the police would have something to act on. Her plan was one part exciting and two parts terrifying. If he saw her, she'd have put herself in harm's way big time.

The factory whistle blew. A mournful sound at 7:30 am but a joyful one at quitting time. Saturday morning was, in some ways the hardest day of the week, though it was only four hours long. Pauline grabbed her jacket, strategically placed on the back of her chair, and raced for the door. She had to find Hindmarsh leaving and begin her surveillance. Her heart raced. Detecting was a lot more exciting than typing and filing.

From the window of the office block, she watched the men streaming from the drawing offices. Hindmarsh was one of the earliest to leave and she skipped quickly down the stairs to the ground floor to take up the pursuit. It took a few minutes before she found him again. From the upper floor window, she'd had a view. At ground level, he was just one of many men in dark jackets, gray trousers, and white shirt collars. She quickly threaded her way through the throng to the point where, as they left the Works gate, they dispersed. She could see her quarry making his way westward along the street.

She looked about. No one seemed to be watching her. They were too busy making their way to their homes or their Saturday afternoon sports. It was summer so Newcastle United weren't playing, and the city was too far north for serious cricket -- as a Yorkshire girl she knew that much. But there were still plenty of other things that men did to pass their non-working hours.

Hindmarsh appeared to be heading home. A lonely, disconsolate figure, she thought, before correcting that to 'has no friends and probably with good reason'. She kept a hundred yards behind him and as close to the walls of the buildings that lined the street as she could. If he turned, she hoped to be able to slip into a doorway and hide from sight.

Then came the breakthrough she'd hoped for. From the far western entrance to the factory, men in coveralls were also streaming out, heading for home. Hindmarsh stopped before he entered the line of men, waiting for someone. A brother perhaps?

Two young men left the main group and joined Hindmarsh. The two she'd seen him with that lunchtime on the embankment. Only now they weren't wearing coveralls but their regular clothes, she knew where she'd seen them before. They were among the group of young men fooling around at the bus stop the night Marjorie died. Her heart leapt. Now she saw another possibility. Hindmarsh had, in some way, made these two carry out his plan. It was like a movie or a book where the murderer has a great alibi for the murder because someone else has done it for them.

The three men set off, still heading westward, with Pauline following as closely as she dared. Up until a moment ago, she'd been afraid of one man who might murder her, and here she was following three. Or at least, a potential murderer and his accessories.

They reached a terraced house where Hindmarsh opened the door and went in followed by the others. Pauline glanced around, looking for a place she could observe from without raising suspicion. At the bottom of the street was a small grassy area where two mothers were watching their children play on swings.

Keeping her face away from Hindmarsh's house in case he was at a window, she walked quickly to the play area. With luck, she could watch from there without too much trouble.

She sat on a bench opposite where the two mothers were sitting and angled herself so she could look back up the street. The children and mothers stopped for a moment as she arrived and settled, before going on with their games and conversation. As the minutes passed, Pauline slowly became aware her presence was a concern. The two mothers whispered as they stared at her. Pauline did her best to ignore them, acting as though she didn't see, but the children picked up on the atmosphere and they two began to watch her intently.

"You're not from around here, are you?" one of the mothers said.

"No," Pauline said. "I'm just resting. I'll be gone in a minute." She didn't wish to raise any local interest in who she was or why she was there. In a small community, this would get back to Hindmarsh, she was sure.

Acting as casually as she could, Pauline stood, smiled, and said goodbye. She walked slowly back up the street, keeping as far away from Hindmarsh's house as she could.

Her luck held for, no sooner than she was at the furthest end of the street from the Hindmarsh house, the three young men came out. Hindmarsh had changed from his work clothes into more fashionable wear. They turned south, away from where Pauline was standing. She was undecided whether she should follow. To do so would take her past the two young mothers and they'd realize she was spying on Hindmarsh. Not following, though, would leave her as much in the dark about him and his two henchmen, for that's how she saw them now, as she was at the outset.

When the men had passed the park and the mothers, Pauline set out to continue trailing them. With luck, the mothers wouldn't link her and the men together. She passed the mothers and smiled in what she hoped would be taken as a friendly acknowledgement by an aimless rambler. Their expressions hardened and Pauline feared her thin ploy had failed but it was too late to worry about that. The pursuit must go on.

It ended only minutes later when the three men entered the Saloon Bar of The Black Swan public house. She couldn't follow them there. It wouldn't be safe or seemly. The pub had a ladies' entrance so she slipped in, hoping the men's side would be, if not visible, then at least audible from this more refined side of the house. It was, of course, a vain hope. No pub would want to have the ladies being offended by the men's talk. Another weakness in her fanciful daydream of becoming a private detective became clear. There were so many places women couldn't go without standing out; she'd need a male partner. She could enter and observe in the ladies' places, as she was doing now, but it was a disadvantage. Men were the active sex in almost everything, including wrongdoing, and consequently would form the majority of a private detective agency's business and she'd always be on the outside of their world. Her detecting would be limited to women's lives, for the most part. An agency – her daydreams had been growing grander with the re-imagining – was a foolish notion so that was an end of it.

She ordered and sipped a sherry sitting as close to the door as she could. The room was empty this early in the day, so she had her choice of seats. It was clear, however, even at the door, she was too far away to hear when Hindmarsh and his thugs left. She finished her drink and left, after carefully peeking around the door to see her presence wasn't being observed. The last thing she wanted was to be seen here, so far from her own neighborhood, and without any reason to be here. It might actually *be* the last thing she did, she thought with a sinking feeling in her stomach.

No one she knew was in the street. She stepped outside into the warm sunshine. Inside had felt cold and damp. Unwilling to risk the mothers again, she continued south toward the river. The area grew increasingly rundown, dirty and unkempt with many abandoned, boarded-up buildings. The end of the war had been devastating for so many businesses that had supported the armaments industry and hadn't been able to transition to a peacetime role. At the foot of the street, where it met Scotswood Road, running along the north bank of the Tyne, she stopped. From here, she could see the pub's entrances, but it didn't feel a safe place to wait. They could be in there for hours.

They weren't. It wasn't long before she saw them leave and head north. Now she had to pass those mothers again if she followed. Her luck changed. They turned right, down a small alley opposite the play area where the mothers were still sitting. Pauline walked briskly along Scotswood Road until she reached the parallel street and saw them crossing it and continuing along the alley. She walked on quickly and picked them up again at the next street. This time they entered what looked like a small shop. Gathering her courage, she began making her way carefully up the street. Fortunately, she was near an open gate when the three emerged back into the street. They were smoking. Clearly, it had been a visit to a Tobacconist. She grimaced. She'd wanted to learn more about these three but nothing she'd learned so far could be seen to help her cause at all. Three young men drank and smoked after work; that was what she'd learned. They headed north and she followed, glad she was out of sight of those too observant mothers.

Further hopes, however, were dashed. They stopped at a bus stop and before she could get there, they'd jumped on the bus and it left, heading into town. Even if she caught the next bus, she had no hope of finding them on a sunny Saturday afternoon in the region's biggest city. Everyone would be there. She caught the next bus and returned to her flat, disappointed but not despondent. At least, she felt, she now knew how Hindmarsh had murdered Marjorie: either he did or his friends did on his behalf. She'd go to the police station and lay out her thoughts to Inspector Ramsay. There was now no reason for her to withhold the information from him about Hindmarsh's reaction to his split with Marjorie.

20

RAMSAY

"MISS RIDDELL," Ramsay said when he arrived at the front desk where Pauline was waiting. "I'm told you have some information for me." A witness who comes into a police station on a Sunday morning, especially in summertime, was unusual, in his experience.

"I do, Inspector," Pauline said.

Ramsay gestured her to follow him to his office, where he pulled up a chair for her.

Pauline sat. When he'd taken his chair behind the desk, she said, "When we spoke the other day, I said Mr. Hindmarsh had taken the breakup with Marjorie quite well. And, at the time, I thought that was a fair thing to say because no one takes the end of a love affair well, do they?"

"I think it depends on who does the breaking up," Ramsay said.

"Quite so," Pauline said. "Well, that troubled me because he did try and pressure me to intercede with Marjorie on his behalf and became extremely unpleasant when I wouldn't do so. Again, I feel that alone doesn't necessarily mean anything bad. As I said, failed love affairs are painful things."

"And what has changed your mind?"

"I went to speak to him at work a few days ago and he was talking to two apprentices. That in itself is a little odd because usually office and shop floor workers don't mix. I thought maybe they were family. We have a lot of families where all the men work at the plant."

Ramsay nodded.

"I thought I recognized them but couldn't understand why at the time. Yesterday, I discovered why. I saw the apprentices meet Hindmarsh as he left the factory. They were in their everyday clothes and I knew at once where I'd seen them. They were waiting for the bus to go into town the evening Marjorie was killed."

"Was Mr. Hindmarsh with them on that occasion?"

Pauline shook her head.

"At what time was this?"

"It was after work, say half past four."

"Your friend was murdered around 11:00 pm and a long way from the factory gate, Miss Riddell."

"I know that," Pauline said, blushing hotly. "I'm not saying this proves anything, only that someone who behaved aggressively to me and who had a reason to be angry with Marjorie has friends who dress exactly like one of the gangs mentioned in the newspaper and who I saw getting on a bus into town that night." Now she came to explain it to someone else, it sounded weak.

"I understand, Miss Riddell," Ramsay said. "Is there anything else?"

"Yes. I've since learned that Hindmarsh was convicted of assaulting a girl some years ago. He assaulted me, though it wasn't the sort of assault that left bruises. He just grabbed my shoulders and shook me."

"When did this happen?"

"As I said when he and Marjorie broke up. He wanted my help to reconcile them, but I wouldn't, and he became angry."

"Did you report this to anyone?"

Pauline shook her head. "I thought it wasn't important then, just his frustration and unhappiness. I suppose I thought it a sign of his passion and therefore understandable, admirable even. Now, I see it as a sign of what he might do if the opportunity arose."

Inspector Ramsay was silent for a moment as he weighed the information. His steady stare made Pauline uncomfortably aware he was assessing her earlier withholding of this and wondering why she was now sharing it. Finally, he said, "Thank you for bringing this to us, Miss Riddell. Is there anything you'd like to add?"

"No," Pauline said. His calm manner was more unnerving than if he'd shouted at her. Now, she just wanted to leave.

"Well, thank you for coming in. It will certainly be something we look into as the investigation continues."

He escorted her out and watched her as she stood motionless in the street, as if unsure what to do. He hoped it was because she had other information she was deciding to divulge. He was disappointed when she strode off without looking around.

Miss Riddell had brought new information, that was true, but what to make of it was unclear. Since meeting Hindmarsh, he'd never had any doubt how the man would behave after a breakup he hadn't created. Nor did he doubt he was a blustering type who would push a young woman to do his bidding if he could. That he had friends who enjoyed the new kinds of music and fashion beginning to appear was also not unreasonable, nor that some of those friends may have been at the Red Lion that night. But were they? And even if they were, what were the chances of them happening on their friend's ex-girlfriend and killing her? It was information and he needed all that he could get but it wasn't a very strong lead. Still, it would have to be checked.

21

PAULINE

ONCE OUTSIDE, Pauline's blush grew even deeper as she debated where to go. He thinks I'm a neurotic lunatic, she thought angrily as she left the police station. She needed a moment to think. She'd expected more from the Inspector and now the afternoon stretched out in front of her without a plan. She'd been to church and even her steady character couldn't face going twice in one day. Without looking back, she strode purposefully down the street.

She approached the park, where a line of children were waiting to buy ice cream. As none of the adult businesses other than public houses were open and she needed some reward for the horrible experience she'd just endured, she joined the back of the line.

By the time it was her turn, she felt calmer. The sun, happy crowds lounging and sunbathing on the grass, and merry children all combined to restore her spirits. It was demoralizing that Ramsay hadn't found her evidence compelling, but she knew she was right. She would continue until she had the evidence that would change his mind. She had to because the police wouldn't find it; of that she was sure. They thought they had their man and that was the end of the case in their minds. And maybe that was enough. Could it be enough for her? Could she stop now when she'd set Poppy off researching? She thought not; the game had to be seen out to the end, whatever that may be.

She needed a photo of Hindmarsh. With that, she could ask the staff at the pub where the trouble began, if he'd been there. It was a slim chance, but somebody might remember him. She didn't have a camera, which was a drawback. Poppy would have one, she was a reporter after all. Pauline sorted through her purse for pennies and went to the nearest phone box. There was no answer at the Herald's offices. So much for the press and their vaunted never sleeping bravado, she thought. She'd have to call on her way to work in the morning.

As the afternoon wore on, and a suntan failed to make any appearance despite her best efforts, the smell of fish and chips began to overcome that of exhaust fumes and coal smoke. Just the thought of another cold ham and salad evening meal was enough; she'd pick up fish and chips on the way back to the flat. She rarely ate them, too greasy was her usual complaint, but she couldn't deny one of the best things of being so close to a fishing port was the taste of fresh fish.

22

RAMSAY

INSPECTOR RAMSAY FINISHED UPDATING DS Morrison on Miss Riddell's new statement and waited while Morrison read the notes.

"What do you think?" Ramsay said.

"I think Miss Riddell really doesn't like Hindmarsh, does she?"

Ramsay smiled. "She doesn't. Does any of it ring true to you?"

Morrison shrugged. "That Hindmarsh's friends could have been at the pub that night and involved in the fighting afterwards, yes. That they would murder Miss Armstrong on his behalf over a failed love affair? No. That Hindmarsh could have been there as well, not likely. We checked that and his alibi is weak. But that's the thing, if he'd been there and really the killer, his alibi would have been perfect."

Ramsay nodded. "I tend to agree with you, Sergeant. However, we have to look into it. We can't dismiss it."

Morrison nodded. "You don't think she could have done it?"

"I've been considering this since yesterday," Ramsay said. "She certainly wants us to look at Hindmarsh and nowhere else. And she's the only one to even mention this Eric person. Marjorie's parents thought Marjorie was going about and staying with her friend, Miss Riddell. Maybe that's exactly what Miss Armstrong did and there was a falling out. Miss Riddell might well be trying to direct us away from herself."

"And she was the last to see her alive, that we know of."

Ramsay nodded. "The thing is though, while she could have stabbed her friend for reasons we don't yet know, she couldn't have carried her body and placed it where it was found. I'm sure of that. She's simply not strong enough. And how did she do it when another killing was happening at that same place and time?"

"Could she have guided the victim to the place where she was killed? If they were lovers, for example, and Miss Armstrong had said she was breaking off their affair?"

"It's possible. I saw Miss Riddell with another young woman just the other night. Was it a love triangle or a change of lovers, maybe? Unfortunately, there were no footprints at the murder scene because of the dry earth. Even if there had been, the later downpour washed everything clean. But there's still the stabbing itself. The pathologist said 'expertly done' and as far as we know Miss Riddell has no military training."

"A lucky strike could be interpreted as skillful," Morrison said.

"Again, it's possible. Have uniform look into these two tearaways and their relationship with Hindmarsh. And have our team start looking more closely into Hindmarsh's background. But I want you, and only you, to look into Miss Riddell's background. Let's keep our suspicions between us for now."

Morrison nodded and left the office to set the official wheels in motion.

For Ramsay, Morrison's immediate spotting of Miss Riddell's behavior as opening up a completely new line of enquiry was re-assuring. He'd also seen it but wondered if he was being unfair. She had freely volunteered the information, which was admirable, but it was very pointed. Since his sighting of her with another young woman, whose face was vaguely familiar, he also suspected she was doing some investigating – or was it misdirection? – of her own. Maybe the other young woman was the reporter from the Herald? The one who'd done the story on Miss Riddell. Maybe it wasn't a foolish story. Maybe it was an attempt to bring the murderer out into the open? Or maybe all this was a clever attempt to make her look like a victim rather than the murderer. Whatever it was, it was confusing and worth following up.

He sighed. He hoped she was just an innocent because he liked the girl. He thought she was too earnest, too eager to help, too concerned for her dead friend and the grieving parents, and these weren't bad qualities. Could it be he was completely wrong, and she was actually a clever, conniving, manipulating young murderess? He shook his head. Sometimes, instinct plays you wrong, he knew, but not as wrong as all this. Still, he kept coming back to it, it had to be checked.

23

PAULINE

AFTER A LUNCH of ham and pease pudding on a stotty bun with too much tea because the sandwich was rather dry, Pauline left her office on her way to the ladies' toilet. She rounded a corner in the corridor to find her way blocked by Hindmarsh.

"Hello, Bob," Pauline said, as evenly as she could though her heart was racing. "What are you doing here?" He was a long way from the drafting offices and should have no sensible reason for being here. Had he discovered she'd gone to the police about him just yesterday? Even for the regular gossip mill, that seemed unlikely.

"I came to see you," Hindmarsh said. "I want to know what's going on. Why you're following me."

"Why do you think I'm following you?"

"Because someone saw you doing it."

Those two mothers, Pauline thought angrily. "Does this person know me?" Pauline asked.

Hindmarsh shook his head. "No, but they described you perfectly."

'There are many people who look something like me in

the city," Pauline said. "You have no reason to believe I'm following you, except maybe your own guilty conscience."

Hindmarsh's whole frame appeared to stiffen, and his hands became fists. "Don't play innocent with me," he said. "It was you and it was you who set that reporter on me."

"What reporter? I don't know what you're talking about. Now get out of here. You shouldn't be here, as you well know. This is the Executive Suite, and you are stopping me going about my business. Someone will come soon, and you'll be in trouble."

"Aye, mebbe," Hindmarsh said, his carefully practiced socially climbing accent slipping back into his natural dialect in his agitation, "but ye'd better watch yoursen." He turned and strode quickly away.

When he'd turned the corner of the corridor and was out of sight, Pauline continued her own progress. She had much to think about and she was going to a quiet place to do just that.

Back at her desk, she still had no good plan of what to do. If just thinking she was spying on him made him this bold and aggressive, she hated to think what seeing the Herald article would do. She could only hope the police would investigate and lock him up soon before she was murdered. But were the police investigating? Ramsay's cool dismissal when she'd told him what she knew hadn't been promising. It almost seemed he was considering her as a suspect.

That thought froze her. She was the last person to see the victim alive. Wasn't that what they said in detective movies? He did suspect her. Her eagerness to help the police had made her a suspect, maybe the number one suspect. She could feel terror rising inside and fought to steady herself. She was imagining things. He was just being neutral, not giving himself away before he was sure her information was good. Another lesson, she thought, to add to the one about speaking to the press. This one was – be careful speaking to the police. She must learn to give information in ways that didn't look like she was pointing someone out as guilty, even if she thought they were.

Her phone rang, breaking into her wild thoughts and its normalcy calmed her at once.

"Engineering Director's office," she said.

"It's Janet over at Research," the voice on the other end said. "Is Dr. Enderby there?"

"He is," Pauline said.

"Can you ask if he could join Dr. Mullins and Dr. Wagner in the research conference room?"

"Certainly. Just one minute." She put the phone down and knocked on the Director's door. On being told to come in, she explained.

Enderby thought for a moment and then nodded. "Tell them we'll be there right away," he said. "I want you to come and take notes."

"Yes, sir," Pauline said, pleased at the break in her routine. It was normally only when the Director hosted meetings she got to take notes and do the minutes.

She confirmed the appointment and prepared what she needed. Enderby was there in a moment and they set out for the meeting.

"I want the notes because I don't trust Wagner," he said, as they walked. "And it's not because I was in the RAF and his fellow Germans were trying to kill me only ten years ago." He gave Pauline a fierce look as though she'd been about to accuse him of anti-German feeling. "The last few times he's been here," he continued, "he's been shifty. Don't know what it is but I want whatever is said, particularly by him and me, recorded and kept. Got that?"

"Yes, sir," Pauline said. She understood what he'd said but had no context to understand what was meant by it. All she cared about was that she appeared to be back in his good graces and for that she was truly grateful.

The meeting was uneventful, but there was no comradeship between any of the three main players, Enderby, Wagner, and Mullins. There was even less with Wagner's assistant who sat quietly at his side without speaking to anyone, which Pauline thought odd. He handed Wagner documents when required and occasionally made Wagner aware of items in other documents but took no part, which puzzled Pauline though she couldn't say why.

As they left the meeting, her boss said, "Type up your notes immediately. I want to go through them before I leave today and my memory fades."

"Certainly, sir," Pauline said, "I'll have them to you within the hour."

Back at her desk, she commenced typing, her fingers skipping over the keys as she transcribed the notes. As she did so, the notes took her mind back over the meeting and the people present. She saw what her boss meant. Wagner did seem ill-at-ease and not just because he was pointing out the poor performance of the company's newest armored vehicle in the recent trials. It was something different, personal perhaps, not technical.

She handed over the notes to her boss, who said, "Sit down, Pauline. I may need you to remind me of some of this."

For the next thirty minutes, Enderby read and questioned her. The questions were odd too.

"When he said this, did you see his face?"

"Not really, sir. I was concentrating on my shorthand."

"Did Wagner seem uncomfortable to you when Mullins talked about his last visit?"

"I couldn't say," Pauline replied. "I don't know Dr.

Wagner at all, so I don't know what is normal for him and what isn't."

"What did you think of him?"

"Dr. Wagner?"

"Wake up, Pauline. Who else?"

"I thought him cold and stand-offish. His accent makes him sound very Germanic. He looked at me a lot, I thought."

Enderby snorted. "Trust a woman to think that," he said.

Pauline flushed. "That's not fair," she said. "I never think men look at me a lot. Quite the reverse, actually."

"Then maybe you were the right person to take along," Enderby said slowly. "Maybe it isn't about our weapons and trade secrets, which is what I've been thinking. Maybe it's him who has secrets." He smiled wolfishly. "Well, well, well. Thank you, Pauline." He paused and then added, "Finish up the changes I've made and get them back to me before you go. And, Pauline, say nothing about our conversation."

She left his office and settled at her desk. The changes wouldn't take long and would give her time to think. Wagner had looked at her a lot and she wasn't any 'Force's Sweetheart' kind of a girl. So why?

An idea was forming in her mind that would be easy to check once she'd completed the minutes. Her fingers flew as she finalized the notes and rushed them back into her boss.

He took them and put them in his briefcase. "I'm leaving for the rest of the day," he said. "Tell anyone who calls I'll get back to them in the morning."

When he was gone, Pauline called Janet.

"Dr. Enderby has asked me to type up his notes," she said. "I can't read his writing for Dr. Wagner's first name and he's gone for the day. Do you have it there?"

"It's Gustav," Janet said, "though he goes by Gus."

"Oh, so it is," Pauline said. "I can see it now. Thanks."

She hung up, bitterly disappointed. She'd been sure his name was Eric.

Deflated, she slumped in her chair and returned to the meeting and her boss's unusual behavior, which led her to thinking about her own feelings about the meeting. Wagner did look at her a lot and what was in that gaze? Not lust, she was sure of that. It was a searching examination but of what? Her person? She thought not, but then what? It bothered her she was being so obtuse. There were things about that meeting she should have picked up on and didn't until her boss had asked her opinion. With this level of performance, she could never be a detective. Yet another reason her fanciful dreams of being a private investigator were nonsensical; she had no intuition about people.

She placed the cover over her typewriter and left the office early, something she had never done before. When the cat is away, she thought, the mice, even a small country mouse such as herself, can play.

Once outside, she made her way to the nearest phone box. For the first time, Poppy was in the office and she was put through.

"Have you got a camera?" Pauline asked, not waiting for the usual niceties.

"A camera?" Poppy said.

"Yes, do you have one?"

"No, why?"

"Oh, I thought reporters would have cameras," Pauline said, disappointed.

"Photographers take the pictures. Reporters write the stories. Demarcation, brother, or in this case, sister."

"Could you get a photographer to take a photo of Hindmarsh?"

"He would need paying and it would be expensive."

"I thought maybe you could say you were writing a story or something like that."

"What is this photo for?"

"I want to ask the staff at the pub where the fight was if they recognize him and his friends."

"And you think they'll tell you?"

"I'll tell them I'm a freelance reporter doing a story."

"Maybe I should do this. I at least have some accreditation," Poppy said.

"If you would, yes," Pauline replied, "but you still need a photo."

"It's the Newcastle Races on Thursday," Poppy said. "Our photographer will be going. I'll suggest a story idea and go into town with him. He'll take the photo if I ask."

"Wonderful," Pauline said. "I want to go with you though, to be sure he photographs the right man, and also two more."

"Two more?"

Pauline told her what she'd seen.

"So, three possible suspects then," Poppy said. "I see a story here already. When can we meet on Thursday?"

"If you and the photographer can meet me outside the western gate of the factory, I'll meet you there at three-thirty and we'll see all three as they leave."

The wait until Thursday quitting time felt like a lifetime, but now, as she waited with Poppy and the photographer, watching the men streaming out of the plant, she was dismayed. From where they were hidden, all the men leaving the plant looked unidentifiable and this precious opportunity was going to be lost.

"We have to get closer," Pauline said. The three left the shelter of the buildings and moved down toward the oncoming line of men.

"There," Pauline said, pointing at Hindmarsh as he met his two friends. Her movement seemed to catch his eye and his eyes met hers in a furious glare of recognition. The photographer began snapping as the three men began heading toward them. They backed away with the camera still clicking but the three men began running toward them.

"Run," Poppy said, pushing Pauline.

Pauline ran, though she knew this could only end one way. Her shoes, sensible enough, weren't suitable for running and her skirt was too constricting. She heard Poppy and the photographer arguing with Hindmarsh and the others. She ran on up the street and away from the noise.

At the top, where the street met a wider road, she saw a bus approaching a nearby bus stop. It was heading out of town, but it was a lifesaver. She caught it and it pulled away before Poppy, the photographer or Hindmarsh and friends appeared around the corner.

She'd escaped for the moment, but her life now really was in danger. Hindmarsh knew exactly where to find her and there was no escape when she was entering or leaving the factory gates. By the time she'd left the outward-bound bus and boarded a city-bound bus, she'd decided to go straight to see Inspector Ramsay. Then she'd talk to her boss first thing in the morning about using an executive entrance for getting to work.

* * *

RAMSAY WAS NOT AMUSED when she explained.

"What are you playing at?" he said.

"I could tell you didn't think the information I gave you was important," Pauline said, "so I was gathering more."

"You have no business doing investigations, Miss Riddell. However much you believe this man to be guilty, he's a private citizen who has every right to go about his daily life without being hounded by vigilantes."

"I'm not a vigilante," Pauline said, "and if you'd shown any interest, I would have been happy to leave it to you."

"I have officers following up on the information you gave us," Ramsay said. "They've been doing that since Monday morning. I don't have to tell you how my investigation is being conducted and my not doing so does not give you the right to mount your own."

Pauline bit her lip to stop herself. She couldn't afford to antagonize the Inspector when she hoped he would protect her.

"Will you provide me with protection?" she asked bluntly.

"I will have uniform branch be vigilant around your address, but there won't be a full-time officer placed at your disposal," Ramsay said.

"I suppose that's better than nothing," she said and stormed out of the room.

Her anger was forgotten the moment she arrived at her flat. A bundle of letters, the addresses written in Stephen's distinctive hand, were on the hall table. She grabbed them and rushed to her room to read them. After so many days of anxious waiting, fearing the worst, to have them all arrive at once gave her such a feeling of joy she could hardly breathe.

She sorted them in the order they were sent and began reading. Everything was well. The army was preparing to return home, all the fighting was over. She could hardly see the words; her eyes were brimming over.

The last letter answered her question about cars exactly as she'd thought it would, 'Dearest, every expensive British car has wooden trim and leather seats, and quite a few foreign ones do too. There's no way of identifying a car from that. Did Marjorie not notice the radiator grille, the badge or the bonnet ornament, something distinctive like that?' Pauline laughed. It was so like a man to imagine anyone gave tuppence about those things. Were they even different? They must be, she supposed, but only a man would know why they were and why it was important.

She took a sausage roll and tomato from the pantry and sat down to eat while she answered Stephen's letters. The night was quite late, but she wanted something to go back to him immediately, in the morning mail pick up. Longer letters could follow.

24

RAMSAY

"I HEAR you've asked uniform to step up patrols around Miss Riddell's place," Morrison said, as he entered his boss's office the following morning.

Ramsay nodded. "I have," he said. "She's gone and made things worse for herself."

"Then perhaps she should accept the consequences," Morrison said. "What has she done this time?"

Ramsay explained, and then added, "There are often times when I'd like to let the public experience the results of their own folly. However, it can't be done."

"I suppose not," Morrison grinned, "otherwise we'd find ourselves quickly out of a job."

"The question is, should she be allowed to continue harassing an innocent man this way? She is in the wrong. There's no evidence he did anything to the victim."

"I also don't like the way the press are using her."

"Or is she using the press? Are they using each other?"

"They're trampling around in our investigation, sir. If we do arrest Hindmarsh at any time, his lawyer will use all this even before it goes to trial."

"I've spoken to her and explained the danger she's putting

herself in with respect to interfering or obstructing a police inquiry. There's not much more we can do unless she crosses into clearly criminal territory."

"What's her game, do you think?"

"I think she's a bored youngster who sees herself as a budding Miss Marple," Ramsay said.

"I don't read Miss Marple stories," Morrison said, "but I can't believe she goes blundering around this way."

"As I said, a *budding* Miss Marple. Not the finished product."

"I do have some information on our Miss Riddell's background," Morrison said. "It came in last night. It was on my desk this morning."

"Let's hear it," Ramsay said. He hoped it wasn't ugly.

"Her dad's a tenant farmer at Ormsdale in the North Riding of Yorkshire. She went to a private Grammar School for Girls in Malton, quite a posh one, apparently. Her mum's the brainy one in the family; she was a teacher at the school before marrying and having a family."

"I'm just relieved to hear she isn't some chief constable's daughter," Ramsay said.

"I never thought of that," Morrison said, grimacing. "If we do arrest her, we don't need anything like that."

"Exactly. Anything else?"

"Not really. Large family, all with good jobs, decent hard-working folk basically."

"Folks who like to take the initiative, though," Ramsay said. "Lord spare us from those."

"Amen to that, sir."

"And today?"

"I'm digging deeper into her relationship with the reporter and her role in that armaments factory. I can't see any harm in any of it but who knows, there may be something."

"Keep me informed," Ramsay said, dismissing his subordinate. He returned to his own thoughts about Miss Riddell and her obsession with Hindmarsh.

25

PAULINE

PAULINE HAD MORE success with her boss than she'd had with Inspector Ramsay the evening before. When she explained her difficulty with Hindmarsh, missing out the part where she was working with the press, he nodded and said, "But perhaps we need to speak to this man, if he works here and is threatening other staff."

"I'd rather you didn't," Pauline said. "It's all a misunderstanding and it will blow over soon enough. It just needs some time. May I use the executive entrance to the offices, just until I have this unpleasantness cleared up?"

Dr. Enderby frowned. "Very well," he said, "but only until it is settled and that has to be soon. Your using the executive entrance will cause trouble with others who will feel they should be able to as well."

"I know," Pauline said. "It will just be a few days. He'll cool down and I'll explain."

"Very well but, understand this, if there is any trouble, he's gone. Now, I advise you to make your peace with him as quickly as you can. Things like this rarely heal themselves."

"Thank you, I will," Pauline said.

"Oh, and you should know, every department manager is

going to hold a meeting with their staff and tell everyone about the security issues we've been having. I'll draft a memo later and you can get it circulated. I'm telling you now so you don't think this is about the incident of a few days ago. It is not. Every department, office and factory will be making the situation known to our employees."

Pauline wasn't sure she believed him but said, "Very good, sir. Has something important gone missing?"

"You'll hear what can be shared at the same time as everyone else," Dr. Enderby said.

That really did sound like a snub and Pauline felt a pain inside she wouldn't have thought possible over something that sprang from work. Back at her desk, she had to blink away tears and compose herself before she could continue. Her career, she realized, meant a lot more than she'd understood. Could she give it up when the time came?

It was after work before she could talk to Poppy. Even in the phone box, Pauline's eyes swept the street around in case Hindmarsh and his friends should appear.

"Are you all right?" Pauline asked, when Poppy was brought to the phone.

"I'm fine. Those three are all bluster," she said, "which makes me think we're on the wrong trail."

"Did you get the photos? Are they good?" Pauline was so focused on the purpose of the call she'd skipped right past Poppy's doubts.

"We have photos of all three," Poppy said. "I think they're good enough to use. Are you ready to try the staff at the pub tonight?"

"Tonight, and tomorrow night," Pauline said. "They may have different staff on different nights."

"I'll be at the Haymarket bus terminal at seven," Poppy said.

* * *

THE RED LION was jumping when they arrived. It was Friday night, and everyone was in with their wallets full of money after Thursday's payday. Poppy grilled each staff member behind the bar, showing them the photos and urging them to think hard. It was no use.

"The place was packed for the concert," the barman said. "No one is going to remember these three. They're just regular men. Look around, they all look like that."

It was true, Poppy acknowledged to herself. They did all look much the same.

"Will tomorrow night's staff be the same as tonight?" she shouted. It was hard to be heard above the din.

The barman thought for a moment. "No," he said. "There are some who aren't on tonight. Try again tomorrow."

Poppy returned to Pauline, who was waiting impatiently in The Snug, and told her the bad news.

"Then we come back again tomorrow," Pauline said. Ideally, she wanted Hindmarsh in custody before she returned to work on Monday. She wouldn't feel safe if he wasn't.

26

PAULINE AND POPPY

ONLY TWO MEMBERS of the Red Lion's staff were in on Saturday that hadn't been there on Friday. Neither could say either way as to whether the three men in the photos had been in on the Thursday night in question.

"But you were here?" Poppy asked the barmaid as she was pulling a pint.

"Yes. We all were," she said in exasperation. "There was a group performing and we'd sold hundreds of tickets. It was bedlam."

"But you don't recognize any of these three?"

"How can I? They look like all the men who were in that night. Young, working class, dress and haircut in the latest fashion, cocky, showing off. What can I say? I wouldn't swear to any of them but…"

"Yes?" Poppy asked eagerly.

"That one," she pointed to one of Hindmarsh's friends, "does look familiar."

"From here though, not from home or somewhere?"

"Probably here," she said, "and like I said, I couldn't swear to seeing him. He just looks familiar."

Poppy rejoined Pauline in the Ladies' Bar and told her

what she'd learned.

"It's a start," Pauline said.

Poppy grimaced. "It's not nearly enough. We both know it." She sipped her half-pint of bitter ale. "You don't suppose they were at the Barley Mow, do you? There was a concert there too."

"Unlikely," Pauline said, sipping her sherry. She occasionally drank beer but it was never going to be a favorite. "They aren't the folky kind. Still, we should go and ask."

"Drink up," Poppy said. "And we'll go." She stared at Pauline's half-finished glass and said, "You do know detectives drink whisky or beer. Not sherry."

"Miss Marple drinks sherry," Pauline replied.

"Miss Marple is seventy years old," Poppy said. "It's too soon to be copying her."

Pauline slowly, and with great dignity, drank her sherry and didn't reply. When she was finished, they left to interview the staff at the Barley Mow.

Pauline was right. After looking at the photos, the pub's landlord made it clear he wouldn't have encouraged the three men in the photos to stay even if they had walked in.

"What's next, Sherlock?" Poppy said, as they were walking back to the Haymarket at the end of the evening.

Pauline frowned and said, "If I'm Sherlock, you're Watson – the dim one, remember? Fortunately for you, I'm sure you're not. Seriously, though, did you have any success finding wealthy 'Erics'?"

"I'm making a list," Poppy said. "Only, I'm not sure how I'll know when it's finished."

"Can we start on that?"

"How? You know nothing about him."

"Well, he must come into town often enough to maintain a love affair and he has an expensive car with wood on the dashboard. How many 'Erics' are there?"

"Not many, actually," Poppy admitted. "I only have three right now."

"Tell me who they are, and I'll scout out their homes."

"I'll come into town on the early bus in the morning and we'll go together."

Back in her flat, Pauline placed Stephen's photo on the table in front of her and began her next letter to him. She'd always found plenty to talk about but now she had a mission and was working with Poppy she thought she could write a book.

Only, she couldn't. She dug out all his letters and re-read them one-by-one. Some made her smile; others made her laugh. All made her long for his return. He teased her when she said she was worried about him and she'd stopped telling him. She wished now she hadn't. When she'd said she wanted lots of children, as her family had, he'd reminded her an army pay might not stretch to too many. When he suggested a house in the country, she promptly reminded him an army pay may not stretch that far. He thought Northumberland a perfect county to live in. She suggested the North Riding of Yorkshire was the _only_ place to live. Their letters were like their conversations had been, teasing, pretend squabbles, serious thoughts, and earnest hopes for the future.

Her new letters were different, and it bothered her. She'd hoped for replies saying he approved of what she was doing, or even disapproved of what she was doing, providing advice or ideas that might help, offering encouragement, even if it was just moral support from half a world away. Even a clear instruction to stop what she was doing would be better than the silence. She worried her new letters would make him afraid for her and distract him in some way. The news said the war was on hold while negotiators came up with a lasting solution, but nothing was certain.

She began.

'Darling,

I hope you're getting my letters. I got a bundle of your letters today, but I haven't had any written by you these past two weeks…'

* * *

PAULINE WAS WAITING at the stand when the bus from Morpeth pulled in. The weather had turned, and the morning was cold and damp. There'll be rain later, she thought.

Poppy bounced off the bus waving a sheet of paper and the two women retired to a nearby café for tea and teacakes. Being Sunday morning, the café was almost empty. Only a handful of travelers changing buses sat at alone in the corners.

Pauline read the list. There were only three names, all senior executives in local companies.

"I think we should focus on these two," she said at last. "This one, the sales director of a plastics company, is on the wrong side of town and I don't see how Marjorie could have met him."

Poppy nodded. "I thought that. The other two though are very promising. They live in Ponteland and work in factories on the west side of town."

"Better than that," Pauline said, "and I've just realized it now when reading this list, they both work at companies that probably have done business with us. This one is in the ship-building business and we still make naval guns, though not so many now the navy is scrapping ships rather than building them. And this one is in the building business and we had a refurbishment of one of our office buildings only last winter. That's what I realized. Marjorie could only have met this 'Eric' when he visited our company offices. She and I don't move in the world of the rich and famous otherwise."

"Bus to Ponteland and then we walk and ask," Poppy said. "Come on, drink up. We've a bus to catch."

Ponteland isn't far out of Newcastle but, being Sunday schedule, the bus stopped everywhere, and it was mid-morning before they arrived. By then it was raining.

Huddled under Poppy's umbrella, they walked through the town center looking for either of the two roads where the men lived. It wasn't until they took shelter in The Diamond public house when it opened for lunchtime trade that they were able to get directions to both addresses.

After a filling lunch of pork pie, salad and bitter ale for Poppy and ham and pease pudding on a stotty cake with half pint of mild beer for Pauline (it had taken her some time to like this rather heavy and dry sandwich of thick sliced ham and the mashed yellow split peas but now she chose it often) they set out to find the two houses. The rain had stopped. Rain droplets glistened on leaves and windows in the occasional bursts of sunshine.

Both houses were detached villas, set back off the road and screened by trees. Both had expensive cars in the drive, a Jaguar in the first and a Wolseley in the other.

"There's nothing to eliminate either of them from our enquiries," Pauline said, mimicking a deep male voice.

"No," Poppy said, wistfully. "Both cars have wooden interiors and leather upholstery. Stephen was right the description wasn't enough to identify any particular car."

"Tomorrow I'll see if either of the companies they work for have done work for us recently and if either of these two names are in our company records as visitors."

"Can you do that?"

"Executive secretaries have some weight," Pauline said sharply. As she spoke, an elderly man came out of the second house, where they were still positioned, and got into the car.

"It can't be him," Pauline said. "He's ancient. Past retiring age surely."

"I agree," Poppy said. "He can't have any lust left in him."

As she spoke, an elderly woman came to the door and waved at the car to stop. The driver wound down the window and the couple spoke briefly before he drove off.

"Should we go back to the first one?" Poppy said.

"Why not. It's on the way to the bus stop."

The car outside the first house had already left when they arrived.

"What do middle-aged men do on Sunday afternoons in Ponteland?" Pauline wondered.

"Golf," Poppy said, "and on wet days, they drink at the nineteenth hole."

"Do you know where the golf course is? Can we go and look?"

"I don't know," Poppy said. "I've never been here before. Do you?"

Pauline shook her head. She was glad Poppy didn't know. It meant they could go home and get dry.

They parted at the Haymarket bus terminal, Poppy to return to her place in Morpeth and Pauline to walk back to her flat. She'd have a lot to tell Stephen tonight; it wasn't very interesting, but she could make it funny. As she ate her evening meal, she wrote:

'Darling,

I must tell you about today. Poppy and I went investigating and all we learned was that rain is wet. It rained the whole time we were out. If, in future, I tell you I want to be a private investigator, you have my permission to lock me in a broom closet until I promise never to say so again – unless we move somewhere warm and sunny, of course.'

27

RAMSAY

RAMSAY GREETED the desk sergeant as he entered the station and the man proffered him an envelope.

"This came in earlier, Inspector, for DS Morrison. It's from the lads down at Elswick."

Ramsay brightened. Elswick was the local station to the armaments factory and it should contain useful information about the three 'suspects' from there. Despite Miss Riddell's misgivings, he couldn't take seriously the idea they had anything to do with Marjorie Armstrong's death. If it wasn't Cranston, and he was inclined to believe the man, then it was someone with a much stronger motive than jealousy.

"A delivery before starting time on a Monday morning is going above and beyond," Ramsay said, taking the package.

"Nay," the sergeant said. "The lad were just passing on his way home from the night shift."

"Still," Ramsay said. "It's to be commended. Tell them I said so."

Once he was in his office, he removed the foolscap sheets from the envelope. The local men had done a good job so far as he could see. Interviews with the three men and follow up with their stories. Hindmarsh had told the same story he'd told when they'd interviewed him and the other two had plausible stories for the night, which when checked seemed reasonable.

Morrison entered as Ramsay was still reading and he called him to take a seat. He finished reading and handed over the documents.

"These were handed in from Elswick," he said. "We need some photos to confirm they were where they said they were, but I suspect it will check out."

Morrison read quickly, looked up and said, "I agree. I'll get a photographer to their homes and we'll have uniform do the rounds tomorrow."

"Well, they say they were in town that night," Ramsay said. "Miss Riddell got that right, a very acute observer is that young lady, but her guess they were at the same concert was wrong."

Morrison grinned. 'That's how it is with fashion and music. To an outsider, like Miss Riddell, someone who wears a particular fashion 'uniform' must like the same music as everyone else in that uniform. But to the insider, there's a constant battle about which performers are the true leaders and which the false. The fellows she saw probably like a completely different band, which is why they weren't in the Red Lion."

Ramsay smiled. "When I was that age it was big bands. You were for Benny Goodman or Glenn Miller, or some such nonsense; you couldn't be both. I'm a Harry Lauder man, myself."

Morrison thought it time to change the subject before his boss started lecturing on the superiority of his generation and Scots in particular.

"I'll follow up with uniform to check out their alibis and

I'll continue researching Miss Riddell," he said. "But if it isn't Hindmarsh and friends, we're right back to Cranston."

"Or this 'Eric' Miss Riddell mentions and no one else does," Ramsay said.

"Exactly. My money is now wavering between Cranston and our over-active sleuth," Morrison said.

"But if it's her, she should be lying low, saying nothing. What she's doing makes no sense if she's the killer."

"Maybe she doesn't know that. After all, she's unlikely to have done this before and may not realize what her best option is."

"Have you found anything that looks like a motive?" Ramsay asked.

"Not yet but if she has a motive it isn't going to be an obvious one. She's not rich, the victim was only a work friend, and neither of them seem to be involved in anything remotely illegal."

The phone on Ramsay's desk rang. He nodded dismissal to Morrison and picked up the handset. It was his boss.

"I want to go over this case, Ramsay. I've a meeting with the Chief Constable this afternoon and I want to tell him where we are. Come up to my office."

Ramsay made his way heavily upstairs to the Superintendent's office. He wouldn't have minded telling his boss where they were if only he knew where they were.

The conversation went much the same as his talks with his boss usually went. Him plodding, doggedly outlining his findings and his doubts and the Superintendent growing more exasperated with every passing minute.

'Damn it, man. You have this fellow in custody for manslaughter, how hard is it to get the evidence that links him to the murder?"

"We have looked, sir," Ramsay said patiently, "but it doesn't exist."

"So, what do I tell the Chief Constable?"

"That we have a man in custody for the manslaughter and he has confessed to that. He'll go to jail for many years for that crime, though his barrister will plead mitigating circumstances. On the other death, the investigation continues."

His boss frowned and shook his head. "He's not going to like this. He'll want to call in Scotland Yard to cover his backside and we'll look like fools. You may not care about your future, but I care about mine."

Ramsay said nothing. He understood his boss's dilemma and had expected this conversation long before now. The higher up the organization they were, the quicker they wanted results and for Ramsay this was a problem. He wanted the right result not the result right now. His painstaking work, plodding it could be said, was rarely appreciated by those he answered to.

"Have you any other suspects?"

"We're pursuing enquiries around three other young men and there's always the elusive 'Eric' we've been told about but haven't been able to identify."

"I think the victim told her friend that just to help a conversation along," his boss said. "How likely are these three men?"

"Not likely at all but we have to be sure."

"If we can have what's his name, Cranston, put away for a good stretch and guide the reporting along the lines of him murdering the second victim, people will be happy with that," the Superintendent said quietly, almost talking to himself.

"You may be right, sir," Ramsay said, "and if we leave the case open for fresh evidence…"

"Quite so! Quite so! Very well, carry on."

Ramsay left the office in the same mood he was always in after updating his boss. He hated politics and especially office politics. He acknowledged his lack of ambition made it easy for him to have such an opinion, but it didn't make any of it better. He could see where this was going. An unsatisfactory end. One that left the Armstrongs without an answer and confirmed him a failure in his own eyes.

28

PAULINE

"PAULINE," Dr. Enderby said, as she entered his office with his folders for the morning meeting, "have you had a talk with that young man?"

"Not yet," Pauline said. "I've been letting tempers cool. I'll do it today if I can."

"Don't leave it too long."

Pauline had thought about this all weekend, off and on, and decided that lunch time with lots of other people around would be the best hope of not getting a beating. Still, the thought of going outside to find Bob Hindmarsh after everything she'd done was not a happy one.

The morning dragged and then it flew. One minute it was ten o' clock next thing she knew it was twelve and the factory whistle was sounding. She took a deep breath and headed outside.

Almost the moment she approached the embankment, she saw him. He was with a group of others. Thankfully, not the two he usually seemed to be with. She wished the police had found evidence and locked him up so she didn't have to do this, but they clearly hadn't.

"Bob," she said, as she approached the group. He swung

round in surprise, his face showing his deep anger. "Can we talk?"

"To you? Why? So, you can set the police and press on me again?" He advanced on her menacingly until he was in her face.

"Let me explain," she began, stepping back for comfort. Her comfort was short-lived. He stepped forward and once again pushed his head forward so his nose was almost touching hers. She could smell the tobacco on his breath and, for a second, was pleased Stephen didn't smoke. She didn't step back again. At this point, it was face him down or run.

"Explain what? Why you have it in for me so much? I loved Marjorie, and because of that you've set me up to swing."

"It wasn't like that."

"What was it like then? You tell me."

"I'm trying to," Pauline said, her own temper rising. Hindmarsh seemed to pause as if building up to another rant, so she continued quickly, "I told the police what I saw and heard, as we all should do. I made a terrible mistake with the press, I see that now, but Poppy is a friend of mine and I thought I could manage them."

"You managed them, all right. What are they going to do with those photos? If they do an article fingering me and my cousins, I'll have you and them up in court."

Pauline almost sighed with relief. At least his anger was trending toward monetary compensation and not physical violence.

"I'll do what I can but believe me, I'm not trying to frame you. I just want the truth of what happened made known and the murderer punished."

"Then you'll be happy to know I wasn't anywhere near where it happened, and neither were my cousins. You need to stop spying on me and look somewhere else for this truth that you want so much."

"I am looking elsewhere as well," she said. "I'm not picking on you."

"Then bugger off and let me enjoy my break," he said and turned back to his colleagues who were all wide-eyed at the best lunch time entertainment they'd had in a long time.

"I'll leave you alone if you leave me alone," Pauline called after him. He looked back at her, then nodded and continued walking.

Not entirely re-assured but unwilling to press the issue further, Pauline made her way back to her office.

ONCE AGAIN SITTING at her desk, Pauline could let the trembling that had threatened to overcome her whenever she met Hindmarsh these days play itself out. It did. Every fiber of her body seemed to be shivering. She felt a little nauseous and fought that down ruthlessly. There might be many more of these incidents before she'd unmasked the murderer and she felt she'd have to get used to it.

It took her a moment to realize she'd thought 'she'd unmask the murderer' and what it meant. She couldn't pretend any longer. She would not let Marjorie's death slide out of everyone's memory. She may never be a private investigator, but she would be the concerned citizen who did something to right a great wrong.

By the time Dr. Enderby returned from lunch, she was back in control of herself.

"I spoke to Bob Hindmarsh," she said as her boss arrived in the office.

"Good, good, and is the misunderstanding cleared up?"

"I think so," Pauline said.

"I'm glad. We don't want somebody's future ruined because of misunderstandings, do we?"

"No, we don't," Pauline agreed, though she felt sure Hindmarsh would one day ruin his future with or without her help.

"Then I hope you can go back to using the regular staff entrance, Pauline," Enderby said. "Perceived favoritism always leads to trouble."

"I'm sure that will be fine, sir," she said, though her heart sank a little.

And it was fine. She waited until the men had all gone before venturing out, taking care to look for potential danger. The street was empty, and the bus home was filled only with other late finishing workers.

The weather was no longer warm and sunny. Yesterday's rain had left behind the more usual overcast sky of northern England so she contented herself with staying indoors and writing to Stephen, telling him of her adventures in solving mysteries. She would have to be careful to make today's events humorous; the last thing she wanted was him getting himself killed worrying about her. It concerned her a little that she hadn't had a letter from him in some days now, but mail from a war halfway around the world was always going to be erratic.

After the letter was written and sent, she settled down to read her notes concerning the three possible 'Erics', as she called them. Her day hadn't been busy and had left plenty of time for investigating. Through the company's purchasing department, Pauline researched each of the three companies Poppy had identified and the three names.

She'd been right about the plastics man from the east side of town. The factory hadn't used the company and his name wasn't in their books. The other two were a mixed bag. Both companies had done work with her employer, but the contact names didn't match either of the Erics. What did that mean? Could a single, unrecorded visit to her employer's factory have led to a meeting with Marjorie and a subsequent love affair? It seemed unlikely and the longer she stared at her notes, the more unlikely it became.

By Friday evening, her thoughts still hadn't brought her to a decision. Nothing seemed to lead anywhere. In her flat, the Home Service played its mix of light music and serious talk on the radio while she resumed work on her embroidery. It was a tablecloth for her 'bottom drawer', that place where young women collected the things that would make their future house a home. Blankets, sheets, pillowcases, and soon the table cover she was embroidering. She liked sewing. It was quiet and she liked to see the pattern or picture, lightly sketched on the white cloth, take shape in the vivid colors of the threads. She didn't knit, though she imagined a time soon when she might knit pink and blue booties and jackets, but not yet. It seemed like tempting fate.

Rain pattered against the window and the room grew darker. She rose to switch on the light and gazed out of the window into the wet and now empty street. Only a couple under an umbrella hurried by. The weather and the day, the whole week really, had left her feeling melancholy. Another day without a letter from Stephen had not helped.

At home, evenings like this would have been a time of board games. The oil lamps would be lit, and the family would be noisily, happily, rubbishing each other's luck at the fall of the dice or the turn of the cards. Even Dad, usually so quiet and worried about the farm, would loosen up enough to join in. Sheep farming on the high moors, even with the few fields down in the dale for other crops, was a precarious living for a large family.

Unable to continue with her embroidery, Pauline plugged in the electric kettle to make her evening Ovaltine. It was too early, not even eight o' clock, but her heart was heavy. When the kettle boiled, she stirred the water into the cup working the dry powder into a consistent warming drink. It was one of the few luxuries she allowed herself. All her spare money was in a bank account for that future home.

Putting on her winter coat and boots, she stepped outside and leaned back against the wall, where the eaves above sheltered her from the rain. She sipped her drink and stared into infinity, seeing nothing of the street or the edge of the park opposite. Everything was quiet, no happy children's voices, no adult conversations, no traffic. This part of the city was indoors keeping dry. Far away, she heard the mournful sounds of the foghorn at Tynemouth. When a warm spell like they'd just enjoyed was followed by a cold front coming in from the Atlantic, there was usually fog and tonight was no exception. The booming cry of the foghorn seemed to be answered occasionally by sad notes of smaller boats on the river. On sunny days, their whistles sounded jaunty and alive, tonight they were as melancholy as she was. A blast from the horn of a bigger ship in the river said it was near high tide for it wouldn't be moving otherwise. Mother, who grew up on the coast, said the weather changed when the tide did, and Pauline hoped she was right. She wanted summer to return and soon, if only to lift her spirits. Today had been Marjorie's funeral and she'd watched the Armstrongs' grief with an aching heart. The service and the mourners' sadness were a reproach she couldn't ignore.

Her Ovaltine was done, and her decision was made. She must go see Inspector Ramsay right after work tomorrow and confess.

29

RAMSAY AND PAULINE

AFTER WORK, Pauline was escorted to Ramsay's office by a police constable who looked about fifteen. Can it be I'm already old? He announced her and left.

Ramsay rose and invited her to take a seat, which she did thankfully. She had no wish to stand before him like a naughty schoolgirl while he lectured her on her behavior. She was just about to launch into her prepared speech when he spoke.

"I have some good news for you, Miss Riddell. We have examined the evidence and followed the reasoning you provided. However, after exhaustive enquiries, we have determined that Mr. Hindmarsh and the other two young men did not kill your friend."

Pauline nodded, unable to respond

Ramsay continued, "I said this was good news for you, Miss Riddell, and I hope you will see that it is and leave those young men alone. We have followed the trail and it is a false one. I appreciate this must be a disappointment to you but, as I've said many times now, you must leave this to the police. We know what we're doing. You don't. Please, go home and forget about this. Let us do our job and we will get the killer if we haven't already."

Pauline wanted to say, you haven't. That sad young man may have killed the gang member, but he didn't kill Marjorie. Her mind was still caught on his words and it was a moment before she could hear his continued speech.

"Miss Riddell, please listen to me. There's a law about wasting police time. Now I'm not going to say your information wasn't good but there are plenty who *are* saying that. You must stop interfering or you will find yourself on a charge. Go home!"

Seeing his recently indulgent demeanor toward her had returned to the sternly parental one of their earlier meetings, Pauline decided to leave before their relationship grew worse. And how could she tell him what she'd just learned? He'd arrest her on the spot for trying to pin the blame on yet another probably innocent man.

Outside, she took stock. She'd got it wrong about Hindmarsh, she saw that now. She had to think. If she couldn't safely tell Ramsay – and she couldn't, he'd probably explode with rage – could she point him in the right direction? That nice café in the Arcade would be a good place to ponder her next steps. It was another extravagance but vital to her morale and mind.

Walking to the Arcade, collar up, umbrella up, spirits down, for mother's weather advice hadn't proved to be right, she went over everything again from the start. By the time she had her seat and ordered tea and buttered crumpets – those and the scones were all she could afford on the menu – her determination to do the right thing had once more asserted itself.

She'd learned of her own error only the night before, just as she was ready to leave work. Dr. Enderby had walked in and handed her a large bundle of files.

"I've been walking around with these most of the week," he said. "I haven't had a moment to sort them out. Look them over, let me know if there's anything I should be doing and file the rest."

It was true, he'd been out of the office most of the week. There were problems with the company's new armored vehicle during tests and exercises on the Otterburn Range. The Ministry and the Armed Forces weren't happy, and the company was scrambling to fix the issue. Since the Second World War, the plant had been on a downward spiral. This new war in Korea had given them a boost. They changed from supplying mainly naval guns to supplying mainly armored vehicles and their guns. Teething problems were showing up and the executives were having a torrid time of it.

"Oh," he said, before he closed the door to his office, "the official minutes of that meeting you attended are in there. You should look at them and see how they thought it went versus what our notes said. It might amuse you. I have responded to them, by the way, so they just need filing."

Pauline was pleased to have the opportunity to leave later for she still believed Hindmarsh might be waiting for her. She found the minutes among the papers, dug out the notes she'd taken and began to read. She saw what Enderby meant. The minutes she was reading were carefully written to suggest the company was engineeringly incompetent and had poor quality craftsmen. To someone without knowledge of what was being discussed, a contracts judge, say, it would even read like the company directors agreed that was the case. She hoped Enderby and Mullins had responded appropriately. Her own future career was tied up in these new orders and she didn't want her job to end while it was going so well.

The minutes had been written by Wagner's assistant and it made her even more pleased she hadn't liked the look of him. It made her seem clever to have identified a bad man without knowing anything about him but his name, Jeremy Murdock. And his appearance, pale, peevish and a bad man to cross, though in a sneaky underhand way, she could tell. A light seemed to go on in her head; that's what had seemed wrong to her. He looked like the puppet-master and Wagner, a plump, fussy, genial-looking older man, the puppet.

It was then that the light in her head became lightning. A glance at the attendees had the name Dr. G. E. Wagner. For a moment, Pauline was too uncertain. His middle name could be Edward, Erhardt, Ernst, or any other Germanic name beginning with 'E' and she wouldn't let herself believe otherwise.

She was still sitting staring at the minutes when her boss exited his office.

"I'm leaving for the day, Pauline," he said, "You should too."

"I'm about to, sir," Pauline replied, and then, before she could stop herself she asked, "What is Dr. Wagner's middle name?"

Enderby was puzzled. "How should I know," he said. "Why?"

"I just wondered."

He shook his head, puzzled at her seemingly random question, and crossed the floor to the outer door of their offices. He stopped, "I do know," he said. "I remember now. It's Eric, spelled the German way, with an 'H', but he goes by Gus. Goodnight." He left the office, and she heard his footsteps receding down the hall.

Pauline had continued mutely staring at the minutes for some time after he was gone, unable to believe she hadn't seen the obvious from the start. And unable to believe she'd wasted everybody's time on Hindmarsh.

Her tea and buttered crumpets arrived. She thanked the waiter and stirred her tea thoughtfully. Inside the Arcade, it was dry and still felt like summer. Shoppers were beginning to walk by, chattering in that buzzing way women do when on a mission. Sometimes, Pauline wished she had a group to enjoy a day in town with. Today wasn't one of those days. Today was the day when she'd crossed the line from being an honest citizen who helped the police, though in her own painstakingly correct way, to being a citizen who flouted police orders and withheld evidence while bringing a murderer to justice.

30

PAULINE

SHE WOKE ON SUNDAY MORNING, dressed, and forced herself to go to church, though her mind was still flailing in disbelief at the step she'd taken – knowingly withholding information from the police. When she'd held back telling them about Bob Hindmarsh's behavior, it was because she hadn't been sure it was the right thing to do. This time she knew she was doing wrong but she was doing it anyway. She had her own mission to fulfill. The police could do their own investigating or so they claimed. The service was mercifully short but focusing on the ritual and the hymns brought some relief. Her mind was calmer as she walked home.

Why hadn't she seen the truth before? Because she'd been so sure it was Hindmarsh and/or his pals and she'd missed the obvious person. Why had she been so wrong? Because she didn't like Bob Hindmarsh, didn't like him as a person or a type, and that had blinded her. It was a lesson for the future, whatever her future may be. In truth, the answer had been so simple she should have seen it right away. Wagner, the man who visited the factory regularly enough to meet and woo Marjorie and was likely to be rich enough to have an expensive car. It had to be him, though she couldn't yet see how.

And now she didn't dare tell the police because she'd wasted so much of their time on Hindmarsh and his cousins. It was her own fault. She'd jumped at the first solution that came into her head and, because of her inexperience in these matters, had placed innocent people in a horrible position with the police and the press, not to mention placing herself in a bad light with the police. She blushed at her own foolishness. Like any crank, she'd seen only what she'd wanted to see. That must not happen again, ever. This time, she'd have real evidence before she went back to Inspector Ramsay.

She tried finding where Dr. Wagner lived and couldn't. The easiest way would be to talk with him on his frequent visits to the factory. After all, that's how Marjorie must have met him. That had to be a last resort, after she'd exhausted every other avenue of inquiry. But he wasn't in the phone book and his address wasn't in any of the factory records she could access. He wasn't in *Who's Who* either. All of which made her even more suspicious of Dr. Wagner. Why so very private?

She forced herself to put such thinking out of her head and decided it wasn't sinister at all. He was a prominent scientist working in the armaments field; simple security was enough to explain this apparent invisibility. More than that, however, he was unquestionably foreign, more than foreign, German. One of those scientists brought to the West from the German wartime research centers and therefore likely to be a target for many groups of people still angry about the war. She hadn't been involved in the war, though she'd lived through it, and she knew how she felt about Germans. Anyone who'd lost someone dear to them may be more than willing to exact some personal or political revenge.

* * *

AS SHE WAS BEGINNING to give up all hope, he visited the plant again and she took the opportunity to confront him, in what she felt was a non-threatening way.

"Good day, Dr. Wagner," she said, placing herself in front of him in a narrow corridor.

He looked puzzled for a moment as if unable to recall who she was.

'Good afternoon," he said slowly, then confidently. "Ah, Miss Riddell."

"You have a good memory, Dr. Wagner," Pauline said. She'd decided to be blunt and not allow him time to see where her conversation was going. "Can I ask you if you knew Marjorie Armstrong? She worked here."

"A sad business," he said. "I heard about that. I didn't know her. I know so few people here. The directors only, for the most part. I heard they got someone for her murder."

"A man has been found guilty of manslaughter for a stabbing that happened at the same time," Pauline said, "and they're sure he also murdered Marjorie. I'm not."

"Ah," Wagner replied. "Well, as I said, I didn't know Miss Armstrong. Why do you think I would?"

As he spoke, his assistant turned the corner at the end of the corridor and made his way toward them. In the low light of the corridor, Murdock looked even more creepy, Pauline decided. More of my vivid imagination, she thought, before driving home her point.

"I thought you might," Pauline said, "because she told me she had a rich older lover whose name was Eric. You're the only rich Eric she could have met."

"You think I had something to do with her murder? Why should you think that?" His expression changed and he grew surprisingly agitated. "This is outrageous," his voice was rising as his anger grew.

Before Pauline could respond, the assistant said, "Doctor, the car is ready when you are."

"I've just a few final words with Dr. Lewis," Wagner said shortly. "Then I'll be ready to go."

He seemed to relax. Nodding to Pauline, he said, "I imagine Miss Armstrong was a friend of yours and you look for answers. The answer is not with me. In my life, I too have lost good friends and I know how long it can take to find peace after such things happen. I hope you find such peace. Good day, Miss Riddell." He strode past her, heading toward the research offices. His assistant, with a withering gaze at Pauline, followed him. She almost ran down the corridor, determined to question the driver of their car before anyone returned to it.

She was lucky. The man was bored and happy to talk to a young woman who happened to be passing. A bit too happy, Pauline felt by the end of the interview, because she was becoming frightened that either Wagner or the assistant would return before she could leave.

Finally, she said, "I'm going to be late with these," she gestured to the files she was carrying. "I'll be in hot water with the boss. Bye."

She scurried across the open area between the car and the offices at the far side. Inside the door, she gave a huge sigh of relief. She should have guessed he would live between the factory, where so much of the equipment was made, and the testing site at Spadeadam and the army training grounds near Otterburn. No wonder he wasn't in the city phone directory. She hadn't the address, that was too much to ask, but she could find the location on the map and there'd be few enough houses to make the search successful. She'd start at the weekend.

Through the week, she pored over ordinance survey maps of the area. She was right. There were only two houses in the locality. Both should be easily seen from an old drover's track, clearly marked, that ran from Corbridge out toward the moors.

The following Saturday, after work, she put on her sturdiest walking shoes, her warmest outdoor clothes, packed a snack in a rucksack and took the bus to Corbridge. There, it took some time to find a taxi so it was two o'clock before she'd reached the point where the footpath crossed a narrow country road and headed out between the two houses, both set back from the road and sheltered by trees. The driver was clearly concerned for her safety and almost unwilling to leave her in such an isolated spot but, after some negotiation, he agreed to return to pick her up at four o'clock.

She'd shown the driver the walk she intended to take and though he was mollified by her explanation, he remained skeptical.

"It's a lonely walk even in summer, miss," he said, "If you fall or get lost, there's no one to save you."

She hesitated before saying, "I have a friend in the house over there," she pointed to one of the old farmhouses nestled among the trees, "but I can't just walk up to the door, do you see?"

"I don't want to see," he said, suddenly cold. "Four o'clock it is." With that, he turned to look forward and avoid her gaze. When she shut the car door, he drove off.

"I hope he does come back," she said to the sheep watching her over a low stone wall. "Otherwise I've a long walk back to Corbridge."

She climbed the stile over the wall, folded her map to show the footpath stretching out before her, pulled up her collar and set off. The path brought her close to the houses where she hoped to learn more about Dr. Wagner and his household. The first house was empty, its inhabitants long gone, which meant he must live in the other. She surveyed it from the trail. What she saw wasn't promising; it was open country and to get closer she would have nowhere to hide until she reached the trees that crowded in around the house. It wouldn't be easy to do that without being seen if anyone was watching.

Fifteen minutes walking brought her alongside the house. It had few windows looking out toward the trail. There was no one in the wide cobbled yard in front of the house or in the garden at the back. Screwing up her courage, she quickly crossed the two hundred yards of coarse grass and into the copse that shielded the house from north and west winds.

The shrubs around the trees were dense and the trees were evergreens. Both gave her cover and shelter from the wind. Taking her binoculars from her pocket, she studied the house and grounds in detail. A large black official-looking car, a Humber maybe, she was beginning to recognize cars, stood outside what was once a stable but now a garage. There were bicycles in a shed beside the garage. Four bikes: two big enough for adults, two smaller for children. That fitted with what Marjorie said. She remembered that now. He had a wife and family he couldn't immediately leave. Pauline suspected he would never have left, and Marjorie's murder was the result.

It began to rain lightly and immediately a woman ran out from the house to gather in laundry from the line. She didn't look like a wife, more like a housekeeper. She went back inside, and the house returned to its former quietness. As the time passed, Pauline began to feel the cold rain seeping through her clothes and against her body. The rain was soft but incessant and seemed to go right through her mackintosh, which had been bought for short showers and an air of fashion rather than an hour of surveillance in the open country.

She shifted to relieve the stiffness growing in her legs and back. A car drove into the courtyard and parked alongside the black car. Pauline stepped back behind a tree hoping she hadn't been seen. Wagner got out of the car and his assistant out of the driver's side. They walked to the house, heads down against the rain, and through the door, which had been opened to greet them. Pauline checked the time. She still had another hour before she had to meet the taxi back at the lane, but she couldn't imagine anything interesting happening now everyone was inside. The weather would keep them indoors. It was going to be a long wait.

The thought of waiting determined Pauline into action. She began to circle the house, keeping among the trees. Maybe she would see something through a window. Anything was better than standing still for another forty-five minutes. Slowly, she crept through the trees, leaving the side of the house and bringing the rear into view. A large glass patio door, or French window, was visible on the farther side and she made her way to a point where she hoped she could see in.

Although the sky was lightening and the rain was moving away, it remained overcast and it was obviously dark enough in the house for lights to be on. The lights showed two men through the patio doors, Wagner and Murdock, facing each other, talking. It didn't look a friendly conversation, but in Pauline's mind, they were men and so probably just arguing over trifles. She crept further forward until she was far enough past the view from the window to allow her to cross the empty lawn between the trees and the house. No one was about and she ran swiftly to the wall, sidling along it to the French window.

Inside she could hear the two men talking, much of what they were saying was too muffled to be clearly understood and the bits she could hear seemed to be technical. Then some snatches of talk about upcoming meetings and the difficulties of dealing with certain people. Time dragged by and Pauline was considering her next move; she was cold, wet and this eavesdropping was providing nothing of value, when the men obviously came closer to the French windows and she could finally hear what they were saying all too clearly.

"You're sure the driver understood what you were asking?" she heard Wagner say. "That woman wanted to know where I lived?"

"Yes, I'm sure."

"I don't like it," Wagner said.

"As you keep saying, but there's nothing she can do. Knowing you live out here isn't going to help her."

"I don't want my family upset."

"Quite so," the assistant said and even through the glass she could hear the irony in his voice.

"What should we do?" Wagner asked.

"None of this is anything to do with us," the assistant said. "We should do nothing. The police will warn her off and that will be the end of it."

"That's your advice?"

"It is."

"We just go on as before?"

"Yes."

"You English are too relaxed about things. We would act."

"Unfortunately, your people would act, did act, and it was a disaster. We prefer to wait, and yes, we waited. Usually, it's for the best."

Wagner snorted in disgust. "Had you acted sooner, the world may have taken a different turn," he said. "Your waiting allowed a dangerous situation to grow worse."

"This is England, Doctor. We play by our rules so what happened in the wider world shouldn't happen here. We wait."

"Ridiculous. I'm to let some crazy woman bring the law down on me? No, I won't let that happen. I will act!"

Pauline heard them moving and stepped back from the window, hugging the wall. A break in the clouds to the west was allowing golden rays of afternoon sunlight to pierce the gathering gloom. If they stepped out to enjoy it, she'd be seen. Throwing caution to the wind, she ran back into the trees and waited.

No one emerged from the house. Pauline decided it was time to head back to the rendezvous with the taxi driver and slipped through the shrubs and branches to regain the open ground and the path.

As she waited for her taxi, she practically buzzed with excitement. She could hardly stand still. She paced back and forth, unable to believe her good fortune. She'd hoped to hear something significant, hadn't believed she would, and yet she did. She learned Wagner was frightened and it was her he was frightened of. It was practically an admission of guilt. If she hadn't been Pauline Riddell, she'd have danced for joy, even in the rain that had begun again. She'd done it. She'd solved the mystery. She hadn't been completely wrong about Hindmarsh, but she was now completely right about 'Eric'.

The taxi was on time, though the driver made clear his disapproval of young women meeting friends in lonely places of a Saturday afternoon by being even more silent and grim than northern English men normally were. That suited Pauline for it allowed her to think. She'd had no fixed plan about today, only to see where he lived and where he may have taken Marjorie but wherever that was, it wasn't to his home. The children's toys in the yard almost certainly ruled out any lovers' meetings there.

Another thing she'd learned was that Wagner's assistant wasn't just for work. They may work on Saturday morning, most people did, but much of the conversation she'd heard was not work related. What did that mean?

They reached Corbridge and she paid off the taxi. The bus stop had a shelter, but the wind blew through the sides and she began to feel truly chilled. By the time she was on the bus, and the excitement that had buoyed her up was gone, her teeth were chattering. Now she could only see the danger she'd placed herself in. She'd been fortunate to learn where he lived. He could much more easily learn where she lived and if he could kill one girl and dump her body, he could kill another. He would act, that's what he'd said, and she was sure she knew how he would act.

She reached home and entered her flat. It felt colder inside than the world outside. Putting on both bars of the small electric heater, and all the shillings she had in her purse into the electricity meter, she stripped off her wet clothes, toweled herself dry to stimulate some blood flow, dressed in nightgown and jumper, and cleaned her teeth before sliding under the blankets. Minutes passed, her teeth chattering and her limbs still shivering, she rose, put on her dressing gown, and threw a greatcoat on top of her bedclothes before jumping back into bed. It was long past midnight before she was warm enough to sleep. Even then, wild dreams flashed through her mind. Feverish nightmares of savage men with knives or squalid lonely death by fever and cold woke her intermittently throughout the night.

Morning light came late, for the sky remained heavy, leaden with rain, but she felt no urge to leave her bed. Yesterday's cold had settled into her and now she was prey to an uncomfortable cold sweat that felt like flu. Realizing her life really could be in danger, which had done so much to end her excitement yesterday, now crowded upon her. She was a sitting duck, unable to fight or flee and out there was man who'd killed once and could easily be on his way to do so again before she could expose him. As she lay, her mind in turmoil, one simple sentence rolled around in her mind, she couldn't stop hearing him say, 'I will act.'

She looked about the room for something to use if she was attacked. A poker would have been perfect but electric fires didn't need pokers and the fireplace had nothing so useful. One thing she could do, she realized, was jam a chair under the outside door's handle to stop it being forced open. She sprang out of bed and did that before returning under the covers. With the electric fire being on all night, the room was warmer than she'd expected, though how much longer the shillings would last, she didn't know. Reluctantly, she got out of bed and made her way down the hall to the house's shared bathroom. Being Sunday, no one else was up. Being an early riser was her normal Sunday treat to herself for it meant she could have first call on the small reservoir of hot water the old house's boiler could supply. She ran water into the old bath and stepped in.

At home, she could have lain in the bath relaxing even with siblings and parents outside. Here, there was no such luxury. Even the act of running the bathwater inevitably woke someone who immediately, and urgently, needed the toilet. She bathed quickly and was almost toweled dry when the knocking on the door began.

"Just a minute," she called and quickly cleaned up before opening the door and wishing the elderly lady from flat three, wriggling uncomfortably on the landing, a good morning. The woman shot past her and locked the door without a word.

Back in her own room, Pauline took stock of her situation. She only had one wooden chair and that had to brace the outer door. She'd have to use the small chest of drawers to do the same for the inner door. She had scissors that would just about do for a knife. They weren't big but they would inflict a shallow wound that may deter an attacker, though in this case she doubted it. She put the scissors in her bag and dressed for church, reflecting on the conflicting emotions she harbored. Part of her longed for the peace she could have if she would give up her investigation and part of her was enjoying the thrill of the chase, even with all the potential harm to herself. Like the Psalm says, 'not forever in green pasture would we ask our way to be but for strength to face the danger and live our lives courageously'. Well, that's what she would do, live courageously, at least until Marjorie's murderer was caught.

Inspector Ramsay had repeatedly told her that tracking down a murderer may well put her own life in danger, but it hadn't quite registered the way it did now. Even when she'd overheard that snippet of conversation, she'd been elated, happy even. Only when she'd grown cold and depressed had the enormity of what she'd done hit home. It was the adult equivalent to being rapped over the knuckles by a school-teacher. Pain really is the best teacher, she thought. Locking the door carefully behind her, she set out to church. It was too early but the walk in the cold, damp air would awaken her. She'd have to be always awake from now on or she wouldn't live to finish the investigation. It's funny, she thought, she never felt that when she was sure Hindmarsh was the killer, not with the certainty she did now. It showed her instincts were good. She'd listen to them more in future.

Tomorrow, she'd call Poppy. Before her foray into the wilderness to investigate Wagner's home, she'd determined she'd keep Poppy out of everything. The press were too blunt an instrument for private investigations and anyway, Poppy was a reporter and couldn't be trusted. Unfortunately, reporters really could find things private citizens couldn't and Pauline wanted answers. Somewhere there must be information on Wagner, Murdock, and the exercises going on at the Otterburn Range, even if it was just a press release.

31

RAMSAY

RAMSAY SLOUCHED in his office chair. And, as he did every weekend at this time, he thought how much he hated Sunday more than any other day. Everything was closed. Watching people going to church still made him angry, even after all this time. He didn't play sports so had no interest in Sunday leagues of anything, and the pubs didn't open until late. Work was his only escape.

Yesterday's bollocking from the Super rankled. It should have made him angry at Pauline bloody Riddell, but it didn't. She had provided good information that proved to be real when his people examined it. The only problem was, like so many good leads in any case, it turned out to be a dead end. What made him angry was the people above him had taken the opportunity to bury the unsolved murder by re-assigning him and his team to a new murder, which is why not only he, but all his officers, were in so early on Sunday. Jennifer Middleton had been strangled last night at a private home in one of the city's better suburbs. A nice girl from a nice family had been murdered in her own home while her nice parents were at a nice dinner party with their nice friends.

For Ramsay, this re-assignment was a source of deep

unhappiness because he knew his superiors wouldn't have reassigned everyone if the new murder victim hadn't been a daughter of one of their own. Jenny Middleton wasn't the daughter of a senior police officer, exactly, but the daughter of someone who moved in their circles. Ramsay was no radical, but it offended his notion of fairness. Marjorie Armstrong may have been just a regular kid with pretensions above her station, but she didn't deserve what happened to her and accepting the easy way out was letting her down.

He rose from his chair and paced the room, unable to settle or work. The new investigation was to go on every day, all day, until the killer was found. No expense was to be spared. He could no longer spend time on poor Marjorie Armstrong; she was yesterday's news.

The new killing had spared the blushes of his superiors, and his own too, by changing the public's focus away from the old unsolved murder to this new one. It was in his best interests, of course, to let the earlier one slide out of the public's consciousness. He knew he should, but he couldn't bring himself to take that seductively easy route. And he knew someone, however, who was equally determined to go on. Only, she'd now been very officially warned off by the police, with him as the messenger, and for her to investigate further could get her into serious trouble. He had no right to ask that of anyone.

He grabbed his coat and left the building, telling the desk sergeant he'd be away only a couple of hours; he had a lead he wanted to follow up. Outside, he walked quickly out of sight of the station and then, taking a narrow alley, headed for the bus terminal.

32

PAULINE

BEING SUNDAY, everything was closed in town and Pauline had no choice but to return to her flat for lunch. Church had been longer than usual, the vicar taking this opportunity to wax eloquently on the perils of modern life and how even our fair city was now a place of frequent murders. Pauline enjoyed the sermon well enough; she just felt the vicar might take a more active role in solving the perils rather than simply sermonizing about them. She kept her thoughts to herself, however.

As she approached her flat, she slowed and observed closely. There were a number of cars parked in the street but none that looked like Wagner's. She saw no one suspicious in the street. It was too raw a day for people to be long outside.

When she could see no one near her door, she went quickly to it but chose to look inside through the small, net-curtained window before inserting the key in the lock. No one was visible and she unlocked the door, removed the scissors from her bag and stepped inside. Everything looked as it had been when she left, which was reassuring. After the noise of opening the door, there seemed no point in tiptoeing to the small kitchen area that was partially screened, and where an intruder might lurk, so she didn't. She crossed the floor swiftly, the scissors foremost, and stabbed around the partition. She was mightily relieved when the scissors didn't contact anything.

Her apartment being empty of intruders, she returned to the outer door and jammed the chair under the handle. Believing she'd have to do this every time she returned home until Wagner was in police custody made her future terrifying.

Lunch was a sad affair of Scotch Broth and bread. At least the soup was warming, for the day was cold and wet. Just walking back to the flat, the rain had chilled her. Even if she'd been home in Yorkshire, it would still have been a day to stay indoors with a fire, helping Mum with the roast beef, Yorkshire puddings (eaten the Yorkshire way, before the meat with rich beef gravy) and the vegetables and potatoes. She shook herself; now she was just getting maudlin. Her home-made broth was hot and tasty, and her flat was finally warm. What more could she ask for?

What she could ask for was inspiration to solve the puzzle of Marjorie's murder. She was certain she now knew who murdered Marjorie. Wagner had a real motive, not like Hindmarsh; she'd jumped to conclusions there like a true amateur. All she needed was proof, evidence, and she had all afternoon to think up a way to get that. Her first priority though was to ensure she wasn't murdered too, but she hadn't yet thought of one sensible idea how that might be done.

She was no closer to a plan when there was a knock on the outside door. Pauline moved quickly to be out of sight of the window before peeping around the frame to see who it was. It was someone she least expected and found she was heartily glad to see, Inspector Ramsay.

Removing the chair against the handle, unhitching the security chain, and unlocking the door took only a minute but

Ramsay was already knocking again before she had the door open.

"Miss Riddell," he said. "May I come in?"

She stepped aside and he entered quickly, like a man who didn't want to be seen at a place like this and certainly not calling on a single woman in her flat, alone. There were names for men and women who behaved that way and even a suggestion of such behavior would be the end of his career in the police.

"Inspector Ramsay, I'm pleased to see you. What brings you here?" She pointed him to the only armchair while she sat on the edge of her bed, thanking providence she was a neat, tidy person who didn't leave an unmade bed for visitors to see.

"I'm not here in an official capacity, Miss Riddell, if that concerns you. I came to discover your intentions regarding your friend's murder."

"Inspector Ramsay, the police have told me I must not have any intentions regarding Marjorie's murder."

"Quite so, Miss Riddell, and that's how it should be. However, if you were to learn of something that would help, I want to assure you the investigation isn't closed. You will have seen the morning papers I expect. We're re-assigned to this new murder but we're still very much pursuing the truth in your friend's death."

"I haven't seen the morning's papers but I'm glad to hear that, Inspector," Pauline said, "and if I should have some new information, who should I speak to?"

"Me, Miss Riddell. For now, I think it best if you only communicate through me. The others at the station are all fully engaged elsewhere and would likely be upset at being sidetracked."

"I see," Pauline said. "What should I do if it seemed

likely I'd put myself in danger by my providing the police with information?"

"Have you reason to believe you have?"

"I might," Pauline said, "and I don't know how to make myself safe, if that is the case." She pointed to the flat's two doors and the poor attempts she'd made to increase their strength.

"That's what comes of civilians interfering in police business," Ramsay said soberly. "We receive threats as well, but we're better placed to deal with them. What nature might this threat take?"

"I think the murderer may try to kill me. I overheard him say something of that nature."

"That he'd kill you?"

Pauline blushed. "He didn't say 'kill' but I don't think he meant anything pleasant."

"What did you hear exactly?"

"He said he would 'act'," Pauline said, uncomfortably aware it wasn't quite as horrific as she'd come to believe it to be.

"He could have meant report you to the police or anything, really," Ramsay said. "Aren't you being overly anxious?"

Pauline shook her head. "No," she said, "I'm not. He couldn't do anything like you suggest because it would alert the police that he was Marjorie's lover, and he hasn't come forward. He meant kill me. I'm certain of it."

Ramsay frowned. It wasn't altogether implausible, people had been killed for less, but was she really that close to unmasking the murderer? Without wishing her any harm, he very much wanted it to be so. For him to fail in this investigation would be doubly painful; he'd wanted to prove to himself, and others, he could succeed on difficult and serious cases. To have that happen he'd dissuaded his superiors from calling in Scotland Yard. He would never live with himself if Marjorie Armstrong's murderer got away scot-free because of his inadequacies.

"And the person you suspect now isn't Hindmarsh, the person you were sure was the murderer only a week ago?"

"That's correct. It's not," Pauline said sharply.

"Is it the 'Eric' that your friend told you of?"

"It is an 'Eric'," Pauline said, "I don't know for sure it is 'the Eric', which is why I'm not giving you any more information right now. I've learned from my earlier mistake, you see."

"And you're making a different mistake this time by not letting us investigate your suspicions."

That made Pauline angry. "You can't investigate my suspicions while you're on this new case, Inspector, as you've told me already. Can you protect me if this man intends me harm?"

"We've already been through this, Miss Riddell. I can't give you a police guard, but I can have the beat officer keep his eyes open in this neighborhood."

"Wonderful," Pauline snapped. "With luck, he'll be able to give valuable evidence in court when my murder is being judged."

"I sincerely hope it won't come to that. I will give you my phone number for the office and at home. You can phone any time." He took a notebook from his pocket and wrote the numbers on a page. He tore off the page and handed it to her.

"Will my killer give me time to get to a phone box, Inspector?"

"I hope that, if you find any new information, you will call me," Ramsay said, refusing to be drawn into her determined effort to quarrel.

Pauline took the page and nodded. "Very well" she said. "Will you do something for me in return?"

"It depends. What is it?"

"Look into the background of Doctor Gustav Wagner and his assistant – a man called Jeremy Murdock."

"And who is Dr. Wagner?"

"He's employed by the War Office and works on the Testing Ranges at Spadeadam and Otterburn. He's a German who came over at the end of the war and his middle name is Erich."

"Anyone working for the government on military testing ranges is generally beyond the likes of me to look into," Ramsay said. "A German scientist will be even more difficult, many have such interesting war records, but I will look. Good day, Miss Riddell."

"Good day, Inspector."

"I hope I can rely on you not to do anything foolish," Ramsay said, as he walked toward the door.

"Of course, you can."

"And if something should come your way, you will phone me?"

"I will, Inspector, have no fear." She closed the door behind him and locked and chained it immediately. This visit, while enraging her, had raised her spirits beyond her expectations. Wagner may be angry with her, she hoped so anyway for he may make a mistake if he was, but Ramsay wanted her help and that gave her a great surge of pride. Pride, of course, was a sin so maybe it was just a feeling of importance, which wasn't sinful as far as she knew.

She went to make her afternoon tea, humming brave, martial songs. After all, she was engaged in a kind of war. A war for justice on the home front while Stephen fought for all of them abroad. They were both soldiers on the side of righteousness.

33

PAULINE AND POPPY

IT WAS the following evening before Pauline could speak to Poppy because, Poppy said, the office was in a frenzy.

"Why?"

"Haven't you heard?" Poppy said. "You people in the city must live in your own little world. Here in Morpeth, we're having a bonanza news spell. We're all out on the trail of rustlers and car snatchers. And to make it better, we have a department store opening this week. Not as big as your Binns in Newcastle, but still big news for us."

"And this has you all out of the office all day?" Pauline asked, unable to grasp the full picture.

"All of us amounts to the boss, Allan, and me. Three stories, three reporters. We've never been so busy or the town so horrified at the crime wave rolling over us all. It's great." Poppy's excitement was so infectious, Pauline laughed with her.

"You couldn't find time to research the press records for a Dr. Gustav Wagner, Jeremy Murdock, and anything about what's going on at the Otterburn Range right now, I suppose?"

"Why?"

"Because Gustav Wagner's middle name is Eric with an 'H', and he visits our offices regularly. He works for the War Office at the Range. Murdock is his assistant," Pauline said.

"Let me write this down," Poppy said. "Give me the names again."

Pauline did so and waited for Poppy to finish before saying, "And forget Hindmarsh and his two cousins. They didn't do it."

"How do you know?"

"The police told me."

"And you believe them?"

"I do, actually. I was way off course there but I'm right this time."

"I'll be wrapping up my articles on the store opening tomorrow," Poppy said. "I'll look into your latest suspects and I'll phone you at work as soon as I have something. But just remember, when this is all over, I get the story, *How I Did It by Pauline Riddell, Amateur Detective*."

"I promise," Pauline said. "Just find something. I'm frightened." She told Poppy what she'd done and heard.

"Hindmarsh and his cousins said much worse than that," Poppy protested.

"And I never felt the way I felt when this man spoke. I'm telling you, Poppy. I'm frightened."

"Tell the police."

"I have. They can't give me a full-time guard. I bought more bolts and chains for my doors at lunch time today, but they won't stop a full-grown man who wants to open the door."

"I'll be as quick as I can, but these things take time. We only have our newspaper records here in Morpeth. I'll have to come into the city to search the bigger archives, which means I have to persuade my boss I'm onto something big to get him to allow me the time to do that. It won't be this week, Pauline."

Pauline's heart sank. "All right," she said, "just be as quick as you can."

She returned to her flat and began fitting additional bolts and chain to the inner and outer doors of her apartment. If a man did try to break them down, at least he'd make enough noise to alert the other residents, she thought, and that may be enough to deter him.

34

RAMSAY AND PAULINE

"MISS RIDDELL," Inspector Ramsay greeted her as she entered the station. He'd been crossing the hall on his way from where his office was located heading to the police mortuary, which was in the opposite wing of the building. "Have you come to see me?"

"Yes, Inspector," Pauline said. "You said I wasn't to return unless I have fresh evidence and I have." She'd spent days arguing with herself. Should she tell Ramsay or was all her updating him actually being counter-productive? Was he growing tired of her interference?

"I can't stop now," Ramsay said, checking his watch, "and I'll be tied up all morning, I expect. Can you come back after lunch?" He tried to keep his voice as neutral as he could and not let his anger show but what was the woman doing? He'd told her to phone him, not come here. He'd hoped, when he'd told her in such plain, though not explicit terms, she would understand the position he was in.

"I will return at seven o'clock, Inspector. Is that accept-able?" That should give her time to go back to her flat, eat and return.

"Good, good," Ramsay said, and abruptly continued his

journey to the mortuary where the police surgeon was waiting for him.

* * *

BY THE TIME Pauline returned to the station, after walking from her flat on another miserable evening, she was cold, wet, and unhappy. The desk sergeant took pity on her and took her through to Ramsay's office without waiting for her to explain her business.

"Ah, Miss Riddell, punctual as ever, I see," Inspector Ramsay said, looking up from the papers he was reading as she entered his office. He didn't smile but thought her bedraggled appearance served her right for going against the instructions he'd so carefully given her. How was he supposed to discuss her new evidence when everyone in the station knew he was only one slip away from being shunted aside, and there were many here who would happily ensure anything he said in the next minutes became that 'slip'. He had to make sure this was by the book and nothing more.

"I've been thinking about the evidence and I've something new to share," Pauline said. "Not about Hindmarsh, obviously, but about one of the other people we know about."

"Miss Riddell, let me stop you there. Did I not tell you about the new murder we're working on?"

"You did," Pauline said, "and you said to come only to you if I had new information. I have new evidence so here I am."

"You did right but, at present, we're focusing on this new crime. The murder of Marjorie Armstrong is likely solved. Derek Cranston did both killings and we have him locked up for one so there's no danger to the public by switching the team. Though, as I said, new evidence will be carefully considered."

Pauline was angry. "You said you wouldn't forget about Marjorie."

"And we won't, Miss Riddell. We're keeping the case open; we're just letting it take a back seat while we solve this new one. Speed is everything in any criminal investigation, as I think I told you."

"I don't remember that."

"No? Well, I have now and here's what I mean by it. Most cases are solved soon after the crime is committed because witnesses still have everything fresh in their minds, evidence is still where it was left by the criminal, and so on. As time goes by, all these things fade and are lost. We believe we have your friend's killer safely locked up, but we haven't closed the case because we can't be entirely sure. So, Marjorie's case will go on, gathering fresh evidence if any comes to light, until we have enough to send that murderous little bugger to the gallows."

"I have new evidence and it doesn't point to that stupid boy," Pauline said.

"I'll have a PC come and take your statement, but right now I have another meeting with the Superintendent. That's all I can do at this time," Ramsay said, rising from his chair.

"You will act on what I give you, won't you?"

"If there's anything we can act on, yes. If not, we'll wait and let the evidence mount."

"How will the evidence mount if no one is working on it?"

"Ah, well, Miss Riddell," Ramsay said quietly, walking to the door and checking there was no one in the corridor outside his office, "with you keeping your eyes and ears open, something may. I have to work on this new case but if you continue to find evidence or information about your friend's murder and provide me with the results of anything you find, the case will move forward. You have my word. But you must phone me and not come here."

Pauline looked puzzled and he could understand why. She was too young to understand how organizations worked and how people sometimes had to act to protect themselves from those around and above them.

"You'll want to think over what I've said, I'm sure," Ramsay said. "Now, I'll send someone in to record your new evidence." He left the room and, after a brief discussion with the desk sergeant, a young police constable was sent to take Pauline's statement.

35

PAULINE

THE PECULIARITY of her conversation with Ramsay at the police station stayed with Pauline over the following days. Was he warning her off or encouraging her on? In the end, she decided he was just covering his tracks, saying one thing to any eavesdroppers in the office while leaving her to go forward. She hoped that's what it was because that's what she intended to do. Her own life depended on it.

Pauline had considered what she could do to continue her investigation when she had to be at work every day. Even when Wagner came to the factory, she wouldn't know of it because he never met directly with her boss. Finally, she found a solution to the problem. She worked on becoming closer friends with Janet, Dr. Mullins's secretary. They knew each other because the two departments so often worked together, particularly in the present time of difficulties. She and Janet weren't friends, but over the days that followed, she visited Janet at least once each day, with any number of excuses, such as 'just passing', 'following up on those meeting minutes' and so on. She hoped this wouldn't arouse suspicion in Janet's mind. Janet was old enough, and bossy enough, to be her mother and a formidable personality when angry.

At every visit, Pauline took care to scan Dr. Mullins's appointment scheduler which was open to the week and always sitting on Janet's desk. Reading upside down soon became second nature. Her persistence paid off for, during one visit to Janet's office ('looking for advice on a meeting I have to arrange') she saw, *1 – 2 pm G.W.*

That was enough. At ten minutes to one, Pauline was positioned where she could discreetly view the comings and goings through the main entrance to the offices. She saw a large black car, not the usual one, park in the visitor's spaces outside the doors and Wagner emerged from the driver's seat. Pauline practically shouted with joy. He was in his own car. Even with the research she'd been doing, she didn't recognize the make of car so she would have to see inside to be sure it had wooden fittings and leather seats, though she was certain it would. Murdock got out of the passenger side and followed his boss indoors. The car was now empty.

Pauline scooted down the steps and out to the parking spaces. She looked around to be sure no one was observing her too closely. They weren't. Passersby were scurrying, heads down, being important in their own minds. She looked inside. It was as Marjorie had described it. Briefly, Pauline wondered if this was where the couple had made love but decided against it. Dr. Wagner was too old and too plump to make love in the back of cars, even ones as big and luxurious as this one.

As she returned to her office, Pauline considered her next steps. She couldn't miss this chance to follow him for he may not come again for some time. She couldn't, however, see a way to do that. She could hardly run after the car and she didn't have her own transport. Taxis were rarely seen in this part of town; people couldn't afford them. From the lookout point on the stairs where she'd watched Wagner arrive, she could see the streets that headed north. Would she be able to see which one he took and trace it out after work? Would that yield any results? After all, all those streets led up to the western road and that was the way to his home and also the testing sites.

Yet he must have had a place somewhere to take Marjorie after their evening out. How Pauline wished she'd listened with more care when Marjorie was talking. She was honest enough to admit to herself that her inattention was quite deliberate. Marjorie was very much in love and gushing like a schoolgirl over her mature lover, 'kids like Bob Hindmarsh and the like are nothing to Eric' she'd said. Marjorie was also sometimes tempted to go beyond what Pauline thought seemly in describing the couple's time together. She didn't say anything actually obscene, but it was still enough to bring a flush to Pauline's cheeks.

Back at her desk, Pauline got out the city map and studied it. There were some nicer neighborhoods off the Great Western Road. That would be the place for their trysts. Wagner could be on the road home the moment Marjorie caught the bus back into the city. Could she ask Inspector Ramsay to see if Wagner owned a property there? She thought not. Not yet. She'd given him some evidence and that would have to do until she had something more concrete.

At 2 pm, she was back at her lookout spot waiting to see which way Wagner went when he left. It was an uncomfortable time waiting because he was late leaving and a great many people passed her by, eyeing her curiously as she tried to give the impression of someone who'd only just stopped for a rest after climbing the stairs. She was ready to give up, when she saw the two men return to the car and drive off.

It left the factory gates and drove north up the street directly opposite. At the top of the hill, it stopped and turned west. Pauline returned to her desk and once more studied the map. The case was hopeless. Without actually following them, she had no way of knowing if they stopped anywhere or drove straight on west and back to their own offices at the testing sites. That was the most likely answer, she knew, but inside she was sure that somewhere in that locale there was a flat in Wagner's name. She needed a bicycle or a motorcycle and she needed one before he visited again.

On her way home, she picked up the evening paper and scanned the pages of articles for sale. As she approached her flat, she was surprised to see Stephen's mother approaching. Pauline smiled.

"Hello," she said, "this is a nice surprise."

Now Stephen's mother was closer, she could see it wasn't going to be that kind of visit. The woman's eyes were red. She was distraught.

"Oh, God, no," was all Pauline could find to say.

The next hours were empty of everything. Stephen's mum and dad sat with her, cradled her, and made tea, lots of sweet tea, but Pauline was barely aware of any of it.

As it grew late, Stephen's father said, "Stay with us tonight. You shouldn't be alone."

Pauline shook her head but allowed herself to be led off to their car and their home and put to bed.

* * *

NEXT MORNING, she rose for work as usual and found herself in a strange house where nothing was where it should be. Before she'd collected her thoughts, Stephen's mother had gathered her up like a fussy mother hen would and sat her at the breakfast table.

"You're not going to work today," she said, as she

prepared toast and tea. "Give me your boss's phone number and extension and I'll call in to explain."

"He'll need his files," Pauline said, numbly. "He has a big meeting this morning."

"He'll manage. Now give me the number."

It was useful, Pauline thought, that Major and Mrs. Bertram had their own phone. One day, she'd have her own indoor phone too.

"I'll call at eight o' clock," Mrs. Bertram said. "He'll be there by then if he has a meeting."

"Seven thirty would be better," Pauline said. She felt as if she was phoning into her own life; it all seemed so far away and inconsequential.

The call was made, and a decision reached. Pauline would take three days of compassionate leave. If she needed more she could use some of her two weeks annual vacation.

"I'll go in on Monday," Pauline said when Mrs. Bertram reported back.

"You'll do no such thing, young lady. Grieving takes time."

"Aren't you grieving too?"

For a moment, Mrs. Bertram didn't speak. Her expression was calm but distant, otherworldly. Finally, she said, "I'm a soldier's wife and mother. I think I've prepared for this day, every day, for all my married life. Like a Spartan mother, 'come back with your shield, or on it' that sort of thing."

"Oh," was all Pauline could find to say and she lapsed back into silent contemplation.

When the following Wednesday came, Mrs. Bertram said no and called Dr. Enderby to say Pauline was still not ready and she'd remain at home until at least the following Monday.

Even the news that her boss had a temporary secretary failed to move Pauline. She found she didn't care. Her old life, so full of interest and excitement only days ago, seemed to be the life of someone else now. With Mrs. Bertram, she walked every morning, afternoon, and evening until she went to bed, tired enough to sleep.

"I shall never marry," Pauline said, one morning as they walked through the local park.

"You must, dear," Mrs. Bertram said, "or you'll become one of those strange old spinsters the wars have given us so many of."

"I won't be strange," Pauline said.

"You would be, dear. Single old women so often are. They dye their hair odd colors and wear ugly clothes. Not like old gentlemen. They drink fine wines, read serious books and become quite attractive."

"The wars have made me a strange spinster too," Pauline said, then she smiled sadly, "but I promise not to dye my hair or wear funny clothes."

"Now you're being silly. You're not yet twenty-one and have lots to live for."

"That's not how I feel."

"I know, dear, but it will pass, I promise."

"Major Bertram came back from the war," Pauline said.

Mrs. Bertram studied Pauline carefully before saying, "Major Bertram came back, Captain Carsley didn't."

"Oh."

They walked on in silence for some time before Pauline said, "I should go back to my flat."

"You shouldn't be alone just now, Pauline. I was waiting for the time to suggest you stay with us for a few weeks and this seems to be the moment. It will be best for you and for us. We'd like some company right now as well."

Put like that, it seemed churlish to refuse, so it was decided. Major Bertram would take Pauline to her flat to pick up more clothes and she would move in with the Bertram's, at least until she was herself again.

* * *

"I'M glad to have you back," Dr. Enderby said when she arrived for work.

"Thank you, sir. It's good to be back."

"Not that Mrs. Forsyth, who stood in for you, didn't do a bang-up job, because she did, but we make a good team you and I."

"It's kind of you to say so," Pauline replied. Though once she would have been ecstatic to receive such praise from her boss, for he wasn't a man to be fulsome in compliments, today she felt nothing. It was just words. "Has anything happened I need to be aware of?"

"No, nothing unusual. It's summertime, most people are enjoying their holidays so it's been quiet really." He smiled as he spoke, but he was clearly worried about her, and no wonder. Even to herself, when she looked in the mirror she looked dead on her feet, expressionless, empty. She knew what he was thinking, 'poor kid, what a thing to happen.' It irritated her just a bit.

"I saw there was some filing on my desk," Pauline said. "I'll start there."

"Of course, work your way back in," he said. He turned away to enter his office and then stopped. "I've just remembered; something happened."

Pauline waited.

"You remember you said Wagner studied you closely in that meeting you attended with me? Well, last week he turned up here at this office. He asked Mrs. Forsyth if I was in, but he must have known I wasn't because we'd been in the same meeting only minutes before and I'd said there that I was going on to another one. Anyway, he then asked where you were."

Only two weeks ago, this would have chilled Pauline but now it seemed harmless. At least, she felt no fear or any emotion.

"When Mrs. Forsyth told him you were on compassionate leave, and she didn't know when you would be back, he left. I'm pretty sure it was you he came to see. Are you sure you haven't met him somewhere before?"

"No, never. Maybe I remind him of someone," Pauline said.

"Probably that's it," Dr. Enderby said, before entering his office and ending the discussion.

Pauline sat at her desk deep in thought. This was all about who killed Marjorie, which seemed so important only two weeks ago. Now her thoughts were about who killed Stephen and why he had to die. She was sure neither Stephen or anyone else in this country knew or cared about Korea. It made no sense at all.

By the end of the day, she was exhausted. Well-wishers came by frequently, offering condolences and help. She needed neither but thanked them anyway.

"Go home, Pauline," Dr. Enderby said. "You look all in."

"I think I will," Pauline said. "The first day back has been tiring. Good night, sir."

On the bus back to the Bertram's, she realized accepting the Bertrams' invitation to lodge with them and give up the flat had the advantage of distancing her from trouble for no one would know where she was. The idea of being killed no longer frightened her, sometimes she almost wished for it, but deep inside she knew that was wrong and moving in with others was the right thing to do.

* * *

THE FOLLOWING WEEKEND, Major Bertram and Pauline drove to her flat and emptied her belongings into the back of his car. Pauline kept a wary eye on the street in case Wagner was around but saw nothing to alarm her.

As she paid her last rent and handed over the keys, the landlady said, "There was a German gentleman came looking for you last week."

"How do you know he was German?" Pauline asked, only mildly curious and faintly alarmed.

"I know the accent. I worked with enough of them during the war. I was a land girl and we had a lot of prisoners of war working with us. Mainly German but some Italians too. They were all nice people. Well, they wouldn't have let them out to work if they weren't but still, it goes to show folks is folks everywhere."

"Yes, I suppose it does," Pauline said. She said goodbye to the landlady and left. During the drive home, Major Bertram was his usual silent self and that suited Pauline. She was still uninterested in who killed Marjorie, but she could still grasp that she may have narrowly avoided being killed herself.

By Monday, her room in the Bertram's house was made her own by unpacking her personal things. Her photo of Stephen in his uniform she placed on the dresser. His steady gaze into the camera held her eyes as it had done since it was taken before he'd left for Korea. She couldn't yet fully accept he wasn't coming home. After all, mistakes happen all the time in war, she'd heard everybody say this since she was a child.

Getting to work was easy, Major Bertram took her to the city center bus stop on the way to his office and she took the bus to the factory. Getting home was not as easy. She had to take two buses, one to the city center and then one to the north where the Bertram's lived. That reminded her she'd toyed with the idea of a motorcycle before her life was upended. The idea was even more appealing whenever she stood in the rain waiting for buses each morning and evening. September had arrived with a miserable week of cold, wet weather.

"Oh, no, dear," Mrs. Bertram said, when Pauline told her of her thoughts. "You couldn't arrive at the office in dripping oilskins and windblown bedraggled hair. You're in the executive suite, not the factory floor."

"I could buy a fetching leather outfit. I've seen them in photos."

"But not, I think, worn by executive secretaries," Mrs. Bertram said forcefully. "Why not a small car? You're not paying rent anymore."

This was true. The Bertrams had refused to accept rent, only letting Pauline help out with the housekeeping and groceries.

"And," Mrs. Bertram continued, "you haven't the cost of gas and electricity you had before. A small car might be quite affordable."

Pauline considered the idea. It was far beyond what she'd ever expected to own but now she wasn't saving for that home and children anymore, she had money to spend.

"I'll look at that," she said. "Maybe I could afford it."

"My husband can help you there. He's quite the expert on motors and machinery."

Pauline was puzzled. She'd never seen the Major working on his car or reading about them. His occupation was in management. "I didn't know he had an interest in cars."

"He was a Major in the Royal Engineers, dear. Not the cavalry."

"Then I shall get him working on my behalf," Pauline said, "for I don't know one end of a car from the other."

"He can teach you to drive as well, while the two of you

are looking for the right vehicle," Mrs. Bertram said, ruthlessly handing her husband's free time to the cause.

Pauline smiled. Major Bertram may have been a wartime leader of men, but he was remarkably compliant on the home front.

"Will he really want to do that?" she asked.

"He would love to, dear. Middle aged men like to show pretty young women how to do things. It's in their nature."

Pauline shook her head in disbelief, but Mrs. Bertram was right and her driving lessons began that evening in the Bertrams' car and continued every evening until the light went and they were confined to the weekends only. By the time Pauline had bought an old Austin Seven, used but in very good repair, she had her provisional driving license and a driving test scheduled for early October.

She couldn't yet drive without a qualified driver in the car but now she was almost free from riding in buses, the journeys to and from work didn't seem so bad. In fact, she thought she might even miss listening to conversations among the passengers. It was one of those conversations that jolted her ever so slightly from the torpor that crushed her every waking moment.

"Yon killer's up for trial soon, I hear," a woman in the seat in front said to her companion.

"He lives on our street," her friend replied. "His mother's worried sick."

"I'd be worried sick if he came home," the first one said.

"Nah. He was always a nice lad, a bit soft like, but he shouldn't have bought a knife."

"A bit soft," her friend exclaimed.

"Aye. I know how it looks and how they write in the papers, but I understand why he felt scared and why he thought he needed the knife. He just should never have gone to that show."

"Well, mebbe you know best," the first one said, "but I hope they lock him up so he can't murder me."

"Manslaughter," the second one said.

"The fellas dead, isn't he?"

"Aye, he is that. And young Derek will be too if he goes to jail. He's not cut out for it. Poor kid."

The first snorted in complete disbelief. Their stop was next, and Pauline heard no more. She bought a paper while she was waiting for the second bus and found the details of the case on the front page. It wasn't often a case involving killing came up in Newcastle. She read the article and tried to remember her feelings on that day that seemed so long ago. She couldn't. Stephen had wiped all that away, leaving her empty, she thought. Until she reached home.

THE MOMENT she entered the house, Pauline knew something was wrong. There was no smell of cooking, no cheery, welcome-home greeting, only an eerie silence. She took off her wet shoes and went quickly into the living room. Mrs. Bertram was sitting on the couch staring at a box of personal possessions, Stephen's personal possessions.

She looked up. "They arrived in the mail today," she said simply. "I'd hoped…" her voice failed her. She covered her face in her hands and wept.

Pauline realized she too had hoped and joined Stephen's mother on the couch. She put her arm around the older woman's shoulders and hugged her. The personal items lay where they'd spilled from the box: Stephen's cufflinks, tie pin, the engraved fountain pen she'd bought him last Christmas, his watch, signet ring, and cigarette case.

As the time drifted by, Pauline felt a growing wave of anger. Men! Callous, unfeeling, stupid men. Their cold natures may be wonderful in the face of danger but surely, even in their minds, they could understand sending a box of a dead son's or husband's personal belongings back to his mother or his wife would be heartbreaking for the receiver? Somewhere in the dim recesses of their minds they must retain some trace of when they were young enough to have feelings. Somewhere in them they should understand a human touch was needed at a time like this. She trembled with the rage that threatened to spill over into violent action.

Fortunately, for the Bertram's furnishings, Major Bertram arrived home from the office just then, and in sharing her grief with him, Mrs. Bertram diverted Pauline's attention.

"I'll make some tea," Pauline said, when she saw Major Bertram had sensibly taken his wife into his arms.

When terrible things happen in England, everyone makes and drinks copious cups of tea. And maybe its gentle flavor really was soothing to the soul.

After they'd eaten a scratch meal, Pauline retired to her room to mourn again her own lost man. Clutched in her hand was the pen she'd given him only ten months ago. For weeks now, she'd felt as if she was dead. Now, unbelievably, it felt worse. She lay on her bed staring at the ceiling as the light faded and slowly returned, her heart aching with grief.

The following day at work she spent in a dream, a nightmarish empty space where she barely heard a word spoken to her or understood anything she read or typed. After lunch, her boss called her into his office.

"Pauline," he said, "you need to take some time away. You still have holidays you can take."

Pauline felt tears prickling her eyes. "Are you unhappy with my work?"

"No. Your work is excellent as always, it's you I'm worried about. You need to get away from here. That damned trial and your grief are overwhelming you. You need to get away for a time."

"I'd rather be at work," Pauline said. "I'll brood if I'm sitting in my room."

"Then go back to your parents for a few days. I'm sure they'd love to see you. Or go hiking in the Highlands or The Lakes with friends. You must try, Pauline. You must or you'll soon be seriously ill."

Pauline nodded, unable to speak. She felt rejected, unwanted.

"I have a reporter friend," she said. "Maybe we could do something together."

Enderby smiled. "That's the spirit," he said.

Pauline left his office lower than at any time since this whole nightmare began.

That evening, she called Poppy and asked if she would be interested in a short trip away. Poppy had visited a number of times since Pauline had moved in with the Bertrams. They'd talked, but the link between them seemed gone. Pauline wasn't sure Poppy would even be interested in re-establishing it.

"It's October," Poppy said, when Pauline finished speaking. "We'd be crazy to hike in any hills at this time of year. Let's go to London and see shows. We need life not solitude."

London it was, though Pauline realized she was going to struggle paying the bills after just buying a car. The hire-purchase payments on the car and the insurance costs were more than she'd expected which left little money for the high life and high prices they could expect in London. Even the train fare seemed outrageous.

36

PAULINE AND POPPY, OCTOBER 1953

LONDON WAS OVERWHELMING. She'd thought Newcastle a big place when she'd first moved there but it was nothing to London. The fact hit her right away as the train entered the suburbs and then kept rolling on for what seemed like an hour before it reached King's Cross station. As it neared the city center, she saw the open spaces where blocks of bomb-damaged buildings had once stood. Cleared now, they awaited investment to return them to life. Pauline felt she was just like one of them.

They walked the parks, rowed on the lake, took a boat trip along the Thames, and saw shows. The week flew past and by Friday, Pauline suddenly realized she was enjoying herself window-shopping in Oxford Street. Oddly, this spark of pleasure hurt more than anything that had gone before. The heartache was so intense she stumbled and had to grab Poppy's coat to stay upright.

"Are you all right?" Poppy asked, holding and supporting her.

It was a moment before Pauline could answer. Straightening up, she said, "Yes, I think I am. It was just a moment, but it has passed."

"We need to sit and you need to eat," Poppy said, guiding Pauline toward a large nearby store.

They lunched in the store's restaurant. While they were finishing their tea, Poppy said, "I did learn some things about your Dr. Wagner. Are you still interested?"

"Not really," Pauline replied. "Marjorie's death hit me hard. I suppose it was because it is the first violent death I've known. Now, I can't remember what I was thinking of."

"Then I'll throw the stuff out."

"Well, let me read it," Pauline said, and then added, "He came after me, you know."

"You said."

"He hasn't been back to our office and he no longer knows where I live so it isn't important, but I'd still like to know, I suppose."

"When we get back, I'll get them for you," Poppy said. "He's quite the scientist, by the way. Recruited from Germany at the end of the war. He only just escaped East Germany before the wall went up."

"Lucky him," Pauline said.

Poppy laughed. "I see you're impressed," she said. "We'll talk of something else, like has the rain stopped enough for one last walk down Oxford Street before we catch our train?"

37

RAMSAY, NEWCASTLE. OCTOBER 1953

INSPECTOR RAMSAY GAVE a quiet sigh of relief. In the end, everything had gone as it should, though the court appearance and sentencing had been delayed all week. Still, it was over now.

Cranston had entered a guilty plea on the advice of his lawyer and had thrown himself on the mercy of the court. His barrister had made a moving speech explaining how the young man had been in fear for his life when he'd bought the knife. How, on what should have been a pleasant evening out with friends, he'd been confronted by the deceased in a threatening manner and how, in the entirely uncalled for struggle, the deceased had accidentally been stabbed. The court had taken all this under advisement and the judge had sentenced Cranston to ten years in prison with the possibility of parole after six if his behavior warranted it.

Ramsay felt some sympathy for the young man, he could even accept much of the lawyer's excellent speech, but at the end of the day someone had been killed and it wasn't truly an accident. There was no mention of the second killing that night; the police had no evidence to bring for that crime. It was still an open investigation, though growing stale now the newer murder was taking the public's, and that meant the police's, attention.

He'd heard nothing further from Miss Riddell and assumed she too had lost interest. As she was the only hope he had of any serious focus on Marjorie Armstrong's death, he felt it would now only be solved by a lucky accident. Something that would come up in some later crime investigation; it sometimes happened that way.

It was the end of a long day. Proceedings had been slow, there'd been much negotiating between the lawyers and the bench to drag things out. He decided to call in at Miss Riddell's flat to see if she had given up or was still in pursuit.

Outside the court buildings, it was a fine October evening. A pleasant change to the weather they'd been having. At Miss Riddell's flat, however, he found a new tenant who didn't welcome strange male visitors and he had to quickly show his identification to pacify her.

"I never met the last tenant, Inspector," the woman said. "You'd best ask the landlady."

He did. Miss Riddell was gone and left instructions that no one was to be given her forwarding address and she wasn't going to share it with him, police or not.

"Did she give a reason for leaving?" Ramsay asked, alarmed that she may have been right about the danger to her life.

"A death in the family, is all I know," the landlady said.

"Oh. And there was nothing else?"

"Why should there be?" the landlady said.

He'd obviously phrased himself badly, Ramsay realized and tried again, "I meant she hadn't been bothered by unwanted visitors or threatened in any way?"

"There was a German man came asking for her, but it wasn't that made her leave because I only told her about it when she was settling up her rent."

"What was this German man like?"

"Middle aged, a bit plump, with one of those pointy beards they like, wore specs, gray hair though his beard was black, smartly dressed. A proper gentleman, I thought. Why? Has he done something wrong?"

"Not that I know of," Ramsay said, with what he hoped was a convincing laugh. "It sounds like someone both Miss Riddell and I know. I wonder why he didn't let me know she'd moved. Thanks for your time." He nodded, still smiling and easy, and left the house.

In the street, his expression hardened. Miss Riddell may have left for good reasons, but she'd thought someone was on her tail and someone was. If it had been the mysterious Eric, and she'd caught his eye in some way, she really could be in trouble. He needed to find her, but how?

38

PAULINE

AFTER SPENDING time with Mrs. Bertram on the day after her return from London, Pauline met Poppy in Morpeth the following day. Major Bertram was still needed to provide oversight in the car until she had her full driving license but they sent him off to find his own amusement in town while Poppy gave Pauline the details she'd learned about Wagner.

Pauline read them without feeling any desire to find out more.

"Thanks," she said, when she'd finished. "He does seem an admirable character, from these papers."

"One of the good Germans in the war and an escapee from the Russians after, too. He's like a character from a spy novel," Poppy said.

Pauline smiled wanly. "I'm sure it's fine. It was just the way he said 'I would act'. It sent shivers down my spine."

"It's the accent," Poppy said. "Their language is so harsh, so many hard syllables, everything they say sounds like a threat. I've often thought they'd be no good as lovers."

"It was 'act' that frightened me. If he'd said, 'speak to her' or 'tell the police' or something, I'd have been fine."

"You have to make allowances for it being his second

language," Poppy said. "He may easily have meant 'speak to her' by 'act'."

"You're right, of course. Anyway, it doesn't matter now. He thinks I'm gone from work. I've left my apartment, and I'll be sure to keep out of his way if I see him again at the factory."

"Do you want the papers?" Poppy asked. "If you're not interested any more, I can put them in my work files. You never know when things like this come in useful."

Pauline handed them over. "You keep them," she said. "I know where they are if I need them."

Poppy took the file folder and pushed it into her shoulder bag, all the while watching Pauline's vacant stare into infinity.

"You're going to hate me for saying this," Poppy began, "but I have to. I've thought about it a lot. Stephen died fighting for us and international justice, whether we understand the why of it or not. We, and by that, I mean *you* must show the same courage in the fight for personal justice. It's the same fight and we must continue it, as his fellow soldiers will do if the need arises."

Pauline stared at her in disbelief. What a thing to say and what a time to say it. Now, when she was overcome with grief, her friend, Stephen's favorite cousin, was urging her to pursue a common murderer because it was her duty? Or was it therapy? "It's a job for the police," she replied slowly, trying not to give vent to her true feelings.

"I knew you wouldn't like it," Poppy said. "Now, let's forget I ever said it."

AFTER A LEISURELY LUNCH, Pauline, with Major Bertram in the passenger seat, drove back to the city through the countryside. Away from Newcastle, the country looked serene on this crisp autumn afternoon. Though most trees were bare, there were still enough bronze leaves on the oaks to shine in the sun and complement the blue sky with its scudding white clouds. It looked so good, Pauline almost regretted having to return to work on Monday. Life, she felt, should be lived in nature not in factories and offices. Perhaps she should never have left the country. Being a farmer's wife seemed very attractive today.

They drove past the common camp where, Major Bertram told her, wartime refugees had been housed and clearly many were still there for smoke could be seen rising from chimneys. Pauline turned left at a junction and they drove along a narrow road between woods and an abandoned airfield, its buildings demolished but its concrete airstrip still solid in the field to the right.

"It was a training field in the war," Major Bertram said, "and here on the left is the shooting range where the men practiced their marksmanship."

Pauline nodded. Behind the range, a tall tower rose above the treetops, strangely out of place in the rural setting. "What's that?" she asked.

"St. Mary's Hospital," Major Bertram replied. "It's a mental hospital for the insane of Tyneside."

"It seems a long way out of town."

"I think the idea is that tranquility is part of the treatment," Major Bertram said.

Pauline nodded. "Major Bertram, do you think I'm doing the right thing?"

"In what way, my dear? The right thing when you were trying to find Marjorie's killer or the right thing now, when you are not?"

Pauline considered. "I'm not sure which I meant," she said. "Both seem right but for different reasons. Poppy said something that has made me uneasy when everything seemed so clearly finished."

"Then it wasn't finished," Major Bertram replied. "It was only awaiting your return."

"It may be dangerous to continue. Is it fair to my family and friends to go on?"

"Julius Caesar said 'Everyone is at the mercy of a falling roof tile' and the world hasn't changed since he said it. Do what seems right to you or you'll never forgive yourself."

Pauline didn't answer. There was a lot to think over. The car wound its way up to the top of a hill and she stopped to take in the view. Ahead to the west, the Whin Sill and the Roman Wall stood out in the far distance while the Tyne valley with its urban sprawl occupied the middle distance. Left and right were fields, harvested now, some with corn sheaves still awaiting collection. Across the land, an autumn haze softened the bright sunlight overhead. That was her mind at this time, she thought. The right thing to do shone clearly but her way forward was blurred and hard to see. She sighed and slipped the car into gear.

"I'm nervous about my driving test on Tuesday," Pauline said, to explain her awkwardness and this roundabout way home.

"You have no need to be," Major Bertram said. "You'll pass easily," he paused, "thanks to my excellent teaching, of course."

It wasn't often he made jokes, so Pauline smiled appreciatively. "You've been very patient," she said.

"I haven't needed to be," he said. "You have a knack for driving. It comes naturally to you."

"I feel it does too. I only hope the examiner agrees."

* * *

WHEN TUESDAY CAME, it was as Major Bertram predicted. Pauline passed and with a feeling of excitement, removed the learner plates before driving back to work.

"How did it go?" her boss asked.

"I passed. I'm now a fully qualified motorist and can terrify lowly pedestrians and cyclists whenever I feel so inclined." She really did feel alive for the first time in weeks.

"Perhaps not right away or they may take your license away again."

"I shall be the very model of a responsible motorist," Pauline said. "Having a car and a license to drive it gives me feeling of freedom I wouldn't have thought possible."

Dr. Enderby laughed. "Well you certainly look happier," he said.

His comment jolted her. She'd forgotten for the brief time of her success that her heart was broken, and she immediately felt guilty.

"Forget I said that," Enderby said, seeing her changed expression. "I didn't mean to spoil your well-deserved pleasure."

Pauline took a moment to recover her poise. "It wasn't your fault," she said, "I'd have come down to earth with a bump quickly enough anyway. Do you have anything you need me to do before we finish today?"

Their conversation turned to office matters and she returned to her desk with a pile of papers and a meeting to arrange, which returned her to a state of calm by the time she drove home in solitary splendor, smiling unsympathetically at the unfortunates waiting at bus stops along the way.

She parked in the short drive of the Bertram's house and almost ran inside to tell her good news. The living room door opened as she closed the outer door behind her and Mrs. Bertram said, "There's a policeman to see you."

Pauline felt the blood draining from her face. She felt

quite sick. What could she have done wrong driving home? Her mind desperately raced through the journey and found nothing that would excite the police's attention. She walked into the living room in dread of what she would hear.

"Miss Riddell," Inspector Ramsay rose from the couch to greet her. "I'm so glad to see you again."

"Inspector," Pauline replied. She was so relieved she couldn't actually find anything else to say.

"I was just explaining to Mrs. and Major Bertram how I'd found your flat with a new tenant and how, when last we spoke, you were concerned for your safety. It made me wonder if all was well."

Pauline was overwhelmed with relief. "It was nice of you to come," she said, "but as you see, I'm quite well."

"Good," Ramsay said, nodding his head. "May I say how sorry I am to hear of your loss."

"Thank you. You're very kind."

"You have suffered no harassment by any of the people you suspected, I hope?"

"No, nothing at all," Pauline said, "and I've given up taking an interest to be honest. A much greater loss has washed away all that nonsense from my mind."

"I understand. While I'm saddened for the cause, I'm glad to hear you are finally leaving your personal investigations behind, Miss Riddell. It really is best to leave it to the police."

Pauline nodded. "I heard that man was jailed for the first killing."

"Yes, there was never much doubt in that case," Ramsay said. "An awful business; one life ended and one ruined over nothing at all."

"You must see that often, Inspector, do you?" Major Bertram asked, breaking into the conversation.

"Not so much with killing in our city, sir," Ramsay said, "but yes, plenty of lives ruined by people behaving stupidly for a moment with a lifetime of regret to follow. Particularly, from young people drinking."

He turned back to Pauline and continued, "Your landlady said a German man had been looking for you. Is that the Eric your friend had told you about?"

Pauline hesitated, and then said, "Yes. As I told you, I discovered that a scientist who visits our offices frequently is called Eric. I foolishly made myself known to him. When I was on leave, he came looking for me at work. I thought I was lucky to escape him at the time."

"Why did you think that then and not now?" Ramsay asked.

"After I'd made myself known to him, I overheard him talking about me to his assistant. I was frightened and took what he said as meaning he meant to kill me. I see now that was foolish as well."

"Why do you say that?"

"My friend Poppy is a reporter. She researched information about him for me," Pauline said. "This was before I learned of Stephen's death, you understand. Anyway, she showed me what she'd found and he's a very respectable man. I'm not surprised he was angry at my insinuations."

"What is the gentleman's full name, Miss Riddell. As you say, he may well be a perfectly respectable man, but I should confirm that rather than ignore it. Two uninvited visits may have no real sinister intention, but it is best we be sure."

Pauline sighed. He'd clearly forgotten their previous meeting and ignored the information she'd given him. She gave him Wagner's name and as much as she could remember from Poppy's notes and she escorted him to the door.

"If this man turns up at your door again, you will be in touch won't you, Miss Riddell?" Ramsay said, as he left.

"Of course, Inspector, but I'm sure he won't."

"You're quite sure you're not in any danger, dear?" Mrs. Bertram asked, when Pauline re-entered the room.

"Quite sure," Pauline said, smiling confidently at them as they anxiously gazed back at her.

"This man came looking for you at work and at your home," Major Bertram said. "He knew where you worked but had to research where you lived, which in itself says it's important to him. I think the Inspector is right. It needs looking into."

"Dr. Wagner was very angry at my confronting and accusing him," Pauline said. "As I'm sure you would be if someone accused you of a murder when you had done nothing wrong."

"But he had done something wrong, dear," Mrs. Bertram said. "He didn't make a statement to the police about his involvement with your friend. It may not be criminal, I'm not sure about the law, but I'm sure it was wrong in every other sense. I also think the Inspector must look into this and you need to be more careful. Don't go anywhere alone."

Pauline could see she was in for a period of time where getting out of the house without an escort might be difficult.

39

PAULINE, NOVEMBER 1953

IT WAS A MISERABLE DAY: wet windy, with rain blowing into Pauline's face as she crossed the factory yard between two office blocks. She'd only just stepped outside, pulling her raincoat tighter around her neck, when she saw the car in the visitor car park. She stepped quickly back inside the small porch that protected the door. It was Wagner's car; she was sure of that. She may not yet know cars definitively, but she could recognize that one.

With her long raincoat and waterproof hood, he wouldn't recognize her even if she did walk past his car on the way back to her own office block, but she was reluctant to do it. She was beyond all that now and she meant to keep it that way. Slipping back inside the office building, she made her way to the side door. From there it was a longer walk in the rain back to her own office, but it was safer than being recognized and that's what counted.

Her outer clothes were dripping by the time she reached her offices and climbed the stairs up the executive floor. She removed her coat and hood, shaking them out. From where she stood, she could see Wagner's car and it reminded her that it was only a few weeks ago, though it seemed like years now, she'd stood here and dreamed of buying a motorcycle or bicycle in order to follow him when he left. Now she actually could follow him in the safety and comfort of her own car. She smiled sadly, reflecting on the ways of fate.

At her desk, she tried to focus on her work. It was impossible. Her thoughts went back to the car and the questions that had set her mind in such a ferment of activity weeks ago and throughout the afternoon her mind strayed constantly to Wagner's car and the office clock. She decided she'd leave early and get away before Wagner left. That way she wouldn't be seen, which would keep herself out of harm's way as the Bertrams and Inspector Ramsay wanted. It would also reduce the temptation to act badly in regard to Wagner, as she now believed she had done before.

Her boss returned to his office, clearly upset. As he passed her desk, Pauline said, "The meeting didn't go well?"

"No, it did not. Those fools in Research have no idea how to talk to customers. They constantly harm our case with their oh-so-professional doubts and dithering. They should be stopped from attending these meetings."

Pauline had guessed that would be the problem; he'd gone to the meeting already thinking this would happen and she knew he would hear harm every time the researchers spoke. Relations between the two departments were fraying daily as the vehicle trials continued to be below expectations.

"Will you want a conference room to meet and discuss?" she asked.

Enderby nodded. "Yes," he said, "do that. I'll phone around to see what can be done to repair the damage." He moved toward his office, then stopped.

"By the way, your friend Wagner was there," he said. "I'd forgotten to tell you that he came looking for you again when you were in London."

Pauline thought she was finished with that fear for her

life, but her insides told her they still wished to live. "What did he want?"

"I wasn't here. I think he waits till I'm out of the office before he comes looking for you. I told you that man is shifty. Mrs. Forsyth said he wouldn't leave a message."

"She didn't tell him where I was, did she?"

"She didn't know but she's a sensible woman and doesn't give out people's private details to strangers."

"I don't like this at all," Pauline said. "If he's here now, he might come looking for me again."

"At least you'd know what it is he wants from you. His going behind my back to talk to you is bad form. I wish I'd remembered about his behavior in the meeting, I could have talked to him about it, but those research idiots put everything else out of my head."

Pauline knew exactly what Wagner wanted from her and didn't want it discussed here in the office.

"Maybe I should find him and see what it is," she said, rising from her chair.

"He's in a meeting with sales and legal right now. You might catch them as they leave."

"I'll try and do that," Pauline said as Enderby went into his office and closed the door. She should do that, of course, but she wouldn't. She'd leave the office right on time and avoid him.

At four-thirty, she practically sprang out of her seat and grabbed her coat and hood. She walked briskly to the stairs and looked out. Wagner's car was still there. She put on her outdoor clothes and made her way down to the ground floor. Turning away from the main entrance, where she might accidentally bump right into Wagner and his silent assistant, she made her way to the side entrance. She looked outside. People were streaming out of the building, heads down against the wind and rain but she couldn't see the two men.

With quick strides, Pauline soon reached her car and jumped in.

Disconcertingly, as she was turning the ignition key, she saw the two men leave the building and get into their car. It backed out and drove slowly away. Pauline pulled out behind it. It stopped at the gate where they showed their pass to the guard and then pulled out into the street.

Pauline was so nervous showing her own pass, she almost dropped it. She wound up the window to keep out the rain. Though she had meant to keep her promise to her friends and turn right to make her way home, she found herself going straight on in pursuit of the black car ahead. It headed north immediately, as it had done that evening she'd watched from the window. When it reached the top of the street, it turned west. Pauline followed, hoping they wouldn't get too far ahead because she doubted her small Austin could catch the big Humber if they got up to speed on a straighter, less busy road.

They'd only gone another half mile when the car turned right and continued heading north along a road edged with large Victorian homes with well-kept gardens and shrubs to provide privacy. Halfway along the road, the car turned into a narrow driveway of one of the more secluded houses. Pauline drove past and parked a hundred yards or so down the street. She switched off the engine and lights and waited. She saw lights come on in the house and decided it was safe to reconnoiter.

With the heavy overcast sky and the onset of autumn, it was quite dark when she made her way back to the house. She was alone on the street; the foul weather was keeping even dog walkers indoors. From the entrance gate, she could see the bay window of the main floor room was curtained. Light shone around the edges of the drapes, but she couldn't see inside. She crept closer, hoping to hear what was being said as she'd done that day on the moors. She couldn't. The walls were too thick and the wind too loud to make eavesdropping possible.

Cautiously, she worked her way to each corner of the house, hugging the wall as she went. In the growing darkness, there were no signs of light from windows at the sides. Deciding there was nothing to be gained on this occasion, she returned to her car where she noted the address of Wagner's local place to stay where almost certainly, he'd spent passionate evenings with Marjorie. Satisfied she'd put her questions to rest, she drove home.

"You're late, dear. Nothing wrong I hope." Mrs. Bertram greeted her as she entered the house.

"Nothing's wrong," Pauline said. "I just worked late and the roads were bad with the rain."

"They were," Major Bertram agreed. "It was a horrible drive home."

They had dinner quietly and Pauline excused herself after, saying she was going to write to her mother. Once in the privacy of her own room, however, her mind soon strayed to her feelings toward Wagner, Marjorie and the mystery of her death. Poppy's notes said Wagner was a highly respected scientist, a family man, a good man, but that last phrase was what jarred with Pauline. She didn't think she was a prude, but she did believe in right and wrong, good and evil – and adultery was definitely wrongdoing even if it wasn't actually evil. Could Wagner be all those good things and still be a bad man?

His affair with Marjorie said traitor to his wife and children. Had he been a traitor to his country and his people before that? She didn't believe anything good could be said about the Nazis, but as people had learned since the end of the war, our gallant allies, the Soviets, were little, if any, better. Had he been in their pay during the war. If so, was he still in their pay now? It seemed to her it was hard to know sometimes what was right and wrong and that made investigating difficult. Maybe she shouldn't care about the past. Maybe she should concentrate on the events that happened now and leave right and wrong out of it. It hadn't escaped her attention that she was once again investigating Marjorie's murder and this after she'd assured everyone, including herself, that she wouldn't.

"This once, Pauline," she said to herself, out loud, "and no more. Once this is done, this wrong righted, you stop. No more." Having settled that to her own satisfaction, she decided she'd call Inspector Ramsay tomorrow. Maybe he'd learned something new about Wagner.

40

RAMSAY AND PAULINE

"MISS RIDDELL, how nice to hear from you again," Inspector Ramsay said when he heard her voice on the phone. "Have you something to tell me?" He carefully rose, and with an outstretched foot, pushed his office door closed before returning to his seat.

"I was hoping you would have something to tell me, Inspector."

"Miss Riddell, I'm sure you will soon hear we've just made an arrest in the murder that has aroused such public concern. At present, we're overwhelmed gathering the evidence and preparing the case. I've had no time to follow up on the inquiries we talked about."

"I see," Pauline replied. "Do you have any intention of continuing your inquiries into Marjorie's death?"

"Certainly, we do," Ramsay said, clearly enough for anyone passing his office door to understand he was fobbing her off. "We will soon be over the hump on this case and then people will be available to return to that earlier unresolved case. But not for some days, I fear. We must get this right. The press has made this a crusade."

"Why is this murder victim more important than Marjorie?"

"You'll have to ask others about that, Miss Riddell," Ramsay replied. His own opinion was severely conflicted on this. While his sympathy lay with both victims more or less equally, most people, press, public, and senior police, seemed not to agree.

"What if another murder happens? Does Marjorie slip further down the ladder?"

"I hope we've had all the murders for this year, Miss Riddell. We're past our annual average already. But, to answer your point, I'm afraid that is what happens. Most crimes are solved within days of being committed if we put all our people on them immediately. With the passing of time, it's harder to solve the puzzles and they lie quiet unless some new evidence comes to light. Have you found some new evidence?"

The silence from Pauline's end of the phone spoke of considerable emotional conflict on her part. She had something to say, he was sure of that, but wasn't sure whether to give it.

"Miss Riddell, please. Something is bothering you. Maybe you think it is so unimportant I'll dismiss it. I assure you I won't. I have not forgotten your friend's death."

"Very well, Inspector. I'll tell you what I've learned recently."

When she'd recounted what she'd seen the previous evening, Ramsay said loudly enough to be heard by any listener, "I thought you weren't going to do anything to put yourself in danger, Miss Riddell."

"I was never in danger and I was just finishing off what I started before," she said.

"Then please leave it there," Ramsay said. "The moment I have men available, I will follow up. What you say is reasonable, the names, the description of the car, and now a nearby place for him to take your friend. This is enough for me to begin some serious digging. You, however, must leave it. I don't want our annual violent deaths statistics to include another young woman just starting out in life."

When she'd gone, Ramsay called in his sergeant and told him what he'd learned.

"I agree, sir," Morrison said, after he'd heard Ramsay out. "It needs following up. Still, I don't see it. Yes, an adulterer might murder his mistress to avoid a scandal, I'm sure it happens, just not very often."

"But think about it, Sergeant," Ramsay said. "This man has a lot more pressure on him than your average adulterer. He was brought here for technical reasons from a defeated regime. Who knows what secrets actually lie in his past? As well, because of his technical knowledge, he has an important position that could be lost if his personal behavior repulsed people. This is Britain where adultery is frowned upon, not France where it is accepted."

"That's true," Morrison said, nodding. "This may well be one of those 'not very often' cases I was talking about. He certainly has a lot to lose position, wealth, family, maybe even his place here. He might even be sent back to East Germany if he loses his job. Maybe he would think murder worth the risk?"

"Exactly. I think we finally have a suspect with a strong motive, as well as means and opportunity."

"Certainly, one with more reason than Miss Riddell," Morrison said.

"Nothing has come up there?"

"If she had a motive it's something incomprehensible to the police mind," Morrison said. "One of the 'they wore the same dresses at a party' or something equally petty to anyone but the perpetrator. Quite honestly, I don't see that in Miss Riddell."

"Nor do I," Ramsay agreed, 'but I don't think we can just dismiss her from the suspect list. She may not have reasons we can see but she had the means and maybe opportunity."

41

PAULINE

WHEN SHE'D FINISHED SPEAKING to Inspector Ramsay, she felt the satisfaction of a job completed and handed over to the next person in the chain. For her, the work was over. Now, with a clear conscience, she'd pointed the police in the right direction, and she could leave it to them. She was done with it. Inspector Ramsay's reticence was discouraging but that was not her problem.

So, on the following afternoon, right after work, there would be no danger of her falling into error if she were to use her newly-won freedom of movement to visit the North's most famous monument to its history – The Roman Wall, by some referred to as Hadrian's Wall.

And the day, when it came, was right for touring the countryside, bright and showery when she looked outside from the office. She'd been in Newcastle three years now and never once been to the region's most famous ancient ruin. Today, and all the days to come would be different. She'd improve her knowledge of history, culture, science, and the arts and all because she had a motor car.

When the clock reached twelve, she left the office in a lighter frame of mind than she'd felt for weeks. From the factory, she headed north and realized she was following the route she'd taken when following Wagner that night. She shook herself. It was nonsense. She was simply taking the shortest way to the western road as she drove slowly past Wagner's city home. Her interest now was purely academic, which was fortunate for no one seemed to be home. She reached the main road and headed west along the other route she'd traced weeks earlier and by bus. The return journey that day, shivering with cold and fever came back to her forcefully and she shuddered. No more waiting in the rain for her from now on.

As if to remind her it was still there, a shower poured down, sending the last few leaves from the trees onto the road and windscreen. The car's wipers struggled to push them aside. Once out of the city, the country opened up, with fewer trees and wider views. Then she reached Corbridge. She could go straight on, but it would get her nearer the wall if she took that same narrow road north: the one that ran past Wagner's home. It was as well this was no longer of interest to her or she might have stopped and walked along that rambler's trail she'd walked those weeks ago. Instead, she simply slowed down to look across the fields to where his house stood. The rain had ended. The sun was shining once more. A column of smoke from the house's chimney rose fitfully into the air before being dispersed by the wind. The evergreens around the house still kept the house's privacy as well as its shelter from the wind.

Wagner's black car was in the yard, but no people could be seen. The rain showers were keeping them inside. She shrugged and pressed her foot on the accelerator. She was sightseeing history today, not watching murderers.

When she drew near to the bare ridge, the Whin Sill, she could see remnants of the ancient wall running along against the sky. Even on this bright autumn day, it looked lonely. As she drove slowly west looking for a place to stop and walk to the wall, she noticed a bank of heavy cloud pushing its way from the west, bringing with it a gray wall of rain. She stopped at an opening into a field, reversed and returned the way she'd come. She wasn't walking out in that. Sightseeing would have to wait for better weather.

She slowed again at the entrance to the Wagner house driveway. The black car was gone. Had the family gone out? Had he gone to the testing ranges? Had he gone to the city house? It didn't matter to her, of course, but she could go back by way of the city house and see. Just for curiosity's sake.

The car was at the city house. Because the day was dark under the heavy clouds that had rolled in, she could see the lights on in the room with the bay window. Wagner was there and so was his assistant, along with a third man. Luckily, none of this was her concern and she drove on without stopping.

That evening, as she tried to read her book and listen to the radio in the living room with the Bertrams, she found she couldn't get the questions around Wagner out of her head. In her mind, she found it hard to understand why she should be so concerned about Marjorie when she was grieving for Stephen who was to have been the man she shared her life and family with. But that's how it was. Maybe the puzzle over Marjorie was dulling the pain over Stephen. It was a kind of therapy.

"I may be late home tomorrow," she said, and almost grinned to see Major Bertram start up from his doze.

"Are you going somewhere, dear?" Mrs. Bertram asked, looking up from her own book.

"I thought I'd visit Poppy and maybe we'd go out somewhere," Pauline said.

"Make the best of the weather before winter sets in, that's the spirit," Major Bertram said.

"Yes, you must," his wife agreed. "It doesn't do to brood too long."

She'd been sure they would object, so had planned good counterarguments for whatever reason they gave. She was disappointed they accepted her plan with so little fuss. However, her arguments she felt would keep for another day, and she left the room quickly before they changed their minds.

After church the next day, Pauline set off for Morpeth. Poppy was still in bed when she arrived and not at all happy to be roused out of it.

"We had quite a night of it at the Blacksmith's Arms last night," she grumbled as she dressed. "You should have come."

"I would have spoiled the party atmosphere," Pauline said, "and, don't forget, I'm staying with your uncle and aunt."

She finally bundled Poppy outside, who visibly flinched at the cold and the light, and put her into her car.

"Where are we going?" Poppy asked when Pauline drove away.

"We're going to spy on Wagner at his city house."

"What are you talking about?"

Pauline explained.

"And you want to sit outside in the street all day watching in case he does something incriminating? Are you mad?"

"Not mad. Puzzled. I'll buy you a nice lunch somewhere before we start. And it won't be all day because it's already afternoon."

Poppy closed her eyes and laid her head on the door pillar. "Wake me when you've found somewhere nice for lunch," she said.

As it was Sunday, a number of the country pubs were open for a Sunday roast dinner with all the trimmings and they soon found one that had a table for two.

"Sunday was always the best day at home," Poppy said, as she stretched back in her chair and finished her beer.

"I agree," Pauline said. "Now I'm living with your aunt, it's like being back at home for Sunday lunch. Eat way too much and then doze gently through the afternoon."

"We can't doze today, or we might miss something important."

Pauline smiled. "I don't want to get your hopes up," she said. "Probably nothing will be going on there."

"Then why are we going?"

"In case there is something. If there's no one there, we can look inside and see what's what."

"Like what? Are you hoping Marjorie will have left a scarf or something there? Something you'll recognize? If he killed her, he'll have gone over the place with a fine-tooth comb to remove any traces she was ever there."

Pauline had already thought of that, but a faint hope lay in her mind that he'd have missed something.

She parked a little way down the street and around a corner. The afternoon was cold but dry and a sharp wind fluttered their headscarves when they stepped out of the car. They crossed the road and walked nonchalantly up the street, slowing even more as they passed the entrance. There were no cars parked outside and no lights on in the building. It seemed Poppy was right.

After watching carefully for a moment, they walked up to the door. It was a solid wooden door without a window. On the wall alongside the door was a small brass plaque announcing this was the offices of the Stirling Engine Engineering Company. Poppy took a note of that and they crept closer to the bay window. Inside, chairs and a long table occupied the center of the room. It was clearly set up for meetings, which seemed credible enough.

No one challenged them and there were no sounds from the house, so they continued around the perimeter, examining each window in turn. They learned very little other than it was a place where office people appeared to work. Rooms had desks and filing cabinets, another a drawing board. Frosted glass on a thin window told them there were toilets too. After fifteen minutes of snooping, they were back to the main entrance.

"I want to see upstairs," Pauline said. "That's where we'd really learn something."

"We'd see more offices and possibly a bedroom where staff stay if they work late."

"The top part of the toilet window was open," Pauline said. "If you boost me up, I could unclip it from the pin and reach down and open the main window."

"And we could be looking at five years for housebreaking by teatime," Poppy reminded her.

"The hedge and shrubs would keep us unobserved," Pauline said.

"No, they wouldn't. Companies have security people who check this stuff out. You'll find the window is visible to the outside world."

"Let's go back and check."

"See," Pauline said, when they were once again beneath the frosted windows. "They've let the shrubs grow up and hide this window from the street. If they ever had a security check, they would have been told to keep this greenery trimmed and they haven't."

Poppy looked all around and nodded. "You're right," she said and clasped her fingers together to make a step.

Pauline held Poppy's shoulders, stepped into her friend's clasped hands and raised herself up. The upper window was only finger-width open, but it was enough for her to push up the handle and open the window. She stepped onto the windowsill and stretched up on tiptoes. Even with that, she couldn't get her shoulders through the small opening. She could get her head in and look down. As she'd guessed, the lower, larger window was the same design as the upper one. A bar with holes and a pin that enabled the window to be locked at various degrees of open. A simple catch, halfway down the window, held it fastened.

She wriggled her arm into the window and reached down to open the catch. It opened easily. Now the bar at the bottom needed to be lifted. Pauline got her head and arm out of the window and took off her headscarf.

"What are you doing?" Poppy said.

Pauline grasped two opposite corners of the scarf in her hands and spun the scarf into a thick rope. She quickly tied a loop in one end and pushed her arm and head back into the small opening. It took two attempts before she was able to hook the bar with the loop. A moment later the bar was off the pin and she gently pushed open the window. She jumped down to the ground and grinned at Poppy.

"I'm opening the window," she said. "Are you coming in?"

"One of us should stay here on guard."

"It would be safer for us both to be inside with the window pulled closed behind us," Pauline said.

"No, it wouldn't. If there's anyone in there, two of us would never get out while being chased. It's better with only one inside."

"Chicken," Pauline taunted her.

"I'm the reporter. I'm the one supposed to do desperate things for a story," Poppy said. "I should go inside. I might get away with it."

Pauline shook her head. "Nice try," she said. "I'm the

detective and this is my case. You stand guard. I'll be back in two shakes of a lamb's tail."

"Lamb's tails are cut off," Poppy reminded her. "Make sure that doesn't happen to you." She clasped her hands again to assist Pauline's step up to the window.

Once inside, Pauline listened carefully in case the noise she'd made scrambling over the sill had alerted someone. All was quiet. She made her way quickly to the staircase of the house and ran up to the first floor. Two rooms had their doors open and she could see they were offices, as Poppy had guessed. A third room, however, had its door closed and she hoped Poppy would be right about that too.

She was. It was a bedroom, nicely though not opulently furnished with all the usual bedroom fixtures and fittings. Pauline quickly searched through drawers, the wardrobe and cupboards. There were clothes – but all for a male. Poppy was right about that as well. It was a place for the men to stay if they worked late or had an early start in the morning. She searched the rest of the room, the trinkets on the mantelpiece, the grate of the fireplace, under the bed, behind the wardrobe and dresser, but there was nothing to show any woman had been here, let alone Marjorie.

Returning to the ground floor, she looked through the rooms, avoiding getting too close to the bay window that looked out onto the street. It was a regular, though remarkably tidy, workplace with everything she would see in the engineering offices at work. Frustrated, she returned to the toilet and its obliging window, through which she saw a frantically waving Poppy who dropped down out of sight a moment later.

Pauline heard rather than saw people just the other side of the hedge. Their conversation was muffled but seemed untroubled, so they hadn't seen Poppy or the open window.

Pauline crouched down below the sill and listened intently. The voices receded.

"Have they gone," she whispered, hoping Poppy would hear.

"Yes," Poppy replied, "but let me check there's no one else about."

She appeared a moment later, saying, "Get out quickly. People are beginning to come out for their afternoon stroll. The street is getting busy."

Pauline climbed back out of the window and pushed it closed. She couldn't lock it again but to a passerby, it would look locked. They crept round to the driveway at the front of the house and peered around the gates. When they were safe, they stepped out into the street and walked quickly, but not so quickly as to arouse suspicion, back to the car.

"Well?" Poppy asked when they were safely inside and driving off.

"It was as you said," Pauline replied. "Two more offices upstairs and a bedroom. I searched it pretty thoroughly but there's nothing there to show Marjorie was there."

"Told you so," Poppy said, "now let's get out of here before we're arrested."

As they drove home, Poppy said, "Did you get anything at all from your spot of trespassing?"

"Even though I found nothing of Marjorie's in the bedroom, I think I've confirmed Wagner's affair with her. His car matches the description I remember Marjorie giving and now I have a local place they could meet. Marjorie could walk from work to that house, even if he didn't pick her up."

"All that proves is they could have had an affair," Poppy said. "Not that they did."

"If he didn't kill her, why hasn't he come forward to the police?"

"Erm," Poppy said, "because he isn't the 'Eric' we're

looking for or, even if he is, because he's a married man in an important position and has too much to lose. In his mind, he didn't kill her and him coming forward won't help. It will just cause him endless, needless trouble."

"But that's not true, it would help," Pauline said. "And he's obviously the Eric we're looking for. Why wouldn't he be?"

"Pauline," Poppy said. "Things aren't so because you want them to be. You may be right and he's the Eric we're looking for, but we don't know that for sure."

Pauline was about to give an angry reply but stopped herself. The Bob Hindmarsh fiasco was still fresh in her mind. After a moment she said, "We have to work on the assumption he is, or we'll never get the evidence we need to confirm it. Don't you see? The only way to prove it's him is to follow the trail."

Poppy frowned. "Maybe you're right," she said. "He's not going to admit it. We have to show he is guilty."

"I know I'm right," Pauline said. "Now, let's carry on with what we do know. She went to meet him that night, which means he was among the last people to see her alive. Even if he didn't kill her, though I'm sure he did, then he should come forward and say what time he dropped her off and where. That's valuable information and he's holding it back from the police."

"In his mind, he dropped her off early and she was killed late," Poppy said. "It's nothing to do with him. I'm playing devil's advocate here, you see."

"I see, but you and the devil are wrong. He had the motive, means and opportunity and his not coming forward confirms his guilt. At least in my mind," she said quickly, before Poppy could start devil's advocating again. She paused, and then said, "There was one thing I found odd during my trespassing."

Poppy groaned. "What now?"

"It was too tidy. No one works that way."

"It's a company, Pauline. They have cleaners who probably worked all yesterday afternoon getting it ready for Monday. It's not odd at all."

"Maybe," Pauline said, "but it was more than that. It didn't look worked in. It says on the door it's a company but there's precious little evidence anyone works there."

Poppy shook her head in mock despair but said nothing. They drove on in silence. But Pauline's knowledge of works' cleaners didn't agree with Poppy's. They may sweep the floor and empty waste bins but that was the extent of it. This office building looked unlived in. Her dilemma was that she couldn't tell the police this without admitting to trespassing on private property. She had to follow up herself.

"You won't write any of this up, will you?" Pauline asked.

"Not right now but I have to some time. I'm paid for stories and I've spent a lot of company time on this one. Sooner or later, a story must be written."

"Not yet though. It's too soon and there's nothing definite," Pauline said.

"I know, but you must understand, this is my job."

Pauline did understand and wished she could have found some other way to get her research done. A journalist was too big a risk to a case that was still in its infancy. As before, she reminded herself that, in a future investigation, if there should be a future investigation, she'd say nothing definite until the end. She smiled to herself. What was she doing? Dreaming of a life of glamor and excitement based on her amateurish stumbling in the dark on this one. Hope really does spring eternal, she thought, remembering a recent sermon she'd found mildly interesting.

42

RAMSAY

INSPECTOR RAMSAY LISTENED while DS Morrison recounted what they'd learned about Wagner. When the sergeant finished, he said, "So basically what Miss Riddell said."

"Yes, sir. The building she mentioned is owned by a London firm that supports various companies in the area with engineering expertise. It's their local office and used mainly for meetings and such. They also do work for the War Office. Dr. Wagner and his assistant are likely to visit there, I'd say, and without any sinister motive."

Ramsay nodded. "Keep digging," he said. "I want a solid reason to interview him not just hearsay and conjecture. If we don't, he'll have the bureaucrats talk to the politicians and maybe even the Secret Service, particularly if he's a bit dodgy as so many of these German fellows are. We have to tread lightly here."

"If he met her at work, maybe someone there would remember them together and if she sometimes walked to that house, which is very easy to do because I did it earlier, someone along those streets may recognize her."

Ramsay nodded. "It's worth a try. Have uniform branch

start on the street first. I don't want to alert this fellow by asking at the factory. I'm serious about this. We had a bad experience with one of the men on the testing range a few years back, before your time. It wasn't my case, but we all heard about it and some lost jobs because of it."

"I'll get them started on the door-to-door questions right away, sir."

Ramsay nodded dismissal and returned to thinking about the killing. The biggest weakness to Miss Riddell's theory was that Marjorie Armstrong was killed on the other side of the city center bus terminal from where she should have been if she'd been coming from Wagner's supposed love nest or even if he'd dropped her off by car. She shouldn't have been where she was found if she'd been meeting Wagner as Miss Riddell supposed. Somewhere, there was a part of the story they didn't yet have. How could they get that missing part?

Maybe the door-to-door search would throw up something new.

43

PAULINE

PAULINE BEGAN SEARCHING company records for Stirling Engine Company in between her duties. It was slow work. The company records included hundreds of suppliers. She soon realized that, even if she was to go through all the records that were open to her in the Engineering Department, there may be others, in Research, for example, she wouldn't be able to check. She needed to find someone in Finance or Accounts Payable and have them search. But who would be mad enough to risk their job handing out confidential information to people who weren't entitled to have it?

"Dr. Enderby," Pauline said, as her boss came back from a meeting that afternoon, "do we have dealings with a Stirling Engine Company?"

"Not that I know of. Why?"

"I just heard the name yesterday and it seemed to mean something to me," Pauline lied. "I couldn't place it and thought maybe it must have been from here."

"Doesn't mean anything to me," Enderby said. "Is it important?"

"No, not at all. It's just one of those irritating things that comes out of nowhere and won't let you rest until you've tracked it down."

"Good luck with the search, then," Enderby said with a wry smile as he entered his office.

Pauline felt deflated. Every question she raised in her own mind seemed to lead to the wrong answer or no answer at all. She'd thought Wagner owned the house. Then discovered it was the offices of a company that he frequented. Now she found it was a company that didn't seem to do business with their company and that seemed suspicious too. We are one of the largest engineering companies in the north-east of England and this engineering company is less than a mile from our door, yet our engineering director has never heard of them?

Would a company allow even someone as important as Wagner to use their offices for romantic trysts? She thought not. Either she was completely wrong about Wagner or this wasn't the place he and Marjorie met. There had to be another one. Did they get together in a nearby hotel?

Fortunately for Pauline, Enderby left early for the day and she was able to go to the company library and looked up Stirling Engine Company in the *Register of Companies* volumes. The books were for 1952 so as up to date as you could expect, but there was no mention of them. Either they were only incorporated this year, or they weren't an actual registered company. What did that mean? Maybe there were lots of small companies that were too small to be noted in the *Register of Companies* but still operated quite legally. Another unsatisfactory answer.

After work, she cruised the streets around the factory looking for suitable hotels. There were very few hotels in the neighborhood and fewer still where a man might impress his mistress – and Marjorie had been impressed by his wealth. That was the little Pauline had gained from Marjorie's conversation. Pauline cursed herself, and not for the first time. She hadn't encouraged Marjorie to talk about her love affair and she bitterly regretted it every time she tried to follow up on anything to do with Marjorie's death. Even when Marjorie, too excited to care about Pauline's cold demeanor, had prattled on, Pauline had studiously refused to take it all in. And now she was unable to remember any small detail that would help.

The hotels proved to be disappointing. The only hotel of any note was the one she already knew about; the one she booked visitors into when they came from out of town to meet with Dr. Enderby. Without a photo of Marjorie or Wagner, there was no point asking at Reception if anyone recognized them. She drove home in a growing darkness that mirrored the cast of her mind – gloomy. Nothing seemed to work out the way she expected, and this wild goose chase seemed as much a dead end as the previous ones had been.

Rain began to rattle on the car and the wipers did their usually poor job of clearing the screen. Streetlights flared brightly in her eyes as if mocking her inability to see. Why couldn't she see what she believed was right in front of her eyes? Hindmarsh had been innocent, and she'd been sure he was guilty. Now she was sure Wagner was guilty, but was he?

By the time she was parking her car at the Bertrams' house, she'd decided finally and forever to let the police do their job. She would have no more to do with this unhappy story. She had her own sad story to come to terms with.

44

RAMSAY

"WE MIGHT HAVE SOMETHING, SIR," Morrison said to Ramsay.

Ramsay was pleased to see such excitement in his subordinate. "What is this something, Sergeant?" he asked with a grin.

"The door-to-door turned up a woman who thinks she recognizes the victim."

"So, they were using that address for their assignations? Miss Riddell was right," Ramsay said.

"Not exactly, sir," Morrison said. "The woman works at the Elswick Arms Hotel and thinks she'd seen the victim there with an older man."

"Do we have a photo of Wagner she can see?"

"Not yet, sir. We're digging one out," Morrison replied, "but if she recognizes both of them, I think we've enough to interview him."

"Let's not get our hopes too high, Sergeant," Ramsay replied, though his own spirit was doing cartwheels.

"No, sir, but it fits."

"Soon as you can, Sergeant. The sooner the better."

"Aye, aye, sir," Morrison said, grinning and lapsing into naval speech.

When he'd left the office, Ramsay rubbed his eyes and sighed. Were they finally getting close? He hoped so. He knew how the Armstrongs felt and desperately wanted to give them some comfort. Not that knowing who killed their daughter would be much comfort; after all, he knew who killed his family and it hadn't comforted him one bit in the past ten years.

Still, a hotel was good. They had registers, which provided tangible proof. Even if they'd used false names, as such couples generally did, the names with their attached addresses would be shown to be false and the handwriting, with the woman's identification, would show they'd been there and Dr. Wagner would have some serious explaining to do. Very satisfactory if it turned out.

"Come in, Dr. Wagner, and take a seat," Inspector Ramsay said, indicating the chair opposite him at his desk.

Wagner sat. He looked angry, rather than intimidated, and Ramsay was intrigued to know how he would behave in this interview.

"This isn't a formal interview, Doctor," Ramsay continued, "it's in the nature of a conversation to clear up some puzzling information we've uncovered during our investigation into the death of Marjorie Armstrong. Did you know Miss Armstrong?"

"No, certainly not. Why should you think I did?" Wagner said.

He's sweating, Ramsay noted. The portly ones always do. Now to hit him with the guest signatures from the hotel registry, sadly not from the night in question but real enough.

"Then how would you account for a hotel registry entry in your handwriting alongside one in the handwriting of Miss Armstrong?"

"I wouldn't try to account for it. It isn't mine."

"Or that a woman who works at the hotel has identified you and Miss Armstrong as being frequent guests there?"

"She is mistaken, of course."

"The porter recognizes your car and its license plate. Is he mistaken as well?"

"I assume you mean the Elswick Arms Hotel," Wagner said. "I have stayed there once or twice when I had an early meeting in town. He remembers my car from those occasions. That's all."

"I see," Ramsay said slowly. "Then I hope you'll have no objection to our forensic team examining your car for evidence. Purely to eliminate you from our enquiries, you understand."

Wagner said nothing. He stared at Ramsay and glanced at Morrison who was diligently taking notes. He licked his lips. The silence in the room seemed to grow and the outside bustle fade. Ramsay could almost hear the gears turning in Wagner's mind.

"Inspector," Wagner said, at last. "I will tell you the truth because it will prove to you I had nothing to do with Miss Armstrong's death."

"That's what we're here for," Ramsay said.

"I did have an affair with Marjorie. I should not have denied it, but I was frightened. A man in my position has to be careful. I'm married and I'm a foreigner, a German. Some people would be happy to see me hanged. Perhaps you would too."

Ramsay gritted his teeth to stop himself saying just how much he'd like that. It wasn't true, he had enough control over himself for that, but he could understand such a wish. Wagner had worked in the German armaments research industry before and during the war. The plane that carried the bombs, and the bombs themselves, were down to the work of people just like Wagner, even if it wasn't him.

"You were explaining," Ramsay said, when he was sure he had control of his anger.

"We did meet at that hotel but not on the night she was killed. My wife called me that afternoon. My son was extremely ill. She needed me to come home, which I did. I left my assistant, Murdock, to meet Miss Armstrong and send her home."

"We shall check this with your wife before you leave this office, Dr. Wagner. I hope you understand."

"Yes, of course," Wagner said.

Ramsay knew from Wagner's expression, his whole demeanor, that he was telling the truth. Miss Riddell's information, good as before, was not going to lead to an arrest.

And so it proved. Mrs. Wagner confirmed his presence at home and a check at the local hospital confirmed they had both taken the child there later in the evening and had stayed with the child all night.

When they interviewed Murdock later, he confirmed that he did wait for Miss Armstrong at the place Wagner had asked him to and told Miss Armstrong what had happened. She had been disappointed but had refused Murdock's offer of a lift home and walked off to a nearby bus stop. That was the last he'd seen of her. The last he'd seen of Marjorie Armstrong

And this, Ramsay knew, was almost certainly the last Ramsay would see of Dr. Wagner and Mr. Murdock. He'd followed the lead hoping for a better result. He knew what would come next. It was more than just this line of investigation that was finished.

The call he was expecting didn't come until late morning. The phone rang; he picked it up. It was the Chief, of course.

"My office, now, Ramsay," the Chief Constable said.

Ramsay made his way to the Chief's office where he found the Superintendent was already waiting. He looked as if he'd had a hard time of it already.

"I'm not going to beat about the bush, Ramsay," the Chief said. "We here know what happened to your family, but other people don't. You can't harass Germans and bully them because you want to. Our job is policing, not oppression."

"I haven't harassed or bullied any Germans, sir," Ramsay said, evenly. "I was given information…"

"And who by? That girl again, I'll be bound."

"I was given information that suggested Dr. Wagner had met with Miss Armstrong on the night of her death. He didn't come forward."

"So, you hauled him in here and browbeat him for a confession," the Chief was practically shouting now.

"DS Morrison and PC Thompson were both present. They will attest there was no browbeating or indeed anything other than a polite exchange of information."

"Morrison is your man and Thompson's a young man. They'll both swear to whatever keeps them clean."

Ramsay fought down the rising anger. He knew the Chief would happily make him a scapegoat if he could.

"DS Morrison is an honest man, and Thompson comes from a Quaker family. Neither of them would have stood by while I abused any witness and they had no reason to do so last night," he paused, "Sir."

"That's not what the home office says. I've just had London on the phone, and they tell a quite a different story, I can tell you."

"As they weren't present at the time, I assume they got their story from Dr. Wagner. Why do you believe his story and not what I, and two other officers of this station, tell you?" Ramsay asked.

Ramsay knew very well why the Chief was taking the line

he was. He didn't believe the story the home office was giving out either. He just didn't like Inspector Ramsay and he had to cover his own behind. Politics was one of the reasons Ramsay was pleased he'd never been promoted. He couldn't stand politics or the people who worked in it. He thought most of the criminals he caught were better human beings than most of the politicians he met or was aware of.

"Any complaint I receive has to be investigated," the Chief said, "and while it is, you will take no further part in the investigation. If there are any further questions to Dr. Wagner or his assistant, I will ask them with you, Superintendent, in attendance. We will not have our station and our personal reputations destroyed by a rogue officer, no matter how well-meaning or personally damaged by his experiences. You may leave us, Ramsay, and hand all your notes and files to my assistant. I'll appoint a more reasonable investigating officer to continue."

"Sir," Ramsay said. He left the room. It was no more than he'd expected. He'd gambled on Wagner being the culprit and lost. If he'd been right, he'd be a hero. As it was, he would be in for years filing papers before being given another investigation to run. Politics was a nasty game, even for those who only brushed against it in the wrong way. His spirits, never very high, had been raised by the information on Wagner and now they were lower than ever. He shrugged. He'd known the risk and taken it with his eyes open; a man could do no more when duty demanded it.

Once his desk was clear, he had time to think. He still had the other girl's murder, which was at the collating of evidence and alibis stage and promising a successful and satisfying conclusion; the Chief hadn't mentioned removing him from that so there was still a chance to redeem himself.

He was still pondering when the Superintendent walked into his office. He looked shell-shocked. Ramsay actually felt sorry for him. He'd had no part in the events, but his career was also hanging by a thread.

"We need to talk to that interfering little madam and quickly before she does any more damage. Get her in here, Ramsay and quickly, man."

"We rely on the public for information, sir," Ramsay protested.

"I'm well aware of that, Inspector. It wasn't a request, it was an order," the Superintendent said, and stalked out, too angry to continue.

45

PAULINE

PAULINE FOUND herself being guided by DS Morrison into a well-appointed office with windows looking out across the houses to the trees of Jesmond Dene. Standing before a walnut desk was an elderly, erect man who looked sternly at her.

"Thank you, Morrison," the man said, nodding dismissal to her escort.

This didn't look good, she thought.

"Miss Riddell," he said, "I'm Superintendent Harrison and I've asked DS Morrison to bring you here because I've something to say that can't be said through an intermediary."

He didn't invite her to sit down and remained standing himself. This clearly wasn't going to be a long speech.

"This latest debacle is the second time you've brought evidence to the police against innocent people and the second time we have, perhaps not foolishly but certainly unwisely, investigated this evidence to the great distress of the people accused and ultimately the demoralization of our credibility in their eyes."

"What debacle?" Pauline asked. "Are you saying Wagner didn't have an affair with Marjorie?"

"We're saying he didn't meet with her that night. He provided us with his movements that night and we have confirmed them with those who were with him at the time and with those he met."

"Marjorie went to meet him, Superintendent. She told me so herself."

"She went to meet Wagner, that's true, but he couldn't be there. He left his assistant to meet Miss Armstrong and tell her of the change of plan."

"What you're saying is my information was good," Pauline said, the moment he paused for breath. "You had new lines of enquiry, to use your jargon, that you hadn't developed on your own."

"We have many calls on our resources, Miss Riddell, that often make us slow in developing our investigations. You say we hadn't developed them, it doesn't follow that we wouldn't."

"Then I helped by developing these inquiries. I saved you many man-hours, if you like." Many of the work documents she typed and filed spoke glowingly of man-hours saved for the company and the rewards the writer expected to be given for them.

"Miss Riddell, you may feel you were being helpful, maybe civic-minded, but you are not. You are interfering in an investigation into a serious crime. It is not a game that anyone can join in. You must desist. If you continue, I shall have no option other than to charge you with wasting police time or one of a number of other crimes. I repeat, you must not continue with this interference. Now, do I have your agreement to desist or at least your understanding that any further interference will result in charges being laid?"

Pauline could barely speak. Rage at this foolish man and his threats, when he knew he'd already effectively ended the investigation into Marjorie's murder, almost overwhelmed her.

With a great effort, she said, "I understand you will charge me if I continue. There, are you happy now?"

"No, I'm not," the Superintendent said, "but what happens in the future is on your own head. I will repeat what I've said, don't investigate this crime anymore. If, by chance, you learn of information you feel is valuable, bring it to *my* attention and I'll decide if it is worth spending our scarce resources on it."

"After this lecture, I would be a fool to bring you anything," Pauline said.

"You would be a fool not to, Miss Riddell," Harrison said. "Remember, I will hear what you have to say in future. Inspector Ramsay is no longer on this case."

Pauline didn't reply. She turned and strode out of the office and into the corridor, heading back to the entrance and the street. She felt if she didn't get there very soon, she'd burst with outraged indignation – if such a thing were possible. Just now it felt like it was possible.

The cold air of the street brought her back to earth and the realization she needed to think. She couldn't do that with her mind raging against the police and her own inability to see what she was sure was obvious: who the murderer was.

Going against her Yorkshire upbringing, though not against the notions of a better life her mother had taught her, Pauline strode to the Central Arcade and the expensive tea shop she'd gone to last time she was this upset and plunked herself in a chair.

A waitress came to serve her. Pauline thought she could detect a supercilious smirk in the waitress's expression. For a moment, she was ready to storm out but then the absurdity of the gesture sobered her. It was life she was angry with, not some poor woman like herself trying to make a living.

Pauline scanned the menu hoping she'd be able to find something that she could afford for she had very little cash in her purse. Afternoon teas, with their selection of elegant cucumber sandwiches and small cakes, were all too much for her slim purse.

"Tea and scone, please," she said, handing the menu back to the girl.

The waitress hurried off. Probably frightened by my expression, Pauline though ruefully. That silly, ungrateful man had quite spoiled her day. She had to put that behind her.

Slowly, as she waited, watching the shoppers passing along the arcade outside the teashop window, her heart stopped racing, her breathing quieted, and calm re-surfaced. It was pleasant sitting watching the world go by. The Arcade was still gay with its bunting from the Coronation festivities, though that was months ago. By the time her tea arrived, she was calm enough to consider her future. It took only a moment, for she knew she was doing right by her own standards and for poor Marjorie who was being abandoned by those whose job it was to pursue justice without favor. It was true she'd been horribly wrong twice and that was unnerving. Two innocent men had been made miserable by her amateurishness, but she could not let Marjorie and her parents down. She must continue her quest.

The difficulty was, she thought, previously she'd been able to see how the two people with motives, Hindmarsh and Wagner, could have done it, even though they appeared to have alibis for the time. Now, there were many people who could have been there at the time, a city full of people to be exact, but none of them had a motive. Or at least not one she knew of. She was back at the beginning; who had a motive and where were they at the time?

Even the tea and buttered scone, superior though they

were, couldn't supply enough creative spirit to answer those two simple questions. They did, however, calm her agitated mind.

46

RAMSAY

WHEN PAULINE HAD EXITED the office and was beyond hearing, the Superintendent turned to his subordinate and said, "And, Ramsay, I expect you to discourage that young woman. I don't deny she's done sterling work and the evidence she brought forward is invaluable, but she could be killed. If we haven't the murderer locked up, then where would we all be?"

"I understand that, sir," Ramsay said. "And maybe what she's proved is that we *do* have the murderer locked up. He's just clever enough to know that should he admit to this one, he goes from a manslaughter charge and years in prison to a murder charge and the gallows."

The Superintendent nodded. "I agree. But that young woman doesn't and you must find a way to stop her, otherwise she really will find herself on a charge of wasting police time and you'll find yourself in serious trouble with those above us both." He sighed and shook his head despairingly. He had daughters of his own and the last thing he wanted was for them to be encouraged into playing mind games with murderers.

"I'll do my best, sir," Ramsay said. "Will there be anything else?"

The Superintendent shook his head. "Not unless you've something to tell me on the Middleton case?"

"Nothing new, no."

"Very well, but mind what I say, Inspector. Stop her before she comes to harm. Even innocent people can become dangerous if they're pushed."

Ramsay left the office wondering how, exactly, he was to prevent a determined young woman from asking people questions about a publicly known event that happened months ago. It may be an unhealthy interest for someone to have but it wasn't against the law and he couldn't arrest her, even if he'd wanted to, which he didn't. She was doing much too valuable work, he thought, smiling at his own small rebellion against the world and its ways.

47

PAULINE

PAULINE WOKE and stared at the ceiling. It was only just light on a gray, overcast morning. The rain pattered against the window in gusts. The wind shook the window frame and the trees swooshed outside, blowing in the gale. Even if she wanted to, she wouldn't be investigating anything today. Again, a sleepless night brooding on what she'd lost had left her in dark despair. She'd lost a fiancé and a friend in quick succession and she could do nothing to right either of the two greatest injustices that had entered and marred her life. She felt too empty to go on. She couldn't even bury Stephen; his body would forever lie in Korea where no one knew him and where no one who knew him could visit. A photograph, some trinkets and a name on a War Memorial would be all she had to remember him by. Her helplessness was galling.

As the light in her room grew brighter, her spirits rose. She couldn't do anything for Stephen, though she'd like to do something unspeakably horrible to the leaders who'd brought this upon him and her, but she could do something for Marjorie. Bringing Marjorie's killer to justice would tilt the scales of justice ever so slightly back to the right side. It wouldn't bring either of them back but Stephen, wherever he was, would understand that she was working for him too.

Yesterday, after meeting the police, she was sure she would never do any investigating again. Now, with recovered drive, she was sure she would. She rose, wrapped herself against the cold morning air, found paper and a pencil and started to list what she knew, what she thought, and what she needed to know. It didn't take too long before she'd catalogued the whole of her meager knowledge. With it before her, she began to think.

If it wasn't Wagner, then who was it? Her heart sank when no other person suggested themselves to her. She really wasn't any good at this. Her mind was a blank with respect to suspects but awash in a whirl of wild tangents that led nowhere. She needed to dress and do something. There was no point in brooding. She had to get a grip on her mind because if she didn't, she'd be driven mad.

Why was Marjorie killed that night? She'd been meeting Wagner for months and now, it seemed, he wasn't even there that night. Is that why she died – because he wasn't there? Then what happened between the time Marjorie stormed out from what was going to be their afternoon tea at around four o'clock until she was stabbed and her body dumped at around eleven o'clock? Where would she have gone after Murdock told her the tryst was off?

She began to realize she hadn't asked enough questions of the police. Had Marjorie been raped? Or was there any kind of sexual connection? Where did Murdock meet Marjorie and at what time? Did anyone see Marjorie that night anywhere along the streets leading to the house or the hotel? Where had she gone after leaving Murdock? There were so many things the police knew, or might know, that she didn't. She was chasing shadows in the dark; a place where no shadows should exist.

With these gloomy, frustrating thoughts weighing on her mind, she dressed and went downstairs for breakfast. After they'd eaten, she joined the Bertrams in attending their church. Since the memorial service for Stephen, she at least knew some of the congregation. The service didn't hold her attention because her thoughts were still on Marjorie, and the vicar's High Anglican service didn't appeal. Her soul found the bells and smells too Roman Catholic for her simple tastes.

As they walked back from the service, she said, "I'm going for a drive after lunch if you'd like to join me." She knew she was safe making this offer for they liked a snooze after Sunday lunch, as all the old people did.

"Mind you don't use up all your petrol allowance," Major Bertram reminded her.

"I shan't be going far," Pauline said. "I just fancy a small jaunt before I settle down for the evening."

"If the rain continues like this," Mrs. Bertram said, gesturing to the steady downpour that sluiced down over their umbrellas, "you won't see anything out of the windows."

Pauline laughed. "It's true," she said, "but I'm too restless to read today."

It was left at that and Pauline drove out of the drive right after lunch, heading for the factory gate, where she stopped to take stock. She and Marjorie had walked out of the gate that evening and made their way to the nearby café, which she could see whenever the gusts of winds blew the rain aside.

They'd settled down to have their light meal in the café. At least that was the plan. Marjorie wanted company until she left to meet her lover at around five o'clock, she'd said. But Pauline had been distracted, thinking how wrong this all was, and about Stephen's letter. Marjorie had stalked out at around four o'clock instead. Pauline had watched her walking up the street until she turned the corner at the top.

Pauline put the car in gear and drove slowly up the street

Marjorie had walked that night. At the top, at the busier road, Marjorie had turned left, west toward the house where Pauline had seen Wagner and his assistant. Unfortunately, the map laid out on the passenger seat beside her showed it was also the way to the Elswick Arms Hotel.

She turned left and cruised slowly along the street. She would have to walk both routes to determine the time each would take but that wouldn't be today. She'd pick dry nights immediately following work. What she wanted to do today was pick a route that kept her away from the terraced houses and the people that lived in them. She knew this was unfair and not something Marjorie would have done. To Marjorie, the people and street scenes would have seemed like home, it was where she was from, after all. Not from this side of the city but an area that looked exactly the same. For Pauline, country-bred and from the North Riding of Yorkshire, the thin, grim-faced men and plump grim-faced women with harsh voices were frightening. It was a sad case of country mouse come to town.

After a few moments, she passed the junction that led to the hotel. Normally, she'd probably be able to see it. Today, the curtain of rain, which was bringing down the coal smoke from every chimney, made seeing even halfway down the street impossible. She drove on until she turned right, drove along the street, and parked opposite the house. She'd expected it to be empty. It was Sunday, after all, but men could be seen through the window. They looked ordinary enough; suits, ties, white shirts, groomed hair and, if they had it, facial hair, but there was something disquieting about it. She waited. Four of the men left the house after about thirty minutes, got into a black official-looking car that had been parked in the drive, and drove off. Moments later, Pauline was surprised to see Murdock leave the house and get into a smaller car before driving off, leaving the house in darkness.

She drove back to the Bertram's perplexed. What was it about the scene she'd witnessed that was off? She saw it. The men looked like the Trade Union leaders, those grim-faced men who regularly descended on the factory to argue the case for their members. She was always struck by their lined faces and how none of the lines were laughter lines. Those people never smiled or laughed. Relieved, she drove home, satisfied she'd explained away her growing disquiet.

* * *

THE AFTERNOON WAS blustery but dry. Overhead, a cornflower-blue sky was studded with high mare's tail clouds. She locked her car, checked her watch and set off walking, heading north, following the route she'd picked out on Sunday that would take her from the café where Marjorie began her last journey to the place she would have run into Murdock. It was still light at three-thirty. If she wasn't quick, she'd be returning in the dark, something she definitely didn't want to do.

Occasionally, children at the tops of each street that joined the western road stood and stared. Some shouted childishly rude comments, but none seemed dangerous and she marched on. She still felt comfortable when the street that led to the hotel appeared on her right. She checked her watch. Fifteen minutes had passed and, as she could see the hotel today from where she stood, she judged only another five to ten minutes walking would take her there.

She continued heading west until, turning north when she reached the junction, she reached the house in a further ten minutes. Twenty-five minutes to each destination. Marjorie could have been at either of them by 4:25 that afternoon. Back then, it would have still been broad daylight on a sunny, though showery, afternoon. Someone must have seen her.

Pauline walked past the house, looking briefly in to see who was there on this Tuesday afternoon. Disappointingly, no one appeared to be. At the next junction, she turned right and followed the narrow road that she knew from the map would bring her out at the Elswick Arms Hotel. It did, in only eight minutes. She marched on. The light was going, and she didn't want to be alone on any of these quiet side streets when it was gone.

At the car, she jotted down her notes on a hand drawn sketch she'd made before setting out. That done, she started the engine and headed home. She had no idea if any of this would help her thoughts take a productive direction, but it was at least something she could do.

"You're late, dear," Mrs. Bertram said as Pauline entered the house.

"Some loose ends to tie up at work," Pauline said. "I'll freshen up and be right back."

"Be quick, tea's been ready a while."

Pauline smiled and headed upstairs. It was wonderful to have a meal ready when one came home but there were times when she wondered if the price she paid in lost privacy wasn't a little too high.

Pauline spent the rest of the week thinking of a plan to get back into that house and have a good nose around. She was sure that something in there would jog her memory of something Marjorie said. Marjorie must have met Wagner there sometimes, even if they didn't go to bed there. Marjorie would never have marched up to the Elswick Arms Hotel without Wagner being already in attendance. It would have been advertising the illicit nature of the relationship and the hotel would likely have reacted in a way the couple wouldn't have liked.

By Saturday, she had a plan. It was a terrible plan, she acknowledged that, but it was a plan. She typed herself an envelope addressed to Dr. Wagner and put it in her coat pocket. When quitting time Saturday finally arrived, she drove away from the factory and parked close to the house where the car couldn't be seen by passersby on the street or by people inside the house. She waited until the street was empty and then, taking a deep breath, stepped out of the car. Her plan was to knock on the door and say she'd been asked to give this letter from the factory to Dr. Wagner. Using the company's official envelope and a typed address should be enough to make it seem genuine. Provided Wagner wasn't there, and she'd have to be sure he wasn't, she hoped she'd be allowed inside to hand it over to some senior person. While this was happening, she could inspect the people, desks, tables, anything really, for clues and the windows and doors for weaknesses. All she had to do was keep talking, and keep them talking, while she spied out what was going on there when people were present. Whatever Poppy might think of what Pauline saw during her last spying mission, Pauline still didn't believe anyone worked in that house.

She had just turned the corner keeping her and the car out of sight, when she saw an old van pull into the driveway. Barely legible on the van's sides was the name 'Clark's Cleaning Services'. Pauline smiled wryly. It seemed even in this Poppy guessed correctly. A middle-aged man got out of the driver's seat and two others got out of the rear doors. She was surprised. Of course, there was no reason men couldn't be cleaners, they just never were in her experience. Maybe this was one of those desperate changes of employment she'd read about where men, returning from the war into a devastated economy, were trying their hands at work they normally wouldn't have done. Whatever the reason, she had to abandon her initial plan and find another. At first, she thought she could just present herself to the cleaners as a courier and get in that way. Watching them move from the van to the house, changed her mind. They didn't look anything like cleaners or not of the office kind anyway.

She stepped back behind the corner and watched. The men took cleaning supplies and tools out of the back of the van and went into the house. Pauline waited. After ten minutes without any one of them returning to the van, she quickly crossed the road and began walking toward the house. She slowed as she came to the entrance and studied the bay window carefully. Inside, she could see one man cleaning a desk and phone. It seemed perfectly normal behavior. Disappointed, she walked on. At an upstairs window, she could see a man watching her and the street. Their eyes met and it gave her a jolt.

She hurried on and turned the corner of the first side street she came to. After a minute, she returned to the corner and peered around it. No one had followed her. Looking around, she saw the narrow alley running down the back of the houses where coal for the boiler would be delivered. Keeping close to the wall in case anyone was on the lookout from the back of the house, she made her way along the lane until she reached the back gate of the house and its coal shed. She took a quick peek around the wall that separated the yard from the lane and saw no one at any of the windows. It made sense. There were only three men and if two were tied up watching, the third would be cleaning all day – hardly a practical process.

The gate was locked. It wasn't high. She could see over it. Hitching up her skirt, she placed her left foot in a gap in the wall where a brick had been broken and lifted herself up. With her right foot on the handle of the gate, she pushed herself up again until she could sit on the gate top. A moment later, she swiveled her legs over and let herself down to the ground. She paused, keeping in the cover of the overgrown shrubs in this corner of the yard. She saw no movement at the windows, so she quickly crossed the yard and pressed herself against the wall beside the rear door of the house. She was sure everyone in the street must be able to hear her breathing and her heart thumping, they sounded frighteningly loud. After a moment, it was clear no one could except her because, almost at once, she heard voices just the other side of the window. As before at the Wagner home, she found it maddening that she could hear people speaking but not clearly enough to be sure of what they were saying. There was no hope of getting closer to the window because there was no curtain or blind on it; she would be seen.

Frustrated, she listened carefully for a few moments before giving up and making her way stealthily down the side of the house. This took her past the toilet window she'd climbed in before. This time it was securely closed. She continued to the front of the house with its open driveway looking out to the empty street. She could only hope it stayed empty as she continued eavesdropping When she was sure no one was outside, she peered around the corner to the bay window. Here there were curtains and they were closed. This, at least, meant she could get much closer to the glass to listen, provided no one came along the street. In this, she was helped by the weather. A thin afternoon mist was settling in and capturing the smoke from the chimneys. Visibility was still too good for Pauline's comfort, but most people would stay indoors where it was warm and dry. It was worth a try.

Silently, she made her way to the window. A movement, at the point where the curtain and window frame almost met, made her start but in another step, she passed that line-of-sight and was securely hidden by the curtain. No one was talking in this room. The only thing she could hear was a clicking sound. Intrigued she moved closer to the point where she'd seen the gap between the curtain and frame. Carefully, heart thumping, she leaned forward and peeked inside before jumping back. A man was taking photos of papers on a desk. That awful briefing they'd been given at work about industrial spying and international spying came back forcibly.

Now, it seemed, she'd stumbled upon one or the other of these two groups of wrongdoers. Her thoughts were in turmoil. It was too incredible. Surely spies weren't so obvious and open about their work. Shouldn't all this be happening in darkness, away from the gaze of honest citizens? Anyone could walk by here and see what they were doing; it was madness. After a few moments, her mind and heart settled, her breathing returned to almost normal and she could see that it wasn't as mad as it seemed. What would a passerby see? A cleaning van in the drive and people moving about inside the offices. The spying part was hidden from the street by the curtains and even that may have a perfectly innocent explanation to a passerby. And while most people would understand such things as spies existed, they'd never imagine they were watching a gang of them at work. It was so extraordinarily ordinary a sight, no one would be suspicious at all. She only stumbled upon it because of the unrelated death of a friend.

A new thought crossed her mind; was it unrelated? Did Marjorie arrive at the house too early that night and see or hear something that she knew at once was wrong? Did she realize it too late? Or not even notice it at all but the spies couldn't take the chance she'd realize it later and tell someone?

She heard voices in the room and now she could hear snippets of what was being said. Her stomach felt like lead. She was a patriotic, rightminded person but she fervently wished someone other than herself had stumbled on this and she was at home sewing and listening to the radio. She forced herself to stay and listen, afraid the men inside were preparing to leave, and she would be seen. Torn between the competing needs of staying or running, she found she was trembling. Her knees felt so jelly-like, she wasn't sure she could run. She looked around the garden. There were bushes and a hedge, but not enough of either to hide in. Her best hope lay in getting to the other side of the bay window and listening from there. If she heard them leaving for sure, she could run down the short drive, cross the street, and hopefully reach her car before they caught her. While the men were talking, she quickly made her way to what she thought was a safer spot and pressed her ear against the glass.

"Is there anything else?"

"No, this is it."

The clicking stopped. Obviously, he'd taken all the pictures.

"Now we clean and make it good. Last week, there were complaints."

"Yeah, we know."

The conversation ended. Pauline was utterly deflated. All her fright for a conversation that was utterly worthless. With one last look around to be sure she was safe, she walked quickly down the drive, through the gate and turned immediately right so she was behind the hedge as she went down the street. Her only thought was to reach her car and get as far away from here as she could. She wouldn't stop shivering until she'd put five miles between herself and this house and these men.

She drove quickly, much too quickly for her comfort, but soon, when she'd seen no white van in her rear-view mirror for fifteen minutes, she pulled over and let herself relax. Slowly, the trembling eased, and calm returned. She got out of the car. Even the icy wind blowing the thickening mist was a joy to feel on her face. She walked to a stile she'd seen from the car, stepped across it, and set out into the field beyond, to the bemusement of a small herd of Jersey cows who eyed her with deep suspicion.

Their gentle expressions, however, made her smile. They watched her go by, munching placidly and she felt at peace again. Their presence was such a contrast to what had gone before; she now realized the other nagging fear that had been behind her loss of control. It had been obvious immediately. Even if there were men doing cleaning in these desperate times, they weren't men like those lean, grim creatures. Those men were straight out of the wrong side in a Hollywood thriller.

Eventually, the cold seeped into her frame. She hadn't dressed for walking in the damp countryside. She turned back with a puzzle to solve. Who to tell? Dr. Enderby said their employer didn't do business with Stirling Engine Company, so the spies weren't getting secrets from her employer. Inspector Ramsay had been removed from his position as head of the murder investigation, which was her fault so she could expect no welcome from him, and the new man, Harrison, clearly wouldn't be willing to risk his position following any new evidence she provided after what had happened to Ramsay. The most likely outcome of her approaching Superintendent Harrison was she'd be the one arrested. There was only one person going to bring this out into the open and, however frightening the thought, that person was her.

48

RAMSAY, DECEMBER 1953

SUNDAY again and Inspector Ramsay sat at his desk staring at the pile of folders he was supposed to be doing something about. Harrison was really making him pay for his wrong step over Dr. Wagner. In his mind, he replayed the interview with Wagner. There was information there they should have followed up but didn't because someone in London got to the Chief Constable and stopped it. Now their second murder case was wrapping up, he was left with dotting the 'I's and crossing the 'T's. Most of it, he'd delegated. The files in front of him he'd saved to make work during yet another Sunday spent alone. They were not holding his interest.

The assistant, Murdock, had confirmed he'd met with and fobbed off Marjorie Armstrong. He said it was at the junction of two streets near the hotel. He said it was minutes before five and he'd waited for Miss Armstrong there as ordered by Wagner. But, and this was the part he wished now to follow up, Miss Armstrong should have been there already. After all, she'd left Miss Riddell in a huff almost an hour before and it was no more than fifteen minutes' walk, even in those party shoes the victim was wearing. So where was she for the other forty-five minutes? She didn't wait at the hotel. He knew that because he'd interviewed the receptionist just before he'd been pulled off the case.

And where did she go after she'd been told there was to be no meeting that night? This one was a real puzzle. Somebody would have noticed her, dressed as she was. He knew little about women's fashion but even he would notice someone wearing that coat and those shoes, even if they didn't see that brooch. She would have stood out like a lighthouse on a clifftop anywhere except in the very best establishments in Newcastle. Nobody had recognized her at the places where they'd interviewed staff, when they were still hoping to find where Wagner might have taken a young woman to dazzle her. He wondered if Miss Riddell had given any of this further thought or if had she done as she was told. There was only one way to find out. He rang the Bertrams' and Miss Riddell was soon on the phone.

"Yes, Inspector," she said, "have you called to check up on me? Make sure I'm staying well away from the police investigation?"

"In a manner of speaking," Ramsay said, quietly. He didn't need anyone in the station listening in. "I wondered if we might have a chat. For old time's sake, you might say."

"Now?"

"If it's convenient. I could drive up and we could find a quiet pub to talk."

"Later this afternoon. I'm about to sit down to Sunday dinner and it would not do to miss that."

"I will pick you up at two, then," Ramsay said.

* * *

"INSPECTOR," Pauline said, when she closed the door of the car, "before we go or talk, I want to say how sorry I am that you suffered for investigating the information I gave."

Ramsay smiled. "Miss Riddell," he said, as he drove the car out of the Bertrams' driveway, "there's no need. Into every policeman's life there comes a moment when we tread on the toes of some powerful person, even here in a quiet backwater like ours. This will blow over and all will be forgotten."

"Is Wagner so powerful?"

"Not here," Ramsay said, "but there are people in London to whom he is important. Politicians and civil service people who have interests of their own and will close their eyes to almost anything to get their way."

"Surely not, Inspector!" Pauline sounded aghast.

Ramsay smiled again. Twice in one day was almost a record for him.

"Forgive me, Miss Riddell, if I'm attacking your belief in your fellow man and our country. I have reason to dislike politicians that has nothing to do with my job and it clouds my judgment of their nature sometimes."

"I hope that is so, Inspector," Pauline said. "I can't accept our leaders are doing anything but acting in our best interests. They may not always be right, but I have to believe they are doing their best for us all."

Ramsay laughed, a genuine feeling of humor that he'd thought himself unable to have any longer.

"If you have such faith in the authorities, Miss Riddell, why are you doing your own investigation?"

"When I said 'not always right', I include the thought they may not always act quickly enough or with clear enough vision," Pauline said, "which is what is happening here."

"Forgive me, again, Miss Riddell. I'm really not mocking you and your faith does you credit," Ramsay said. He paused and added, "When you have worked for a few more years, you will see why I've grown cynical about our leaders."

He could see Pauline had become silent; her expression

remained guarded and cold. Exactly the opposite of what he'd wanted. He gave himself a mental kick.

"Let us talk of less contentious things," he said, as he pulled into the pub parking lot. "Have you thought any more about what happened to your friend?"

He could see immediately from her expression, the way she didn't catch his eye, that she had something to share. Now, he realized, he'd given himself a mountain to climb to get it out of her.

"I think of it often, Inspector. After all, I blame myself a lot for what happened. If she'd had a more sympathetic listener, a less censorious friend, she'd have stayed until five o'clock, which was what we'd planned. Was it me sending her away early that caused her death, for example?"

Ramsay didn't answer until they were seated in a small, isolated area of The Snug with a sherry for Miss Riddell and a pint of bitter for himself.

"I don't think you should blame yourself in any way for what happened, Miss Riddell," he said. "There were many hours between you and your friend parting company and undoubtedly many events happened in those hours. Anywhere during that time, someone could have made different decisions and saved Miss Armstrong's life. Including Miss Armstrong."

"You may be right, Inspector, but you can see why I fret over this," Pauline said.

Ramsay nodded. "I do indeed. It's called survivor's guilt and we all have some of that."

"Why did you want to talk to me, if not to scold me for further interference?"

"The other murder case is wrapping up and I find my mind wandering back to this earlier one. Somewhere there's something we've missed." He studied Pauline's face as he said this but detected no change in her expression. Either she had grown warier than before or she really had given up.

"Why do you think I may have something that could help you find this missing piece?"

"You knew Miss Armstrong better than anyone, so far as we could tell," Ramsay said. "I know you shut out what she told you, but I'd hoped some memory, something said, would have come to mind since the murder."

Pauline shook her head. "I remember some of what she said. Only it was romantic twaddle, for the most part. 'Eric was so mature, so knowledgeable, so sensitive, so cultured, so…' well you get the picture."

"She was really in love, you think?"

"Oh, yes. A real schoolgirl crush but with an adult woman's emotions." Pauline shook her head in despair.

"You met Wagner. Was he in love, do you think?"

"No! I spoke to him, spoke Marjorie's name to him, he showed not a hint of feeling. Like all those over-educated men, they have shallow feelings. I see many of them at work. Brilliant scientists and engineers but cold personalities. He was one of that kind."

"And nothing since has happened that sheds more light?" This time, he noticed, Pauline hesitated before replying. Only a millisecond but enough.

"Inspector," she said, "I have given you information twice and you followed up on it. I'm very grateful but it has cost you dearly in your career, I'm sure of that, and if you do so again, you may well lose your job. I've no doubt you have a family that needs your income, so I won't put your livelihood at risk again."

"My family can't be hurt by what happens to me, Miss Riddell, don't concern yourself over that. And, as I said, like many police detectives, I will occasionally upset someone in power and be punished because of it. It's part of our lives."

"But this time it's from London the power has reached out to punish you."

"In this country, London is where the worst people live and work. We have to accept that. After all, we elect many of them."

"You don't like politicians, Inspector?"

"I don't, Miss Riddell, and I don't discriminate. I don't like any of them."

Pauline smiled. "A strange sentiment from a servant of the Crown and Parliament," she said.

"You work in an armaments factory," Ramsay said. "Does everyone there like what their products will be used for?"

Pauline frowned. "To be honest," she said. "I'm not sure it ever sat easily with my own Christian principles. And now I have even more reason to dislike what I do for a living, though I see we have to defend ourselves if we are attacked."

Ramsay laughed. "Then, Miss Riddell, we're both rebels in our own way so don't worry about my future and tell me what you have discovered."

Pauline smiled. "I assure you I'm no rebel, Inspector, just someone trying to do what is right, but I take your point. To answer your question, I think I've found another motive for Marjorie's murder."

"Aha!" Ramsay said. "My missing piece."

"Well, maybe. I'm reluctant to press this too much. I was so horribly wrong before."

"All investigations go down wrong paths ninety percent of the time, don't let that put you off. And when you find the right answer, you'll think you are the dimmest person in the world. Believe me, I know. Most of my work has been routine. Silly people doing silly things that turn out badly and they end up in court. Since I became a Detective Inspector, I've only had five truly major cases to solve and each time, when I solved them, instead of feeling elation, I was plunged into despair for my stupidity in missing right away what at the end seemed so obvious. I've no doubt when this one is solved I shall feel the same way."

"I hope not. I certainly won't. I'll be ecstatic to know someone will pay for Marjorie's death."

"Then shall we talk about what you've learned and pool our resources?"

Once again, Pauline hesitated, and then asked, "First, tell me where Murdock said he met Marjorie."

"He said he waited at the four corners at the top of the street that leads straight from the factory gate," Ramsay said. "Miss Armstrong arrived just about five, as he'd been told she would, and he explained the change of plan."

"It doesn't make sense," Pauline said. "From the café, I watched Marjorie walk up that street and turn the corner at the top and that was not long after four o'clock. Even if the meeting place were around the corner, where I couldn't see, she wouldn't have waited there for forty-five minutes, She wasn't the type. And, if she didn't, then Murdock is lying."

"I agree, however, we've found nobody who can tell us either way; that is, whether they were there or not. If he sticks to his story, and at this point he has to, there's nothing we can do."

Pauline again hesitated. Finally, she said, "I've been wrong on the two most obvious suspects so I'm reluctant to tell you my new ones. You'll think I'm mad."

"I can only repeat, share what you have and let me be the judge."

Pauline told him of her recent visit to the house. When she'd finished, waited silently for his opinion.

Ramsay found it hard to say anything. His mind was whirling through many computations of what he'd just heard. At last, he said, "Spies, Miss Riddell? Here in Newcastle?"

"I said you'd think I was mad."

"It seems unlikely, that's all. Traitors generally live in London, by all accounts, not out here."

"But here we have an arms factory and two military testing ranges," Pauline said. "Even spies must come to see these things sometimes and why not now? After all, we're in a war and we're testing new armored vehicles and jet planes. Why shouldn't there be spies?"

"I see you've given this some thought," Ramsay said.

"Recently, we've had reminders at work about spies," Pauline said, "so I may be a bit pre-disposed to see reds under the bed where others don't. Still, I saw what I saw and I can't explain it any other way."

"But why would they kill poor Marjorie?"

"Because she went there on her own when she wasn't supposed to be there. My guess is they didn't decide to kill her at once but at some time that night they realized they had no choice."

"Then how did she come to be where she was found? No, this won't do, Miss Riddell. Even you must see this doesn't fit. Marjorie was stabbed at the same time as that idiot, her body dumped nearby. How could any of these spies have done that?"

"I've only just discovered these people exist, Inspector," Pauline said. "I haven't put all the pieces together yet. I hoped you, at least, could help me do that. I wouldn't have told you otherwise."

Ramsay nodded. "My apologies, Miss Riddell. I'm treating you like a detective sergeant and I shouldn't. I will see if any of this can be verified from the official channels and we will talk again."

"Clark's Cleaning Services should be easy to check."

"It should, if it's a legitimate business. You saw this on Saturday, but your friend went to the house on Friday, if she went there. Is it likely that spies would be at the house stealing secrets every day?"

"I don't know, Inspector, but I plan to find out. After all, if they only came to the house once and then vanished, they'd rather give the game away don't you think? If I can see them photographing papers and get some evidence, a photo of my own perhaps, maybe then you'll believe me."

"I do believe you, Miss Riddell. I'm not saying you didn't see what you saw but this is a huge jump from an isolated murder to an industrial or military spying ring. It needs some time and effort to confirm. This is probably our last chance to get justice for your friend and her parents. If we get it wrong, the two of us will be the ones who suffer."

"Of course, you're right, Inspector. Forgive me, I'm just so frustrated that I can't do more."

"You have done more than any others would, Miss Riddell. Now let me do some investigating and we'll move on from there."

"I will await the results of your investigations, Inspector. I hope by 'we'll move on from there' you really do mean we will move on together?"

"Yes, Miss Riddell, I believe for better or worse we are harnessed together in this to the end, whatever that might be."

"One for all and all for one, Inspector," Pauline said and held out her hand. They shook hands on their newly created pact, both with wry smiles on their faces.

"More like Nick and Nora than Musketeers," Ramsay said, "without all the cocktails, of course."

49

PAULINE

AFTER INSPECTOR RAMSAY had dropped her back at the Bertrams' house, Pauline tried to get back into the book she'd been reading when he'd phoned. She couldn't. Daphne du Maurier's hero was still refusing to see what an awful woman Rachel was and that this whole thing would end badly for him if God, or nature, didn't intervene. Pauline had enjoyed the film when she'd seen it only a few months before, but the book was harder going. Now it wasn't going at all. She'd more or less promised Ramsay she wouldn't do anything to put herself in danger, and she agreed with that in the main, but she needed to do something.

His point that she jumped to conclusions, however, was well taken. She had to start thinking strategically – it was wonderful the words one learned when working for an arms manufacturer – rather than tactically. Now she looked back, the plan she'd made about turning up at the house with an empty envelope in order to gain admittance wasn't just a poor one, it was suicidal. The thought of what would have happened to her if she'd gained admittance and the deception exposed while she was still inside gave her the shivers.

The first thing she could do was look into Clark's Cleaning. She wished she'd noticed if they'd had a phone number on the side of the van, but she hadn't. That wasn't a problem because the first thing she could do was look them up in the city phone book. They weren't there. Inspector Ramsay said he'd check them too so maybe he'd have better sources. It occurred to her they may not be a local firm at all. If they did important clients across the country, security-minded firms possibly, they may be in the *Register of Companies*.

The following day at work, she checked in the *Register*. They weren't there either. The rest of the morning was spent trying to decide what that meant. Did it mean she was right and they were spies using a bogus company name? But why would any company working in a sensitive field use a cleaning team that had no offices or registration? In which case, they probably weren't spies at all, just some friends of the owner or manager of Stirling Engines, working for cash in hand. There was only one way to find out and that was to go back after working hours and watch for the van to return. Provided she did that safely, she would still be keeping her promise to the Inspector.

At lunch time, she phoned Mrs. Bertram from the call box outside the factory gates and told her she was working late that night and would be every day this week. She explained it as being a frightfully hush-hush project that couldn't be mentioned to anyone so Mrs. Bertram mustn't talk about Pauline's late nights either.

Back at her desk, nibbling on a rather soggy egg and cress sandwich in the palest, whitest bread she'd ever seen, Pauline hoped her explanation would keep Mrs. Bertram happy because she was still being overly protective and would try to prevent her from investigating further. She finished her sandwich and decided she'd stick to pastries from the tea trolley in future; they were much less likely to wilt when kept in a desk drawer until lunch time.

After work, Pauline drove to the same spot she'd parked on Saturday and waited. It was already dark and the street lamps had haloes of misty light around them when she stepped out of the car. She walked to the corner and peered round the edge. There were still lights on in the house and a car in the drive, so she returned to her own car, pulled her coat closely around herself and sat back to wait.

Fifteen minutes later, unable to contain her impatience, she returned to her observation post – the military phrases were popping into her head readily now. Again, the car was still in the drive. There was no sign of cleaners. She returned to her own car in frustration. It was too cold to sit any longer, so she started the engine and drove slowly around the corner and past the house. A man was exiting the door. His back was to her and she only had a second as she drove by the entrance, but she was sure it was Murdock, Wagner's assistant. She drove on and pulled over to park at the curb. In her rearview mirror, she saw the car back out of the driveway and head toward her. She slipped down in her seat hoping not to be seen by the driver as the car passed. Unfortunately, that meant she couldn't confirm who the driver was and the car was turning onto the main road before she'd started her own car.

Her first thought was to follow him, whoever he was. Then she remembered she was now doing strategic thinking, looking for the bigger picture, and settled down again to wait for the cleaning van she was sure would soon appear. By six o'clock, with no van in sight, she gave up on strategy and drove home.

50

RAMSAY AND PAULINE

INSPECTOR RAMSAY LEFT the office and headed home. He'd no sooner reached his house than he changed his mind and drove to the Bertrams' house where he discovered Miss Riddell was working late all this week. This should have made him angry, knowing she was quite clearly putting herself in danger when she'd said she wouldn't, but he wasn't angry – or surprised.

He was invited in and spent a comfortable hour talking with the Bertrams about the state of the world and their city. Ramsay knew enough about people and interrogation to know when he was being sized up. Mrs. Bertram, he was sure, was considering his suitability as a partner for Pauline, even though there was such a difference in their ages. It amused him to keep them guessing as to his motive in visiting. Was he here as a suitor or as a policeman? Even his steady temper, however, was growing stretched by the time they heard Pauline's car enter the driveway and park.

His annoyance vanished when he saw how guilty she looked when she saw him.

"Good evening, Miss Riddell. I hope you don't mind me calling on you uninvited, as it were."

"Not at all, Inspector. Give me a moment to hang my coat up and I'll be right with you." She hurried upstairs before he could answer.

When she returned, Mrs. Bertram said, "You and the Inspector will want to be private, I expect. Use the good room, my dear."

Pauline led Ramsay into the good room, kept for best occasions, and signaled him to sit. The room was cold for there hadn't been a fire lit in it for some days.

"Have you brought news, Inspector?"

"In a manner of speaking," Ramsay said. "Though it's no news also. There's no such company as Clark's Cleaning. Are you sure you remember the name right?"

"I am," Pauline said. She paused, and then said, "As I'm sure you've guessed, I've been watching the house to see if they come back."

"I take it they haven't?"

"Not yet but I have hopes for tomorrow and Saturday."

"Then I shall join you, if I may, for those watches."

"I'd be very grateful if you would, Inspector. It isn't comfortable being on my own in the dark in a strange part of town. Where shall we meet?"

Ramsay gave her directions and Pauline wrote them in her diary.

"Do you have any better news?"

"Not exactly," Ramsay said. "I know more about Murdock, the assistant you dislike so much."

"Tell me."

"He's single, from a good family, went to a minor public school followed by Cambridge University, and, interestingly in support of your feelings toward him, he's not generally liked by men or women. He was in the Spanish Civil War as a volunteer and in our Intelligence Services during the war. He wasn't much liked there either and was moved out to the regular Civil Service where he got the job of assisting Dr. Wagner to liaise with his British counterparts in the academic, industrial, and political world. It's generally considered he's done all right in that role."

"Not a glowing reference or career," Pauline said.

"It isn't. I find it interesting no one seems to know or like him. Usually someone has a kind word, even for an obvious loner like him."

"He looks like that kind of person who has a permanent grudge against the world," Pauline said. "You know what I mean. In his mind everyone is picking on him and nothing is ever right. I've only spent one meeting in his company, and seen him occasionally in the company of Wagner, but his expression was always the same, a disdainful sneer. I don't like him."

Ramsay nodded, smiling. "I got that," he said, "and while I'd normally tell you not to judge a book by its cover, I also got the same sense when talking to him as well, though he managed to answer our questions openly and, so far as we can tell, honestly."

"Until tomorrow then, Inspector," Pauline said, as he left.

51

PAULINE AND RAMSAY

"I'M pleased you're here, Inspector," Pauline said, as they pressed together under his umbrella peering around the corner to the house. "Otherwise I'd be soaked."

"This is December, Miss Riddell, how could you forget your umbrella?"

"I'm not an umbrella sort of person but today may yet change my mind."

"I think we can return to the car for now, Miss Riddell. Our friends Wagner and Murdock are still there and there's no sign of your mysterious cleaners."

"I agree. My feet are freezing," Pauline said.

"You're dressed for a heated office and not a sentry post. I feel you will have to be more practical if this game goes on much longer."

They walked quickly back to the car and jumped in.

"It wasn't raining when I left home this morning," Pauline protested.

"I hope this isn't how the winter is going to be," Ramsay said, gloomily staring out of the window at the downpour. "It was bad last winter, the flooding and all those people killed. We don't need another."

Pauline nodded. She knew people who'd lost family members along the Yorkshire coast in those storms. The weather since the war ended had been awful, terrible snow and cold in 1947 and then devastating flooding earlier this year. It made her wonder about mankind's effect on the world; did all those bombs have something to do with it?

They sat in comfortable silence for some minutes while Ramsay made notes and Pauline watched the rain sluicing down the car windows. Their warmth began to steam up the windows inside, reducing their visibility even further.

"People will get the wrong idea about us," Ramsay said, watching Pauline clearing the condensation so she could see out.

"That will be to our benefit. After all, people can understand something of that kind, while sitting staring out of a car window for an hour is suspicious."

"Time to get back to our post," Ramsay said. "I'll go if you'd rather keep dry."

"This is my investigation, Inspector. You're only here to observe." She opened the door and stepped out into the downpour.

Ramsay exited the car, opened his umbrella and quickly walked to her side. They crossed the short distance to the corner and peered around. Pauline hoped that Ramsay's suggestion of people misunderstanding their intentions would come to their aid here as well. To a passerby, she felt, they'd look just like a courting couple enjoying being romantically isolated in the rain, lost in a world of their own.

"They're here!" Pauline could hardly contain her excitement.

The white van was now in the drive, parked behind Wagner's official car and preventing it from leaving.

"I can't read the sign on the side," Ramsay said.

"We have to get closer," Pauline said. "Here's where our couple disguise will really work for us."

"Unless they look closely. I'm old enough to be your father."

"Wagner was old enough to be Marjorie's father," Pauline reminded him.

They walked quickly across the narrow street and then slowly made their way to the entrance and the van. The company name was clearly marked but there was no phone number or address.

"A strange sort of business that makes it impossible for customers to find them," Ramsay said. Their pace slowed even further as they passed the narrow gap where the bay window was visible. The curtains were drawn but shadows could be seen on them from the lights inside.

"They're all talking," Ramsay said. "It's a regular stand-up meeting. Do managers and engineers regularly talk to the cleaners, do you think?"

"I think they might give orders, even explain the standards they expect, but not, I think, stand around talking like they were doing."

They continued walking to the turn and the narrow alley Pauline had followed on her previous visit. She pointed out the gate where she'd climbed in, then through the shrubs to the window where she'd trespassed.

"It would be too conspicuous for us to saunter down there today," Ramsay said. "The brolly would give us away."

"We can wait at the corner and see what happens," Pauline said. "Having them all here is too good to miss."

They returned to their original lookout position and waited. Pauline's teeth were chattering before the van driver exited the house and backed the van out of the drive. Wagner and his assistant backed their car out and drove away. The van returned to the drive, its driver returned to the house, and the activity was over.

Deflated, Pauline and Ramsay returned to the car. She switched on the engine and turned up the heater to warm herself. In minutes, the windows were again misted over.

"There's nothing more we can do here tonight, Miss Riddell, and to continue will only make you ill. I suggest we leave and return tomorrow afternoon when we might have a better opportunity of observing their activities."

Pauline nodded. Her teeth still chattered too much to speak.

"And tomorrow, you'll be dressed more warmly, I hope."

* * *

SATURDAY WAS ALMOST the opposite of Friday, as far as the weather was concerned. The day was bright and icy. Yesterday's rain was now frozen puddles when they returned to watch the proceedings.

"I've set some of my team digging into Clark's Cleaning and Stirling Engines," Ramsay said as Pauline parked her car, continuing the conversation they'd had while driving. "We've looked at Stirling Engines before but clearly neither of these are quite what they seem."

"At least you don't think I'm mad anymore," Pauline said.

"I've never thought you mad, Miss Riddell. Your information has always been good. Your analysis has been good too. It's just been the conclusions you've drawn from both that have been too quickly reached."

Pauline nodded. "I'm still only learning, Inspector."

He smiled. "Are you thinking of a change of career?"

Pauline shook her head. "As a police detective, how much

freedom do you have on cases? I suspect much less than people imagine. No, that wouldn't do for me."

They left the car and made their way to the corner, where Ramsay leaned against the wall and Pauline leaned against him. This really was a useful disguise, she thought, blushing faintly as Ramsay's momentarily surprised expression gave way to a sly grin.

"I'm merely making our presence more understandable to observers, Inspector," Pauline said, in case that grin meant more than just amusement.

"I'm pleased to hear it, Miss Riddell. I'm too old for such goings-on."

It was still too early. There was a car in the drive, not Wagner's, and no van. They were about to leave when the car driver appeared from out of the house. It was Murdock. He rooted around inside the vehicle and returned to the house with a briefcase.

"I wish we could get inside that house," Ramsay said in frustration.

"Do police have listening devices?"

"Yes, but we have to have a warrant and for that, we need a reason."

"Can we get the device and place it ourselves?"

"That's illegal, Miss Riddell. I'll pretend I didn't hear it."

"My earlier point about how much freedom you have is demonstrated, I think, Inspector," Pauline said with a smile.

They continued watching, whiling away the minutes in small talk. Pauline was ready to return to her car for warmth when the van arrived. It parked at the curbside and the men climbed out. She couldn't tell if they were the same three as last week or not. They entered the house and the street settled once again into its quiet state.

"We'll warm up, I think," Ramsay said. He could obviously feel her starting to shiver. They returned to the car and waited with the engine running and heater on. Pauline didn't like to think of the fuel she was wasting, her weekly ration was small enough as it was.

"I'll go back and check," Ramsay said. "I'll signal if there's anything to see."

He left the car and was soon peering around the corner. He stepped back and motioned her to join him, which she quickly did.

Murdock was leaving and the van was pulling into the space his car had just left. Once again, the street and house settled into a Saturday afternoon state of mind. Men would be at the game, Pauline thought idly. Newcastle United were playing at home today. The women were shopping, had their feet up or were visiting family, a normal Saturday in December.

"I'm going to knock on the door," Ramsay said.

"No!" Pauline said. "You're the only remaining hope I have of getting justice done. If those men are spies from our side, they'll report you and you'll be drawing the dole by Monday."

"I fear you could be right, Miss Riddell, but we have to know and that would be the quickest way. They don't know who I am. I could be the Electricity Board's representative come to trace a fault we have in the area."

"If you can make that look plausible, fine," Pauline said. "But today you don't look like anything other than a regular citizen or a policeman. So, I insist, Inspector: You don't do anything."

Ramsay grinned. "Yes, boss," he said, and then added more seriously, "You have a point. I too think I'm the last hope for justice for your friend, so I'll watch and wait and think."

"Exactly, Inspector. Strategic thinking is what we need here, as someone once told me."

"A man of considerable intellect, I'm sure, and one whose advice we should certainly follow," Ramsay said.

"Quite so, Inspector."

"It's infuriating to be standing here watching when I should be doing."

"As do I but we must think before we act."

"You are wasted as an executive secretary, Miss Riddell. You would be an excellent headmistress of a school."

"Keeping executives in order is enough for now. When I have more experience, maybe I'll apply for the Headmistress position at Roedean."

"I'm sure you would be a credit even to such an august academy as Roedean but I fear you will need some good references to climb that high without some academic credentials, or do you have those as well?"

"I don't, but my mother was a headmistress. She could teach me enough to bluff my way into it."

Ramsay was intrigued. Was she being serious? "Are you considering a change of career, Miss Riddell?"

"Not really and certainly not into teaching," Pauline said. "My mother's stories, mild though they were, were enough to point me in a very different direction. I fear I'd be the sort of teacher who ruled by fear. I have strong views on what is, and what isn't, to be tolerated."

"Like the murder of a friend, for example?"

"Yes, exactly. I won't accept Marjorie's death being left unresolved. Justice must be done, Inspector. I insist on that."

After an hour, when their lurking was becoming noticeable to local people making their way in and out of the street, they were relieved to see the van drive away. They followed at what Pauline hoped was a safe distance. It made its way westward, as if heading out of town.

"Are they going to the testing ranges, do you think?" Pauline asked.

"I have no idea where they're going," Ramsay said, equally puzzled.

They weren't kept in suspense long. The van pulled into a garage attached to a large house on the edge of town. Ramsay noted the address.

"I'll find out who owns that place," he said, as they returned to the city center and his car.

"And I'll do more thinking. We've done enough observing for now."

Pauline found the days of waiting to hear from Ramsay almost unbearable. Work continued as before. She occasionally observed Wagner and Murdock at the factory but kept out of their way. The evenings she spent at the Bertrams' listening to the radio and sewing or reading. It was a lot warmer than her evenings had been during the previous week but almost as tedious. The quiet evenings lacked the excitement of witnessing an event that would explain everything.

Finally, word arrived in the form of a phone call to her at work.

"I hope this won't get you into trouble, Miss Riddell," Inspector Ramsay said.

"Oh, phone calls in aren't considered quite as bad as calls out, and in this case it's police business," Pauline replied.

"Well, yes and no," Ramsay said. She could hear the smile in his voice. He continued, "That house is owned by a property firm in London, would you believe."

"I would believe, Inspector. Everything about these people is from London."

"While I would never say *all* the evil in any country emanates from its capital city, I believe most of it does," Ramsay replied.

"We don't know they're bad people, Inspector. They might be our people defending our interests."

"They might indeed and that's where we're going to be

stuck. Those you call our people might know they're on our side but to we ordinary folk, the distinction isn't often quite so clear."

"I'm not sure it matters, Inspector. I've been thinking about it and what I've come up with is it could be just a bad apple. Marjorie stumbled into a situation and died because of it. It doesn't follow they were all involved. In fact, I think quite the opposite. I think if they were all involved, it would have been managed differently."

"That sounds reasonable but not particularly helpful."

"I have an idea to make it so. Can we meet later, and I'll explain?"

"You don't want to tell me over the phone?"

"Walls have ears, Inspector, as I'm sure you remember," Pauline said. Her reference to the old wartime slogan made Dr. Enderby smile as he crossed from his office to the outer door.

"Are we in World War Three now, Miss Riddell?" her boss asked, as he reached the door to the corridor.

"No, Dr. Enderby, but the police are still very security minded." When her boss had gone, she returned to the phone call.

"Why don't we meet in the Elswick Arms Hotel," Ramsay said. "It's pertinent to the case and perfectly respectable, even if some of their guests haven't been, or at least two we know of weren't."

* * *

"I DON'T LIKE IT, Miss Riddell and I can't let you do it," Inspector Ramsay said, that evening when she related her plan.

"Unless you're going to lock me up, Inspector, you can't stop me doing it," Pauline said.

"It's foolhardy and dangerous."

"Then you and your men should be somewhere nearby to rush to my aid."

"I can't have men on standby for a case where I'm not the officer in charge."

"Then my death will be on your conscience forever, Inspector."

"It won't, Miss Riddell. I've advised you and you must take that advice or the blame lies entirely on your shoulders."

"If I'm right, the blame won't lie there long so it isn't a problem," Pauline said.

Accepting defeat, Ramsay thought for a few minutes before saying, "I have a plan too. Here's what we'll do."

* * *

PAULINE HAD WATCHED PATIENTLY every night after work, observing the comings and goings at the house. None of the nights had fitted what she was looking for until tonight. Tonight, everything was as she'd thought it was on that night Marjorie was killed.

She crossed the street. It was dark, misty, filled with sooty smoke and subdued street lamps casting eerie shadows of branches and lampposts. She knocked on the door and waited. This whole affair had been about waiting, she thought. Waiting for the police to find the killer. Waiting for them to arrest people whose names she'd given them. Waiting to hear snatches of conversations at windows and doors. Waiting to see what Wagner was doing. Waiting to see what people were doing here at this house.

Nothing happened. She knocked again. Footsteps sounded in the hall and the door opened.

"Good evening, Mr. Murdock," Pauline said.

"What do you want?" he asked harshly, peering out into the street.

"I want to speak to you and Dr. Wagner. May I come in?"

"Dr. Wagner isn't here," Murdock said, still blocking the doorway.

"You're his assistant," Pauline said, "you should know if he's going to be here soon."

"He's not going to be here tonight, so I advise you to come back another time. Maybe I could set up an appointment when next I see him."

"Excellent. Then I can tell you and you can tell him what I have to say. May I come in?"

"Just say what you want to say and go."

"I think you'll want me to be more private," Pauline said. "Anyone passing may hear me and you definitely don't want that."

Murdock shook his head in frustration but stepped aside to let her pass. They went through the small hall at the door and into the large room with the bay window.

As the door closed behind Pauline, Ramsay stepped out from their usual observation point and signaled to his two colleagues, Morrison and Thompson, one in the shadows at each side of the house. Like him, they were off duty. If anything went wrong, they were just three coppers out for the night, heading for the Elswick Arms Hotel for a convivial drink, and hearing cries of distress, jumped into action to save a woman in distress. They disappeared further into the darkness and Ramsay quickly crossed the road. He crept into the driveway and up to the bay window.

Through the place where the curtains didn't quite join, he could see Murdock and Pauline. He raised his whistle to his lips ready for the moment if it should come. He saw Murdock pointing to the papers on the table, apparently assuring Miss Riddell of his honesty. Murdock then left his field of vision and all he could see was Pauline staring at the papers with a puzzled expression. Then Murdock reappeared, he spoke, Pauline looked toward the window, and he was on her. His right hand pressing a rag to her face. Ramsay blew the whistle and, with his elbow, smashed the windowpane in front of him to startle Murdock. He heard glass breaking at the side and rear of the house and knew the others were on the move too.

Murdock dropped Pauline, who flopped to the floor like a doll, her head bouncing off the corner of the table. As Ramsay had expected, Murdock ran for the entrance. Ramsay, however, was already there when the door flew open.

"Going somewhere?" he asked, his service revolver pointing steadily at Murdock's middle.

Morrison and Thompson arrived together and grabbed Murdock's arms. In a moment, he was handcuffed and bundled back into the room where Pauline lay.

"You'd better hope she's not a second murder on your conscience," Ramsay said.

"She's not dead and you can't prove I killed the other one, either," Murdock replied.

"I think Dr. Wagner might help us there, even if it's just to save himself."

Murdock laughed. "I think you'll find no one is going to help you, Inspector. Your best hope for the future will be traffic duty."

DS Morrison put down the phone. "Ambulance is on its way, sir," he said.

"I'll wait for it. You take this creature to the station and charge him with assault. That will do as a start."

52

PAULINE

INSPECTOR RAMSAY FOLLOWED the nurse into the room. Pauline lay on the bed, under the covers, eyes closed as if asleep, an ugly purple lump on her forehead where her face had hit the edge of the table as she'd fallen, leaving a hairline fracture and concussion. Hearing the sound of their entry, her eyes opened and she stared at him.

"Did you get him?" she asked.

"You were right, Miss Riddell," Ramsay said, politely waiting for her to invite him to sit down.

"Then you did get him?" Pauline asked eagerly. The knowledge Murdock was in custody and not waiting to kill her was a huge relief.

"Yes and no."

"But he is in custody?"

"He won't be able to hurt you, Miss Riddell, that I can tell you."

Pauline stared at him. "Is he dead?"

"No. He and Wagner have been apprehended and are being held in a secure location."

"Will I have to give evidence at the trial?"

"There won't be a trial, Miss Riddell, and you won't ever see them again."

Pauline frowned. There was more going on here than she liked. "Inspector Ramsay, can we stop this question and answer game. Please tell me what has happened without further delay. I'm not getting a good feeling about this."

"I'll tell you what I can, which isn't as much as I think you deserve but it is out of my hands. Nothing I say here can be repeated and I will deny saying it if you do tell anyone. Is that clear?"

"This wasn't just about saving Wagner's marriage then. I thought it couldn't have been."

"And you were right. That day your friend went to join Wagner, she arrived early."

"That was my fault," Pauline said. "I'd upset her by telling her she was behaving unwisely."

"You couldn't have known and nor could she," Ramsay continued. "She saw Wagner's assistant, Murdock, through the window. He was talking to those 'cleaners' but she thought he was talking to Wagner who was out of her view. The window was open a little for it was a warm day."

"She heard what they were saying and they killed her for that?"

"Not at once. She hadn't really understood what she'd heard and Murdock, apparently, thought he could let her go after passing on Wagner's message. Then she said the wrong thing and one of his contacts, one of the cleaners, grabbed her and pulled her into the house. She became frightened and angry. They had to subdue her. From that moment on, there was no going back.

"Still, he didn't kill her right away. His contacts left and he was left with Marjorie, trussed up and unconscious but still alive. It wasn't that he was squeamish; he was just trying to devise a realistic 'accident'. By eleven o'clock, as he was driving Marjorie out to the coast, where this accident was to take place, he heard on the police radio, which they monitored all the time for safety, there was a street fight and someone had been knifed. He realized he had the perfect cover. He parked in a quiet place and waited until he heard the police had finished at the scene. He came through the park from the other side, away from where the street fight happened, dropped Marjorie where it would be thought the rioters might have done, knifed her and left."

"Tell me she didn't suffer," Pauline said, "and that she was drugged when it happened."

Ramsay nodded. "That's pretty well true, I think. Poor kid. Your reasoning got us there. Now, how do you feel? You could have been the next 'accident'."

"I'm fine," Pauline said. "Though I feel sickly. It's revolting stuff, chloroform, and I have a splitting headache. And now, why won't they stand trial?"

"It seems we have some people on the other side of the Iron Curtain we want to bring home and now we have two prisoners to exchange."

"So, they go home heroes and Marjorie is dead without any justice being done."

"I'm afraid so, Miss Riddell. We live in awful times and occasionally the awfulness reaches down even to this small city in our country."

"Will you tell Mr. and Mrs. Armstrong?"

"No one will tell them what *really* happened, Miss Riddell. This can go no further."

"It's unfair, unjust," Pauline said.

"It is both of those and more, Miss Riddell, but don't make the mistake of trying to correct this injustice. The shadowy people who keep us safe often do so in horrible ways. Another death would serve no one."

Pauline frowned. "Threats make my hackles rise, Inspector. I'm like a guard dog."

"I'm not threatening you, Miss Riddell. Remember, I'm not here and I've not told you anything so how could you be threatened?"

Pauline rose unsteadily from the bed and stretched out her hand. "Thank you for telling me, Inspector. It doesn't satisfy my desire for justice and I'll have trouble saying it does or explaining why I've stopped investigating."

"There will be no difficulty there, Miss Riddell. Tomorrow's newspapers will tell the world that the two miscreants who were wanted by the police in connection with the murder of Marjorie Armstrong were killed resisting arrest and credit you with identifying them. The Armstrongs will have something to cling to and you will have your 'justice', however unsatisfying it is. I can only beg you to accept that result."

As he put on his hat, he nodded and said, "Goodbye, Miss Riddell. Please return to your life and forget this awful business."

"I'll try, Inspector. Oh, and thank you for believing in me all these months. I know how much it has cost you. Will you get any credit for arresting them?"

"I will have some credit, Miss Riddell, but you may be surprised to learn how little. It seems you, and by association I, broke up a clever disinformation campaign by our side. They aren't pleased. In fact, they're very angry but my heroic mentions in the newspapers will keep me safely in my job this time, I believe."

Pauline considered this. "Is that true or is someone just protecting their rear?"

"You're a quick learner, Miss Riddell. They have said they were using these people for our purposes and there's no reason to disbelieve them."

"Surely they didn't know about the murder?"

"Who knows," Ramsay said, "and none of us will be foolish enough to ask. I warned you it's hard to know which side they're on. Goodbye again, Miss Riddell."

She sat up to watch through her private ward's window as he walked out into the lobby. When he was out of sight, she flopped back on the bed, staring at the ceiling with its single, bare lightbulb. The murderous nightmare that had been her life these past months was gone, and she felt bereft, as though she'd lost a friend.

53

PAULINE AND POPPY

"YOU PROMISED ME THE SCOOP," Poppy said, in mock indignation, "and it's splashed all over the Sunday papers."

"Not by me," Pauline said. She was back at the Bertrams' and being anxiously waited on by all her friends, who were horrified at how ill she looked. The large, bruised bump on her forehead where her head had hit the table and the swollen lip and black eye where her face had hit the floor made things look worse than she felt.

"Well, I still expect that 'how I did it' story," Poppy said. "Otherwise, I'll never speak to you again."

Pauline smiled. "If you have your notebook, I'll tell you," she said.

Both Mrs. Bertram and Poppy were shocked and said together, "Not until you're well enough."

"I'm well enough now and if Poppy waits, the public will have forgotten."

There was some continued resistance but eventually they agreed, as she'd guessed they would. They were too excited by the weekend events not to want to know.

"Before I start," Pauline said, "you have to know I will deny telling you anything, if you repeat what I say."

"I have to write something, Pauline. I can't put in a blank piece of paper."

"Then you'll have to be clever how you write it," Pauline replied. "I'm sure you'll manage."

Pauline recounted the early part of the investigation. Poppy already knew this but the Bertrams didn't.

"Now we get to the clever bit," Poppy said, when Pauline had brought them up to the start of her surveillance of the house.

"I'm not sure it was clever," Pauline said. "It was more of a growing understanding that something I was watching wasn't right. And when Murdock said he'd met Marjorie at five o'clock I knew that couldn't have been so. She had to have gone to the house and she'd gone an hour too soon. It was that 'too soon' part that set me to thinking and asking why that would be a problem."

"The only answer was she'd seen or heard something she shouldn't have. To kill her for that meant it was something big, really big. Not marital affairs, though I've no doubt people have killed to cover those up too, but there was no married man in the scene when Marjorie arrived that day. I have to admit, I thought only Murdock involved and Wagner as much a victim as the rest of us, but it turned out that was wrong."

"But what happened when you went into the house?" Poppy cried, still waiting for something to draw in the readers.

"It was a complete anti-climax," Pauline said, and grinned when Poppy glared and threw a cushion at her. "It was, really. I thought I'd got it wrong again. He was so calm, so cool, I couldn't believe my eyes and ears."

"Tell me!"

"We walked into the room with the table and desks and he pointed to the large table, which was covered with papers and drawings.

"He said, 'As you can see, I'm very busy so say your piece and go.'"

"I said, 'I've been watching this house for some time', still pretty sure of myself at this point. Then I told him, 'You have some very odd cleaners.'"

"He said, 'Our cleaners are from a firm that specializes in security work. Not that it's any of your business.'"

"So I said, 'That explains why they aren't in the phone book or anywhere else.'"

"He asked, 'What is it you came to say?'"

"I asked him, 'Why did you lie about meeting Marjorie that night?'"

"He looked angry and said, 'What? Are you mad?'"

"Then I told him, 'No, not mad. Just slow on the uptake.'"

"He then said, 'Why would I lie about that?'"

"I explained, saying, 'Because Marjorie came here early. Your 'cleaners' were photographing papers. She saw them, they grabbed and imprisoned her before calling either you or Wagner. Whichever it was, you couldn't risk her telling someone what she'd seen and later one of you killed her.'"

"He repeated, 'You're mad. I hope you haven't told anyone else of these wild accusations!'"

"I assured him, 'I haven't told anyone, but I will tell the police if you don't listen to what I have to say.'"

"'What do you want?' He asked me."

"I replied, 'What everyone wants, Mr. Murdock, even you, I imagine. Money. Not more than your, or Wagner's, paymasters can afford. I'm sure they could add a new contact to their books.'"

"He said, 'You're entirely mistaken in your assumptions, Miss Riddell. Let me show you what I do here. Then you'll see I'm not what you think. Come.' He ushered me over to a table covered with drawings and papers. A camera lay on top of them.

"He told me he worked for British Intelligence and he was keeping his eyes on some of the people at the ranges and at the house we were in. It was his job to keep his bosses informed every week. He was really convincing because what he was saying was as likely to be true as what I'd thought was true. I had no way of knowing.

"Then, casually, he said, 'Excuse me a minute, I've the kettle on for tea. I assume you won't want to take tea in case I've poisoned it.' He laughed and left the room. Like I said, I couldn't comprehend what was happening. I thought he'd have done something by that time.

"He was back a moment later and asked, 'Are you convinced?'

"I was truly perplexed. My whole plan had depended on him attacking me. This bringing me in, showing me what he was doing was all as if it was the most normal thing in the world.

"Then there was a faint medicinal smell in the air. I looked around. The speed of his attack stunned me. I was gripped tightly, hauled backwards with a chloroformed rag clamped over my face. I heard Inspector Ramsay's whistle and the breaking glass. I grabbed at his face, hoping to hit an eye, and then the world went dark."

"It's disgusting," Major Bertram said. "We gave that man, Wagner, shelter when he escaped from East Germany and he betrayed us. As for that other man, he went to a good school; he was of a good family and attended one of the world's best universities. How could he behave like that?"

Pauline thought it time to steer them in a less dangerous direction. "I don't know who they were spying for, Major. We shouldn't assume it was the Soviets. After all, we have plenty of industrial competitors who would dearly love our secrets."

"You can believe what you like, Pauline," Major Bertram said. "I know what I believe."

"Yes, dear," his wife said, "but Pauline is right. We can't accuse people without evidence."

Major Bertram harrumphed in true gentlemanly style.

"I'm with you, Major," Poppy said, "but I can't write that."

"It would be very wrong of you to do so," Pauline said. "All we know is what was in the official statement and all I know doesn't contradict that. I suspect more, it's true, but that's as far as I can say."

What she suspected was that Wagner didn't escape from East Germany, he was sent. And Murdock was the one inviting and receiving. As Inspector Ramsay had told her, Murdock was in the Intelligence Service working on Central Europe during the war and he'd fought on the Communist supported International Brigade in Spain before the war. She guessed the secret services would keep such a man on their staff because he was useful, though they maybe didn't fully understand who he was being most useful to.

"Ugh," Mrs. Bertram said. "It's revolting the way some people behave." She made treachery and the rivalry of powers and ideology sound like a spat between neighbors.

"True, my dear," Major Bertram agreed. "Now, when is dinner. The smell of roast beef is making me hungry."

After lunch, Pauline and Poppy worked on Poppy's article. What could be said and what couldn't. The focus was to be firmly on the 'plucky heroine' of fiction, rather than the reality of a nosey secretary. It seemed to have the best chance of meeting both their needs.

54

AN END AND A NEW BEGINNING

THE DAYS that followed were a blur. Everyone in the factory seemed to want to shake her hand. People she'd never met in all the years she'd been there congratulated her if they met in a corridor. Her boss took her to the Director's meeting room where senior executives of the company gave speeches in her praise. Even Hindmarsh, who'd suffered at her hands in her first sad effort as a detective, approached her. Though she'd feared the worst when she saw him approach, told her how glad he was she'd found the true culprits. She thanked him and apologized for ever believing he could have been to blame and they parted, if not as friends at least no longer as enemies.

At first it was gratifying but by Saturday she was happy to escape them all for a day and a half's peace and quiet. The morning dragged until the factory whistle blew and people began to stream out to their homes. She stayed on, unwilling to mingle with people who would want her to recount, again, how she'd solved the mystery when the police hadn't.

It was almost dark when she covered her typewriter, put on her coat, and left the office. She drove out of the factory gate and turned onto the street heading for home. She passed the bus stop where a group of young men, dressed for a night on the town, were pushing and shoving each other in the rough horseplay they never seemed to tire of. It reminded her of the night it all began. She drove on as a bus stopped and the young men piled on, still jostling one another.

After they'd eaten, Pauline took her tea to her room's one armchair and sat in front of the small two-bar electric heater. It had been gratifying to be so publicly praised by the police but the truth was, she'd been wrong throughout the whole sorry affair. Worse, she'd led the police astray twice, by pointing an accusatory finger at innocent people.

She'd accused Bob Hindmarsh and his two friends because she didn't like them as people, and Wagner because he'd been evasive and foreign. It was unlikely she'd ever be involved in anything like this again, but if she was, she would do better. She'd hold her counsel until she was sure. She must never put people's lives in turmoil, danger even, in future.

Having made this resolution and feeling confident she'd never be called on to live up to it, she tucked her legs under her and sipped her tea thoughtfully.

Did she really want to be a secretary for the rest of her life? Without Stephen, there was going to be no husband, no family, no home, and above all no point. There were a lot of noes in there so maybe there'd be no harm in adding one more. No, she wouldn't follow the life that had seemed so happily mapped out for her but was now gone.

She would begin another. She'd be a younger, more active Miss Marple. How? Agatha Christie never actually explained how Miss Marple kept body and soul together before retirement and that was a long way off for herself. Join the police force? No, they weren't ready for female detectives yet; she'd spend her working life in an office or being called out to domestic disputes as Woman Police Constable Riddell and if a mystery came along she wouldn't be allowed to do anything in it.

Maybe she could open a detective agency, like Agatha Christie's Poirot, or Tommy and Tuppence? She shook her head. In books, detectives worked with nice people and their problems were cleverly uncommon. In real life, detective agencies were owned by seedy middle-aged, friendless, single men who checked out straying husbands in divorce cases. That wasn't what she had in mind. Anyway, the long hours of watching that house told her she didn't want to do this. In the movies, the detectives are shown just moments before the crime happens. The hours of utter boredom they'd endured leading up to the moment had to be deduced by the audience. But no one can really imagine boredom, not really.

She suddenly remembered the letter that Mrs. Bertram had handed to her when she'd returned home. She'd stuck it in the pocket of her cardigan. Pauline pulled it from the pocket, rather crumpled, and stared at it. She didn't recognize the handwriting and that in itself was exciting. Now Stephen was gone, she only ever got letters from her mother. And it couldn't have been from her mother for she wrote on Sunday. A Saturday postal delivery was something out of the ordinary.

She opened it and read:

'Dear Miss Riddell,

I saw the article in the Herald yesterday and your amazing success in unmasking those killers. I have a puzzle the police won't look at, but somebody should. I thought, hoped, you might like to. I can't pay very much, I'm not rich but it may interest you. It's not a serious thing like murder but it is puzzling, and it worries me. Sorry if you think I'm rambling. I just can't get it out of my mind. Maybe it would be better if I explained a little, then you'd see...'

POLITE REQUEST

THANK you for reading my book. If you love this book, please, please don't forget to leave a review! Every review matters and it matters a lot!

Head over to Amazon (or wherever you purchased this book) to leave a review for me. Here's the link on Amazon:

IN THE BEGINNING, There Was a Murder

I THANK you now and forever :-)

READ MORE OF MY BOOKS!

Starting with the second published book in the Miss Riddell Cozy Mystery series, It's Murder, On a Galapagos Cruise

Or the third published book of the series, A Murder for Christmas

Or the fourth published book of the series, Miss Riddell and the Heiress

AND NOW you can pre-order the book that follows *In the Beginning, There Was a Murder*: Then There Were … Two Murders?

Or visit my P.C. James Amazon Author Page https://www.amazon.com/P.-C.-James/e/B08VTN7Z8Y

FOR SOMETHING DIFFERENT, my books by Paul James at: https://www.amazon.com/-/e/B01DFGG2U2

BONUS CONTENT

AS THANKS for reading this far, here's an excerpt from the second book in the Miss Riddell Cozy Mystery series. The book that follows directly from this one., called ***Then There Were … Two Murders?***

Chapter 1: Newcastle-upon-Tyne, England, December 1953

Pauline stared at the letter in her hand, hardly daring to believe it possible. Only minutes ago, she'd been wondering how she could change her life to make something more exciting of it and here it was. A letter from a woman, Mrs. Elliott, who wanted her help and all because she'd been mentioned in the newspapers as having solved a murder when the police had given up. If it wasn't for the letter, which she could clearly see and feel in her hand, she'd have thought herself in a dream. A dream from which she'd wake and be disappointed.

She held up the letter so she could see it better in the light streaming through the window from the nearby streetlight. The words seemed to float on the page, drawing her in.

'Dear Miss Riddell,

I saw the article in the Herald yesterday and your amazing

success in unmasking those killers. I have a puzzle the police won't look at, but somebody should. I thought, hoped, you might like to. I can't pay very much, I'm not rich but it may interest you. It's not a serious thing like murder but it is puzzling, and it worries me. Sorry if you think I'm rambling. I just can't get it out of my mind. Maybe it would be better if I explained a little, then you'd see.

First, you should know I live in an old house on the outskirts of Mitford. It's very quiet, or at least it was. Recently, I've heard noises, particularly at night. I have a good security alarm system and I lock up carefully, so I don't believe I'm in any danger. However, something is going on.

A week ago, I was crossing a stream on my daily walk by a bridge I've used every day, twice a day, since I retired. There's never been any trouble. On this occasion, the bridge had come loose and it tipped me into the stream. Fortunately, though I'm old, I'm not frail and while I'm cut and bruised, I'm not seriously hurt. But I could have been. I showed the bridge to the police and told them about the noises, but our local policeman man says the bridge is old and the bad weather has driven a lot of animals to find shelter in and around houses. What he said is true, but it doesn't explain it. I've lived in this house nearly forty years now and I know every creak – and so does Jem, my dog.

I have more to tell you, however, you may not be interested. If you are, please phone me at this number and I'll explain more fully.

Yours Sincerely,

Doris Elliott

PAULINE PUT down the letter and walked to the window, where the cold December night was lit by the lights of houses opposite and a nearby streetlamp. She told herself she wanted to think about this invitation. Should she raise this woman's hopes and then dash them because she couldn't provide answers or because the answers were as ordinary as the local policeman said? She shook herself. What on earth was she thinking of? Of course, she'd phone and accept the cry for help. After all, it wasn't just Mrs. Elliott who needed her to use her gifts, she needed to use them as well. The new life she'd wondered about was stretching out before her. There could be no question about turning away. She glanced at her watch. It was too late to call now. She'd phone Mrs. Elliott after church in the morning.

If this excerpt has whetted your appetite for more, you can now pre-order Then There Were … Two Murders?

Or you can read more of Miss Riddell's adventures right away:

Starting with the first published book in the Miss Riddell Cozy Mystery series, In the Beginning, There Was a Murder

Or the second published book of the series, It's Murder, on a Galapagos Cruise

Or the third published book of the series, A Murder for Christmas

Or the fourth published book of the series, Miss Riddell and the Heiress

For my family. The inspiration they provide and the time they allow me for imagining and typing makes everything possible.
I'd also like to thank my editors, illustrator and the many others who have helped with this book. You know who you are.

For more information: email: pj4429358@gmail.com

Twitter: https://twitter.com/pauljames953

Facebook: https://www.facebook.com/pauljamesauthor

Facebook: https://www.facebook.com/PCJamesAuthor/MissRiddellCozyMysteries

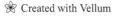 Created with Vellum

ABOUT THE AUTHOR

I've always loved mysteries, especially those involving Agatha Christie's Miss Marple. Perhaps because Miss Marple reminded me of my aunts when I was growing up. But Christie never told us much about Miss Marple's earlier life. When writing my own elderly super-sleuth series, I will trace her career from the start. As you'll see, if you follow the Miss Riddell Cozy Mysteries over the coming years.

However, this is my Bio, not Miss Riddell's, so here goes with all you need to know about me: After retiring, I became a writer and, as a writer, I spend much of my day staring at the computer screen hoping inspiration will strike. I'm pleased to say, it generally does — eventually. For the rest, you'll find me running, cycling, walking, and taking wildlife photos wherever and whenever I can. My cozy mystery series begins in northern England because that was my home growing up and that's also the home of so many great cozy mysteries. Stay with me though because Miss Riddell loves to travel as much as I do and the stories will take us to many different places around the world.

Printed in Great Britain
by Amazon